MEET THE
O
THE LUC

COLONEL STOSSEN is the only commanding officer the Lucky 13th has ever had. He doesn't always like what he has to ask his men to do, but he always knows they'll do it—or die trying.

LIEUTENANT HILO KEYE was finally commissioned from the ranks after joining the service at age thirty. He was overdue for a promotion, but everyone knew it was inevitable—if he survived long enough.

SERGEANT JOE BAERCLAU has been a soldier for a quarter of his life. He's a small man, but unbeatable in hand-to-hand combat. And when his eyes begin to "smolder," his men will follow him anywhere.

CORPORAL MORT JAIFFER is the "old man" of his squad—at twenty-eight. This former college professor turned down a chance at officer school and resisted promotion for as long as possible. But he's just too good to remain a corporal forever.

PRIVATE WIZ MACKEY has a personal stake in the fight against the Heggies. He saw his best friend killed on the Lucky 13th's last campaign, and was badly wounded himself. Now he means to pay back the debt—with interest.

FIGHT ALONGSIDE THE LUCKY 13th . . .

UNTIL RELIEVED
SIDE SHOW
JUMP PAY

SIGN UP FOR RICK SHELLEY'S THRILLING NEW SERIES . . .

SPEC OPS SQUAD: HOLDING THE LINE
SPEC OPS SQUAD: DEEP STRIKE
SPEC OPS SQUAD: SUCKER PUNCH

DON'T MISS SGT. DAVID SPENCER'S MISSIONS TO PROTECT THE COMMONWEALTH . . .

THE BUCHANAN CAMPAIGN
THE FIRES OF COVENTRY
RETURN TO CAMEREIN

FOLLOW THE CAREER OF LON NOLAN AND GO TO WAR WITH RICK SHELLEY'S DMC . . .

OFFICER-CADET
LIEUTENANT
CAPTAIN
MAJOR
LIEUTENANT COLONEL
COLONEL

SIDE SHOW

RICK SHELLEY

ACE BOOKS, NEW YORK

SIDE SHOW

An Ace Book / published by arrangement with
Bill Fawcett & Associates

PRINTING HISTORY
Ace mass-market edition / December 1994

Cover art by Steve Gardiner.
Cover design by David Rheinhardt

For information address: The Berkley Publishing Group,
a division of Penguin Group (USA) Inc.,
375 Hudson Street, New York, New York 10014.

ISBN: 0-441-00123-8

ACE®
Ace Books are published by The Berkley Publishing Group,
a division of Penguin Group (USA) Inc.,
375 Hudson Street, New York, New York 10014.
ACE and the "A" design
are trademarks belonging to Penguin Group (USA) Inc.

PRINTED IN THE UNITED STATES OF AMERICA

10 9 8 7 6 5 4

SIDE SHOW

PROLOGUE

By the start of the thirty-first century SA (Stellar Age), mankind had spread to more than 230 worlds. Apart from a few isolated planets, those worlds were divided into three primary blocs. The Accord of Free Worlds in the Terran Cluster was the newest alliance, even though the seventy-five member worlds were among the first settled by humans. Earth was also a member; the term "Terran Cluster" simply referred to those extraterrestrial worlds nearest Earth. The Accord was founded as a direct result of military and diplomatic pressure generated by a generations-long war between the other two groups of worlds.

The Schlinal Hegemony consisted of some fifty worlds, densely populated and heavily industrialized, with an average distance of little more than three light-years between inhabited worlds. The Hegemony was a tight dictatorship run from the world of Schline, fairly close to the border between the Hegemony and the Terran Cluster.

The Dogel Worlds were more feudal in nature. In theory, they were a loose confederation of about a hundred worlds, but in actuality they were controlled by a half dozen extended families who worked in close concert. The leaders of these aristocratic clans, the Doges, owned everything on their planets. Those worlds were, on average, less industrialized and less heavily populated than the worlds of the Schlinal Hegemony, but there were twice as many worlds, giving the two empires a rough parity.

Beginning in the middle of the thirtieth century SA, both the Doges and the Hegemons had started trying to upset that parity. Diplomacy and economic pressures had proved insufficient, so war had been the inevitable next step.

Stalemate on the frontier between the Hegemony and the Dogel Worlds eventually involved the independent worlds of the Terran Cluster in the fighting. Both sides looked for allies, or additional subjects, among the free worlds of the Terran Cluster, which bordered both empires. Most of the worlds of the Terran Cluster were heavily populated and nearly as industrialized as the core worlds of the Schlinal Hegemony. And the easiest routes for either Hegemons or Doges to outflank their enemy ran through the Terran Cluster.

Over the next several decades, the Doges and Hegemons expended as much effort on the worlds of the Terran Cluster as they did on each other. A dozen worlds fell to one side or the other, to military force if not to diplomatic suasion.

The threat drove the remaining independent worlds of the Terran Cluster to unite in the Accord of Free Worlds, a military and economic alliance that deliberately stopped short of full political union. For twenty years, the power of the Accord was enough to keep the Hegemony and the Dogel Worlds away. But in 3002 SA, the Hegemons started a military drive into Accord space. Two lightly populated Accord worlds, Jordan and Porter, were conquered and occupied. There were several other skirmishes, and Accord forces repelled invasions on three other worlds.

Six months later, the Accord was ready to start liberating the worlds taken by the Hegemons, both in the latest push and in the earlier expansion. Devon and Porter were liberated in the first campaigns. Now it was Jordan's turn.

. . . At least, that was the plan.

CHAPTER 1

War is a noisy business, producing sound levels that can damage, or even destroy, human hearing. Yet men sleep in that noise—not well, or deeply, perhaps, but they *do* sleep. The stresses of battlefield noise and insufficient sleep combine to drain soldiers, to decrease their effectiveness until they become zombies. If they are not given a break from the noise and the stress, those soldiers become useless, malfunctioning automata who can be destroyed as easily as a child might stomp a sand castle into oblivion.

The men of the 13th Spaceborne Assault Team had been in combat on Jordan for two weeks, with no more than six hours at a time away from the front, where they might grab a few hours of sleep in relative security. Fourteen days. Few of the men would have believed that it had been no longer than that. For some, any span less than eternity would have seemed too short by half.

For others, eternity had already come. The 13th had buried more than fifty men on Jordan. Another half dozen were missing, presumed dead, their bodies somewhere out beyond the front lines, on ground that the 13th had contested and lost. Hegemony troops held that land now.

"Ezra, get those new men down and tell them to ease off on the wire!" Even though he was talking over his helmet radio, Platoon Sergeant Joe Baerclau of the 2nd platoon, Echo Company, shouted. Down the line, Ezra Frain turned to look at him. Ezra was the first squad's leader. A quick glance was all Ezra spared before he passed the Bear's orders on to the three new men in his squad. *New men*—all had been in the squad for at least five months, but they had joined after the last campaign, so they were still *new men.*

"If they were down any more, they'd be underground," Ezra said when he returned to the platoon noncom's circuit.

"That's what we're trying to prevent," Joe said, more tight-lipped than usual. Sergeant Baerclau was still short of his twenty-fifth birthday. He had been a soldier for nearly six of those years, first in a defense regiment on his homeworld of Bancroft, then in the Accord Defense Force, the last thirty-three months in the 13th SAT. Jordan was his fourth campaign in eighteen months. He was, physically, one of the smallest men in the company, but there was no one who could feel confident of besting him in any combat sport.

Joe turned his attention to the space in front of the platoon again. It was nearly dawn. For the last several hours there had been no more than intermittent rifle fire along this stretch of the front. What had been an unspoiled forest showed the effects of two weeks of combat. Trees had been uprooted, toppled, split, or burned. Leaves that had been starting to change to autumn colors had fallen. Several small wildfires had burned most of them and charred the trunks and underbrush. Three days of rain had churned the area into a foul-smelling sludge. There was one benefit to that. Mud covered everyone, splotched over the camo pattern that had been tailored especially for this region of Jordan—but tailored for a spring or summer campaign, not for an autumn, when the colors were all wrong.

"Baerclau."

"Yes, Lieutenant?" Joe replied, flicking his helmet radio to the channel that linked him with Lieutenant Hilo Keye, Echo Company commander. The 2nd platoon did not have a platoon leader at the moment. The 13th had come to Jordan short a dozen junior officers.

"Get your men alert," Keye said. "We've got relief coming up. Soon as they're in place, we pull out."

"Which direction?" Joe asked.

"Believe it or not, back," Keye said. "It looks as if we're due for another breather."

"Aye, sir, I'll pass the word." Joe was too tired even to make a bad joke about the prospect of relief. There was an acid aftertaste in his mouth from the stimtabs he had been using to stay alert for the last several days. It would be good to get away from the stimulants for a time.

If everything had been timed properly, the transfer would have taken place in the last thirty minutes before first light. But the sky was already starting to brighten in the east before the first of the relief soldiers, men from the 27th Light Infantry Regiment, moved up to the lines, and the black of night was fading into the gray of morning dusk before the 13th started to pull back. Under fire.

Even in the dead of night, there would have been *some* infantry fire. Night was not a cloak of invisibility. The helmet visors of both armies incorporated sophisticated night-vision systems. At best, those gave only 70 percent of daylight visibility, but even that slight advantage was not one to be squandered.

Withdrawing under fire took time. The 27th provided heavy covering fire, as did the units on either flank, but they could not suppress all of the incoming Heggie fire. It took nearly an hour to get all of the 13th out of range of Heggie small arms. A few mortar rounds chased them even farther back.

Two hours later, Colonel Van Stossen relaxed in the unaccustomed luxury of a staff car. He was trying very hard not to think. After two weeks of combat on Jordan, he was so far short of sleep that he scarcely trusted his mind. A fanciful notion kept nagging at the edges of his attention, telling him that the skimmer was a dream, or a hallucination, that he was still in his command post at the front, with his men being pounded by enemy fire.

Stossen had been commander of the 13th SAT since its creation. *His* men, *his* team. For fourteen days, they had all been suffering. The campaign to liberate Jordan was not going well. That made the order to pull the 13th out of the lines puzzling. Then Major General Dacik, commander in chief of the invasion force, had sent his own skimmer to pick up Van. The colonel had barely had time to get his men settled, to issue all of the necessary orders. He hadn't even had time to wash and shave.

It can't be anything good, Stossen reasoned. He tried not to dwell on possibilities. *I'll know soon enough,* he told himself.

"We're here, sir."

Stossen lifted his head and blinked several times. He looked around as if he had no idea where he was or what he was doing there, which was very nearly the case. Finally, he focused on the driver.

"Thanks, Sergeant. I guess I dozed off."

The driver grinned. "Yes, sir. About a hundred and ten decibels."

"I was snoring that badly?"

"Don't worry, sir. I won't tell. General's office is right through that door, bottom of the stairs, then to the left."

Stossen laughed. "If I could only get another eighteen hours of sleep." He picked his combat helmet up from the seat next to him and got out of the skimmer. While he stretched, the car pulled away quickly, moving into a garage rigged from a thermal tarp.

The colonel stood out in the open for a minute, continuing to stretch, bending to one side and then the other, trying to force some alertness back to his mind by working his body. Just over 180 centimeters tall, his frame was well-muscled. Although he was nearing the middle of his fifth decade, he kept active, holding himself to the same high standards that his men had to meet. His dark brown hair was cut short, almost to the scalp, whenever the 13th went into combat.

"Better not keep him waiting," he mumbled. With a quick brush at the dirt on his combat fatigues, he went inside the headquarters building.

The building wasn't much. It had been the home of one of the leading Accord families on Jordan before the Schlinal invasion nearly two years back. An old structure of pseudo-adobe, the house was, at least, dry and comfortably warm inside. One wing had been destroyed by the fighting during the Accord landing. The roof was partially down on the opposite wing, across the inevitable courtyard. On the outside, there was no obvious reason to suspect that the hacienda was currently inhabited.

Stossen found the stairs and went down into the cellar. Two guards at the bottom nodded him through a heavy door. The first room beyond was filled with a dozen staff people, officers and enlisted men. General Dacik's aide came over and saluted.

"You're to go straight in, sir." He pointed to the appropriate door.

"Thanks, Captain. Any hints?"

The captain shook his head. "Sorry, sir."

"I guess I'll find out soon enough."

Major General Kleffer Dacik didn't bother to stand when Stossen came in, and he quickly waved off the colonel's salute.

"Sit down, Van. Join me in a stimulant?" He pointed at the keg-shaped portable bar open on his desk.

"Thank you, sir," Van said. "There's an ugly rumor in the 13th that I once turned down a drink, but I assure you there's no basis to it."

Dacik's laugh was more of a grunt, short and quickly disposed of. The glasses he set up were real crystal, though nanofactured. The general filled both glasses and slid one across toward Stossen. The two men raised their glasses toward each other and drank. Stossen took merely the lightest sip, but Dacik nearly emptied his. The liquor was brandy, potent but smooth.

"Things that bad?" Stossen asked.

Dacik blinked. "They could be better."

"You must have a real bitch to drop on us. From what I've heard, the last man you offered a drink to in the morning never saw the next night."

"Don't let that booze evaporate," Dacik said. "It costs too much."

Obediently, Stossen took another drink, longer, almost enough to start him coughing. It had been two months since his last taste of alcohol.

"The 13th rear guard ready for an evacuation?" Stossen asked.

"No, it's not that bad—not yet, at any rate."

Dacik didn't seem inclined to continue. After a minute or so, Stossen emptied his glass. The liquor warmed him all of the way to his stomach.

"Things aren't going as well as we'd like." Dacik shook his head. "Hell, that's the understatement of the year. You've seen the situation." He waited for Stossen's nod before he continued. "We've committed all of the forces we could for this operation, and it might not be enough. We won't get reinforcements anytime soon. Intelligence underestimated Heggie strength here. There's nothing unusual about that, but they went to extremes this time. Instead of forty to fifty thousand garrison troops, we found nearly eighty thousand *assault* troops. The Heggies were building up a strike force here. Hard telling where they were planning to strike."

"If we've stopped an invasion somewhere else," Stossen offered, "then we've managed *something*."

"Yes." The word was almost a sigh. Dacik looked off toward the wall for a moment. When he returned his gaze to Stossen, the vagueness was gone from his manner. It was time for business. "I'm afraid I am going to drop a major bomb on you, Van. No way around it."

"Yes, sir."

"The 13th is in the best condition of the three SATs I have here. That's why you've drawn the short straw. You and your men have until sunset tomorrow. Rest the men. Get a few extra meals into everybody. Replenish your stores, munitions, food, the works. You'll have top priority."

"And then?" Stossen asked when the general paused.

Dacik stood. "Come over here." He moved to a large mapboard hung on the wall. He flipped the map on, showing all of the only significantly inhabited continent on Jordan.

Stossen let his eyes travel quickly over the sixty-centimeter board, a dedicated mainframe linked to a central mapping mainframe on one of the ships in orbit, just as his own, smaller, mapboard was. Both Accord and Hegemony positions were marked, as far as they were known. The Accord had landed on the eastern seaboard, just south of the capital, and they had managed to flesh out a significant foothold, a rough semicircle with a depth of seventy kilometers and the ocean at the rear. It had taken only four days to manage that . . . and then some. On the fifth day, the expansion had been stopped cold, and in some areas, reversed.

Dacik stabbed a finger at a point well beyond the Accord perimeter, a third of the way across the continent.

"Telchuk Mountain," he said. "There's a secret laboratory there, inside the mountain. The people there have managed to stay undiscovered the entire time that the Heggies have been here."

"Two years?"

"Roughly," Dacik agreed. "And, yes, we know they're still there. We've had communications with them since we landed."

"Important research, I take it," Stossen said. The fact that the lab had been hidden was enough to make the deduction inescapable. Hidden *before* the invasion, which meant before the war started, since the invasions of Jordan and Porter had been the *casus belli*.

"Yes, but don't ask me what. The immediate concern is that we have to reach them. There's undoubtedly a limit to how long their luck can last, and the facility wasn't designed to provide cover against an occupying enemy. And we don't dare let the Heggies get those scientists."

"Which is where the 13th fits in?" Stossen was already trying to estimate the distance involved. Too far for comfort.

"Yes. We might be forced to evacuate Jordan. If we do, we can't leave those people behind. Three of them. I'll let you scan bios, but you'll have to make do with what you can remember of them. No notes or photos leave this building. Until you get there, only your exec and ops officers are to be told what this is all about."

"Yes, sir."

"The entire landing force will stage an attack tomorrow at sunset. All out, as if we're trying to break out of our foothold and go back on the offensive. The 13th will marshal behind the lines and pop through whatever hole we can open in the Heggie lines. Once you're through that gap, you head straight for Telchuk Mountain. Well, not *straight* for it. Don't give the Heggies a vector they can use to get there before you do. You're to make every effort to rescue the scientists and their staff. If it proves impossible to get them back to us, the vital thing is that they're not to fall into enemy hands, *no matter what*." The stress on those last words was unmistakable. "Is that clear?"

"Perfectly clear, sir. We don't let the Heggies have them, whatever else happens. No matter what we have to do to make certain of that."

"I wish we could bring down landers to drop you closer to Telchuk. It's a thousand kilometers away, across some fairly difficult terrain, but we can't. *Can't*." Dacik pressed his eyes closed, then opened them again.

"We *are* going to try to collect enough armored personnel carriers for you. Make the job of getting *to* Telchuk a little easier. You'll have your Havocs and their support vans. Take half of the ground crews for your Wasps and leave the rest. As long as possible, your Wasps will give you cover from here. When you get to the end of their effective range . . . maybe we'll be able to move them out to you, operating from wherever you can get them to their support crews. Beyond that, once you get through our lines tomorrow night, you'll be completely on your own, and I do mean *completely*. We won't even be able to bring in landers to evacuate your wounded. We're managing local air parity, over the ground we control. There's not a chance we could support landing operations beyond the perimeter."

"I understand, sir."

Dacik nodded. "My staff is set up to give you a complete briefing."

"One question." Stossen waited for the general's nod before he asked it. "How much time do we have?"

Dacik looked away from the colonel. "I can't even guarantee that you'll have enough time to reach Telchuk Mountain, Van, even if you go flat out and meet no opposition. If worse comes to worst here, we'll have to leave you behind if you're . . . somewhere out there. All I can say is, do the job as quickly as you can, but *do* it, no matter what. You are to consider the 13th completely expendable. Just do the job." By the end, Dacik's voice had faded almost to a whisper.

"Hey, Sarge! Who fouled up and gave us time off?" Al Bergon asked. Al was the medic for first squad.

"Don't ask questions," Joe Baerclau replied. "They'll find their mistake soon enough. You check your whole squad?"

Bergon nodded. "Everybody's up to par, medically speaking."

"Get your rifle cleaned, and then yourself," Joe said. "This lark won't last long." Bergon nodded and strolled off, back to his mates in first squad.

Joe was almost finished cleaning his own wire carbine, the Mark VI Armanoc. The zipper fired short lengths of collapsed uranium wire from twenty-meter spools. Joe could take the rifle apart and put it back together in the dark, or asleep, in fifteen seconds. He had had a lot of practice. Right now, he was scarcely aware of what he was doing. He was already thinking ahead to a hot shower, a fresh uniform, and as much sleep as he could fit in while he had a chance. He had no illusions. Whatever the reason why the entire 13th had been pulled out of the lines, it wasn't for a vacation. Not with the invasion locked in a bloody stalemate. The 13th was being prepped for something new, and most likely deadly.

Showers had been jury-rigged some thirty meters off. Outside the entrance were stacks of fresh fatigues with the built-in net armor and the camouflage pattern that had been designed specifically for this campaign. On another field table were stacks of towels and small bars of soap.

While he showered, Joe kept his battle helmet close, upended so that he would hear any calls that came in. Even naked and lathered up, he could scarcely consider himself off duty. He anticipated some sort of briefing, as soon as there was anything to say. Word that the colonel had been summoned to headquarters had spread through the 13th in minutes. And as soon as the colonel got back . . .

A smell of cooking food found its way into the shower tent, strong enough to overpower the smell of disinfectant soap. Joe sniffed deeply and hurried through the finish of his shower.

Field kitchens had been set up, and that was even more unusual than being pulled out of the lines. The promise of something better than the self-heating field rations that were a soldier's normal lot on campaign almost made whatever might come afterward seem worthwhile.

Joe was just tightening the closures on his boots when he got the call from Lieutenant Keye on the noncoms' circuit. "Chow time. Get everybody in for lunch."

Joe donned his battle helmet and relayed the call over the platoon channel. "Let's not have a riot getting there," he added.

Most of the men of the 13th got only the good news that evening, that they had another twenty-five hours (the day on Jordan was ninety minutes longer than Earth-standard) to do nothing but eat, sleep, and take care of their gear. Colonel Stossen only briefed his own staff and the company commanders, and even they got only the minimal information they would need before the 13th reached its target. The rest of the officers and the senior noncoms got the news the next morning, just after their third consecutive hot field-kitchen meal.

Joe Baerclau had his men clean their weapons again before lunch.

CHAPTER 2

The Accord's 15 Spaceborne Assault Teams were the fundamental building blocks of its combined arms organization. Each of the SATs was capable of extended service without support from other units. Besides eight line companies of infantry and four 60-man recon platoons, the team also included a squadron of twenty-four Wasp fighter planes and a battalion of thirty-six Havoc 200mm self-propelled howitzers, with the necessary support personnel. Authorized strength for an SAT was slightly over two thousand officers and enlisted men. None of the SATs on Jordan was at full strength. They hadn't been at the time of the landing, and all had lost men since.

The Accord of Free Worlds had committed more than thirty-five thousand combat troops to the campaign to liberate Jordan. In addition to the three SATs, there were a half dozen regimental combat teams plus supporting artillery and fighters. With the fleet support in orbit over Jordan, the total commitment topped forty-five thousand.

The 13th's Wasp Air Group and its Havoc battalion were the only segments involved in the covering attack for the breakout.

There was always enough work involved in an artillery fight to keep all four men of a Havoc's crew busy. The driver and gun commander sat on either side of the gun barrel, at the front of the turret, about in the middle of the ten-meter length of the gun carriage. The gunner and loader sat farther back, and lower.

Right now, the rear compartments of the 13th's Havocs were more congested than usual. Each gun had taken on a half dozen rounds more than its ammo racks could hold. Those six shells were to be the first expended, in this initial assault.

Gunnery Sergeant Eustace Ponks was the gun commander for Basset two, also known as "the Fat Turtle" after the artwork that decorated the side of the turret next to the commander's hatch. The Havoc batteries were all named after dog breeds, an ancient pun . . . "Cry havoc and let slip the dogs of war."

"Okay, Simon, start moving us into position," Ponks said after the fourth round was out.

Simon Kilgore, Basset two's driver, nodded. Even with radios for intra-crew communication, a nod was a better answer.

Eustace saw the gesture, but he was already relaying the gun's next target to Karl Mennem, the gunner. Jimmy Ysinde, the loader, already had the round locked in.

A Havoc could fire standing still or moving at sixty kilometers per hour with equal accuracy, but the entire gun carriage had to be pointed roughly toward the target. With a low turret, the gun itself could only be rotated six-and-a-half degrees to either side of the vehicle's center line. At a range of ten kilometers, a Havoc could drop a shell within its own length from the aim point. Even at twenty kilometers, it seldom hit more than three meters from the point targeted. Since the suspended plasma shells had an effective radius of destruction of twenty meters, that was sufficient.

The Havoc was ten meters long, armored only heavily enough to stop small arms fire. To escape heavier counterbattery fire, it depended on speed and maneuverability. It also depended on infantry to keep enemy ground troops far enough off that they couldn't use shoulder-operated rockets, and on the Wasps to keep enemy air power out of range.

The 13th's thirty-two remaining Havocs (four had been lost in the first two weeks of fighting) maneuvered near the center of the Accord lines, far enough behind the front for relative safety, close enough to be able to move forward quickly when a hole opened up. After firing six rounds apiece, the 13th's Havocs fell silent. In the continuing bombardment, it was unlikely that the enemy would notice that so many guns had quit participating.

"I hope somebody opens something up soon," Eustace muttered. "I don't like stooging around in one place." The thirty-two guns were far too close together for the comfort of any of their crews. Massed artillery made for nothing more than a large, irresistible target.

"We might be safer getting hit here," Simon said. "I don't think much of this chase."

"Hell, once we put a hundred klicks between us and the lines, there shouldn't be many Heggies around," Eustace replied. He held up a hand to stop Simon's rejoinder. "I'm getting something on the command net."

At a dozen points along the Accord perimeter, infantry and armor units were making forays in strength, probing for weak points in the Heggie positions. Between those probes, smaller patrols were also looking for potential avenues out. Beyond the lines, recon patrols had infiltrated to create diversions and plant mines to disrupt Heggie attempts to move troops. Artillery barrages and consolidated attacks by Wasps worked to create gaps. Unless a usable path through the encircling Schlinal lines could be found or made, the entire plan would fail. Worse, it might expose the Accord to a devastating counterattack, and that might be fatal to the liberation of Jordan.

"Mount up!" Joe Baerclau said over his platoon channel. The men of the 13th had not waited inside the APCs that would carry them. The armored vehicles might be tempting to enemy artillery or aircraft. The battle had been in full swing for nearly an hour and a half before the movement order arrived. A gap—marginal, perhaps—had finally been opened up in the Hegemony's line. Now, all the 13th had to do was get through that hole before someone plugged it.

The Heyer armored personnel carrier was designed for a crew of three and seven passengers, one squad. The Heyers gathered for the 13th were more crowded than that. Some carried twelve men, others as many as fourteen. Crewmen from other units had been replaced by men from the 13th, put into service as operators for the two splat guns each APC sported. Only the original drivers remained. Piloting a Heyer was a little more complicated than driving a skimmer.

The splat gun was a crew-served automatic weapon. It fired the same collapsed uranium wire that the Armanoc zippers did, but at greater speed and from two-hundred-meter reels, rather than the twenty-meter spools the carbines used. On the Heyer, one gun was mounted in front, next to the driver's position. The other was in a turret, top rear, able to swivel through a complete 360 degrees.

Lieutenant Hilo Keye, Joe Baerclau, and 2nd platoon's first squad all crammed into one Heyer with two of the enlisted men from headquarters squad. The lieutenant took the front gunner's position—"So I can see what the hell's going on," he mumbled to Joe, who moved to a spot near the hatch at the rear of the vehicle, close to the turret.

Hilo Keye was old for a company-grade officer. He was a mustang, commissioned from the ranks, and he had not even joined the ADF until after his thirtieth birthday. As company commander, he was filling a captain's slot. His predecessor, Captain Teu Ingels, had been promoted to major and the colonel's staff, as operations officer. It was common knowledge that Keye's own promotion was due "any day now." He had the rare combination of talent, ambition, and family connections to assure him the fast track upward. As long as he survived.

There were four veterans in the first squad of 2nd platoon, Echo Company. Sergeant Ezra Frain was twenty years old, tall and thin with bright red hair and green eyes. His home world, Highland, was one of the places where Accord and local forces had defeated an invasion by the Schlinal Hegemony. Ezra had been serving in his planetary defense force. After that fight, he had transferred to the ADF, and to the 13th SAT.

Corporal Mort Jaiffer was the assistant squad leader, which meant that he ran the squad's second fire team. At twenty-eight, he was the old man of the squad. He was also the intellectual. A large, hulking man with a growing bald spot on the top of his head, he had been an associate professor of history and political science before joining the ADF. He had turned down the opportunity to become an officer and had resisted promotion to corporal for as long as he could.

Al Bergon and Wiz Mackey were still privates. The SATs did not promote men simply because of longevity. Al was twenty-three, tall, thin, and dark. He doubled as the squad's medic. Wiz was two years younger, tall, big-boned, and fair-haired. Both of them had been critically wounded during their last campaign, on Porter. They had been given the option of transferring out of the 13th. Neither had taken it.

The three rookies had come to the squad together, straight out of the SAT training camp. Of the three, only Olly Wytten would have qualified for assignment to an SAT under the old guidelines—combat experience or a year in the ADF. He had been in uniform for a year before volunteering for the elite assault teams. Of average height and weight, Olly Wytten looked hard and angular, and much older than his twenty-one years. Black hair and eyes and a dark complexion made him look even more menacing than he was. In training, he had proved adept at everything demanded of him. He picked up combat skills more rapidly than most. Joe Baerclau and Ezra Frain had tabbed him as the most promising of the replacements.

Carl Eames was from Bancroft, Joe Baerclau's homeworld, but not from the same region. Not yet twenty, Carl seemed rather awkward at everything he did, but—somehow—he did it. Even his speech was awkward, hesitant. As a result, he said very little. He had grown up on an isolated farm. He was tall and heavy, with the muscles of a man who had known nothing but hard manual labor for a lot of years.

Phil "Pit" Tymphe was from Ceej, Tau Ceti IV, one of the very first worlds settled directly from Earth. The nickname came from his initials. He was another quiet one, with nondescript brown hair and eyes, and a vague smoothness to his face. He did have his moments, especially in any sort of competition, whether training or real combat. Almost as short as Sergeant Baerclau, he was ten kilograms heavier, and none of it was fat.

The APC started moving forward almost before Joe got the hatch secured at the rear. Joe tapped Wiz Mackey on the shoulder. Wiz was at the rear splat gun, his head up in the turret. He leaned down to see what the sergeant wanted.

"Make sure that gun's ready to fire," Joe said over a private radio channel. "And keep your eyes peeled. These things are magnets for trouble."

"Don't worry," Wiz said, his voice cold. "I ain't paid off my debt to the Heggies yet." His best friend had been killed in the fighting on Porter.

"Don't let it get personal," Joe told him, his voice almost as hard as Wiz's. "That blinds you worse'n booze."

Wiz didn't reply. He just moved his head back up into the turret and traversed it through ninety degrees, then back to its original position.

Joe squeezed onto the bench seat on the right side of the APC. There was no way this ride could be comfortable, but it would go better on his butt than on his feet.

• • •

Turnaround time was under ten minutes. The ground crews replaced the batteries in the Wasp fighters and replenished munitions. For this fight, the weapons were cannons and rockets.

Lieutenant Zel Paitcher had not moved in the cockpit of Blue two after landing. He hadn't even taken his hands off of the control yoke except to hit the power-down switch. Outside, the ground crew had worked with its usual expertise, as polished as any racing pit crew.

Zel did blink several times. He breathed deeply and slowly, working to keep his nerves under control. It was difficult to move back and forth between the adrenaline rush of combat and the dead time on the ground. Getting back "up" could be a problem, and that was the sort of problem that could prove fatal. The Heggies had plenty of fighters of their own around, and pilots who knew how to work them. For just an instant, Zel considered popping a stimtab. That would perk him up again, but he decided against it. Too much, too soon.

"All buttoned up, sir," Roo Vernon, crew chief for Blue one and Blue two, said. "You're ready to go."

"Thanks, Chief," Zel replied. He switched radio frequencies. "Slee?"

"Let's go." Slee Reston had just made captain, leader of the eight Wasps of Blue Flight.

The two Wasps lifted silently into the growing dark. In the night, the kidney-shaped fighters were almost perfectly invisible, to optics or electronics. The pilot sat in an ejectable cockpit near the center of the leading edge. The twin antigrav engines and their batteries were in bulging pods at either side. Between power pods and cockpit, the rest of the Wasp was given over to payload, in a number of possible configurations. The new Wasps, the Mark IVs, had a couple of refinements to previous models. Two batteries serviced each motor, extending the plane's maximum air time by nearly 50 percent, to just over ninety minutes. And a rear-firing five-barrel cannon had been installed, behind and below the cockpit, a permanent addition to discourage enemy fighters coming up from behind.

The Wasps of Blue Flight each carried two of those five-barreled cannons, one facing rear and, in the current configuration, another facing forward, in a pod just below the cockpit. Their 25mm depleted uranium rounds separated into 15mm-long slivers after being fired. With each barrel firing sixty rounds a second, one Wasp could put a lot of metal on a very small target. Not even the best personal armor could withstand that sort of onslaught, and an enemy fighter *might* be brought down that way . . . with a little luck.

Zel blinked once more, consciously, right before he pulled back on the yoke and took his Wasp into the air, just meters from Slee's. Even this close, the other Wasp was already virtually invisible. In a few more minutes, as evening dusk settled into night, the planes would be invisible to each other even in tight formation. They would rely exclusively on instruments. The final line was an automatic crash avoidance override that would cause the Wasps to veer apart if they came within fifty centimeters of each other. That system was as nearly foolproof as any.

"Our course is two-nine-five," Slee said as the two Wasps cleared the trees surrounding the landing zone. Two more Wasps of Blue Flight landed. As long as possible, each of the three flights would try to keep all but two planes in the air, to cover the breakout and keep the rest of the Heggies in the area occupied.

"Two-nine-five," Zel repeated. Keeping station on Slee, he was already on course, which would take them directly over the 13th, where the SAT was rushing through the lines. One of the other pilots of Blue Flight had been the one to spot the opening. A little help from air and artillery had widened the gap. Now they had to keep the Heggies from closing it too quickly.

"Red Flight still has the high cap," Slee reminded Zel. It wasn't that Slee thought his wingman's memory deficient. Repetition simply made errors slightly less likely. The high cap was responsible for intercepting enemy aircraft. That left the ground support mission to Blue and Yellow flights.

Zel kept his eyes on the heads-up display on his canopy. That would tell him anything he needed to know sooner than he could learn it any other way. The Hegemony's Boem fighters were as nearly invisible as the Wasps. It was unlikely that either side would pick up an enemy fighter until it caught its radar emissions. At night, two fighters might be less than a hundred meters apart before they became aware of each other. That made for tense encounters.

The antigrav engines were silent. Only at full throttle did they make an audible whine. Apart from that, the loudest sound in the cockpit was normally the breathing of the pilot, or his radio transmissions.

"Hang on, Zel, we've got a mission," Slee said. They had only been in the air a little more than a minute. "Looks like a full battalion of Heggie tanks moving to intercept our mudders. Change course to two-eight-six, distance thirty-two hundred meters."

As soon as Zel changed course, the target blips appeared on the heads-up display, twenty of them, moving across his course.

"We'll work from the front," Slee said. "Seven and eight are coming in from the southwest. They'll work up from the tail."

Zel simply clicked a reply. He flipped his weapons selector to rockets and pointed his target acquisition system at the lead Nova tanks. Though he could not actually *see* any of the tanks, Zel could picture them adequately. It wasn't just the photographs he had studied. He had seen Novas on the ground—disabled, but relatively intact. The Nova was heavily armored and carried a 135mm main gun. It only required a crew of two.

The TA system clicked twice, indicating target locks. Two of the blips on the screen were highlighted. Zel hit the trigger twice, and two missiles raced out from under his Wasp. At the same time, Slee fired two of his rockets. Four missiles, four Novas. The two Wasps were almost directly over the tanks when the missiles hit. They flew on and flipped their Wasps around in a high-gee turn, climbing as they did.

For the second run, they came in from high, targeting four more tanks, then peeling to the left as two enemy surface-to-air missiles climbed after them.

Zel dropped decoys and pushed his throttles wide open, climbing straight up. Slee angled off to one side, also dropping decoys. The new Wasps were just a trifle more sluggish than the old models, but the limiting factor in the Wasp's performance was still, generally, the gee-load that its pilot could take. Zel and Slee had plenty of warning of the incoming enemy fire. Their lead was enough to let them outrace the limited fuel supply of the Heggie missiles. Those arced over and started to fall. Zel and Slee turned to make another run at the enemy tanks. Twelve had already been destroyed or damaged, but only seven of them seemed to be completely out of commission.

"Boems coming in!" a voice shouted over the radio. Zel scanned his display. The voice hadn't been any of the pilots in Blue Flight, and he didn't recognize it. It had to be one of the pilots in the high cap. "At least eight passed us."

"Keep climbing, Zel," Slee said.

"I don't have them, Slee," Zel replied.

"Low, clipping trees, due north of the tank formation."

"We're not attacking?"

"Yellow flight has them," Slee said. "We'll go north and down, come in behind, try the Novas again if the Boems are accounted for before we catch up."

At twelve thousand meters, Slee and Zel leveled off and moved north. They were just turning back toward the targets when there were three explosions below them, in the air, followed within seconds by two more.

Nearly thirty seconds passed before Slee said, "Rais got it, and one of the planes from Yellow Flight." Rais was Rais Sivvens, Blue seven.

"They get out?" Zel asked.

There was only the slightest pause before Slee said, "No."

CHAPTER 3

There had not been a single word in the design specifications for the Heyer armored personnel carrier about passenger comfort, and the builders had not gone beyond the requirements. The only real advantage a Heyer provided was speed. Its thin armor might provide marginally better protection than the net armor woven into battle fatigues, but that was more than offset by the fact that an APC was a much more attractive target for enemy gunners. Still, even on broken terrain, a Heyer could make better than fifty kilometers per hour. The night's race in Heyers was mind-numbing but physically almost painful for the infantrymen of the 13th. Riding in a Heyer at speed was as draining as marching with full gear through almost impassable terrain. Sleep was virtually impossible. All anyone could do was hang on and try not to get bounced around *too* badly.

It was nearly midnight before the 13th stopped for a break. That wasn't so much for the comfort of the men as to allow the hydrogen converters to process water into fuel for the engines. Running after dark, the process was less efficient than during daylight, when solar batteries could speed the conversion along.

The 13th had dispersed after clearing the Schlinal lines. The four recon platoons were out front and on the flanks. The eight infantry companies moved in a loose diamond pattern, with the artillery and various support vehicles in the center. The distance from one flank to the other was fifteen kilometers. The distance from point to rear guard was only slightly less. Echo Company was in the rear left section of the diamond.

"Fifteen minutes," Joe Baerclau told his men as second platoon emerged from their three Heyers. "Do what needs to be done fast." Joe knew that the fifteen minutes would almost certainly stretch to at least thirty, but he preferred to have his men ready as soon as possible.

Most of the men started out by going through a series of stretches and bends, trying to work out the kinks that four hours of riding had given them. Ezra Frain came over to Joe and lifted his helmet visor.

"Any idea how long this goes on?" Ezra asked.

Joe shook his head. "I don't even know what we're doing. Head off a thousand klicks or more. Get there as fast as possible. Nobody's saying why, what we're to do when we get where we're going."

"Just something to loosen up the Heggies around the rest of our guys?"

Joe hesitated before he said, "I don't think so. If that was what we were supposed to do, we'd come out maybe this far then turn to move behind them, give them something close to think about."

"Then what?" Ezra demanded. He took his helmet off and ran a hand through his hair. Even in the dark, the red seemed to stand out, almost as if it were luminescent. "I've been trying to puzzle it out since we left, and it just doesn't make any sense. Blow a week's worth of munitions to send us out into the middle of nowhere, a thousand klicks from the action." Wasting ammunition was something that had to bother any veteran of the Porter campaign, where the entire 13th had virtually run out of everything from wire to Wasp rockets and Havoc shells.

"They don't pay us to understand the big shots," Joe said. "We just obey orders." The exhaustion in his voice was only partially physical. He had also been trying to guess what their mission might be, with as little success.

"Hey, Sarge!" Both Joe and Ezra turned.

"I think we've got us a concussion," Al Bergon said.

"Who?" Ezra got it out first.

"Eames. He whacked his head good, early on, while all the fireworks was goin' on around us. I just had a chance to give him the once-over."

"You get to Doc Eddles yet?" Joe asked. Eddles was the company's senior medtech, more than a medic, not quite a full doctor. He could handle anything short of invasive surgery, but the need for that was rare, thanks to trauma tubes and medical nanobots.

"He said he'll try to get to us before we take off, but he's got a couple of others in the same shape or worse."

"Damn buckets," Ezra muttered under his breath. Louder, he asked, "Where's Eames now?"

Bergon pointed. "There against the side of the mixer."

Frain put his helmet back on and lowered the visor so he could use the night-vision gear. "He get cut?"

"Naw, but he's got a lump the size of his nose. I put a soaker over it." A soaker was a bandage impregnated with analgesics and simple repair nanobots, molecular medics.

"Anything more Doc could do?" Joe asked.

"Probably not, but he might be able to tell if there's a skull fracture," Al said.

"You think he might?" Ezra asked.

"I doubt it, but I can't be sure without pictures."

"Neither could the doc," Joe said.

"I'll keep an eye on him," Al said. "But if he doesn't get better, any chance of medevac?"

"Skipper said no way," Joe said. "Whatever this lark is, we're completely on our own."

Whatever this is. Joe turned away from the others. He could make a vague guess. They were being sent to something specific. There had to be some reason for sending two thousand men cross-country on a world still dominated by the enemy. What that reason might be eluded Joe. Something or someone, and neither made a lot of sense. What, or who, could be worth risking the lives of two thousand men?

Twenty minutes later, when the order came to mount up again, Joe had come no closer to finding a guess he was happy with.

The break had scarcely been long enough for Van Stossen to conduct a hurried conference with his staff. Major Dezo Parks, his executive officer; Major Bal Kenneck, intelligence; and Major Teu Ingels, operations—each was riding in a separate vehicle to minimize the effect of a lucky enemy hit. They had their own radio channels so that they could talk privately, but it was never the same as a face-to-face. Those three officers were the only men in the 13th, other than the colonel, who knew virtually all of the details of their mission.

"We've got three really dangerous transits," Kenneck said when Stossen asked for his assessment. "These two rivers." He pointed to a mapboard open on the ground in the center of the group. "And, of course, the last fifteen klicks, in the valley leading to Telchuk, that's too narrow, with too little cover. If we get hit in there by substantial enemy assets, we're finished. It's as simple as that."

"Teu?" Stossen asked.

"One thing is obvious," Ingels replied. "We can't take Havocs into that valley. Not only isn't there room for them to maneuver, in a couple of places they couldn't even turn around. I think we should disperse them to these two areas, here . . . and here." He pointed out the locations on the mapboard. "That way, they can give us effective covering fire while we're in the danger zone. And if we post a couple of recon platoons near the ridge lines"—he indicated those as well—"we'd be in better shape. Warning at least, maybe time to get out. It might be smart to leave the APCs out beyond that valley too. They'd be more trouble than they're worth in that narrow track."

"Bal?"

"Since we have to do this regardless, I agree," Kenneck said. "Those measures do minimize our exposure, especially if we do have Wasp support, but it's still going to be hairy."

"Dezo, you have anything to add?"

Parks shook his head slowly. "I agree about leaving the Heyers outside the valley. As *far* outside as practical."

The laugh the others gave was subdued and showed little humor.

The 13th took one more long break during the night, then, two hours before dawn, they stopped again. The formation was spread out even more than it had been on the march, with units taking advantage of whatever cover the terrain offered—more to hide vehicles than themselves.

It wasn't much. The broad plain between the eastern seaboard and the mountains was mostly flat. Areas of forest were interspersed with prairie. The 13th had reached an area where the long prairie grasses predominated. The stands of trees were mostly small, and widely separated. Heat tarps were spread over all of the vehicles. The combination of camouflage and trees did offer some protection. The men were set to digging holes for themselves.

"I hope they don't hit us too soon, Lieutenant," Joe Baerclau said. "We're all so zapped that it wouldn't take much to roll right over us."

"I know," Keye said. He stifled a yawn. The two men had their foxholes about eight meters apart. Iz Walker, Echo's first sergeant, had his hole thirty meters the other side of the lieutenant, far enough away that a single hit, even from a bomb or 135mm shell, would be unlikely to take out both of them. "Best I can say is that there's no indication of Heggies anywhere close. We're already better than four hundred klicks beyond the lines."

"Coupla Boems could knock the stuffin's out of us," Joe said.

"If they see us. Just make sure that they can't. Get everybody tucked in good, ponchos over the holes. The works." This was the rainy season. Ponchos had been issued. While not as effective as thermal tarps, they would help minimize a man's infrared signature.

"Aye, sir. I'll make the rounds myself." Joe already had his own hole dug. The soil was somewhat sandy and loose.

"Let the squad leaders handle it," Keye said. "That's what they're there for."

"Yes, sir." Joe changed channels and passed the word on.

"Half and half on watch," he added. "One fire team sleeps while the other's on alert. Hour at a time to start. If it looks like we're going to stay put all day, we'll extend that later."

What am I forgetting? Joe asked himself. That was a common question for him on campaign, more as the days and nights dragged on and he got further behind on sleep. It was too easy to forget, and forgetting was as lethal an enemy as any Heggie.

A yawn forced its way out. For just an instant, Joe raised his visor so he could rub at his eyes. They burned from lack of sleep and too many stimtabs. It would be so easy to let them slide shut and sleep . . .

Joe shook his head violently. Not for an hour. He had to take the first watch. Then he would turn the platoon over to one of the squad leaders for the next hour. The price of being a leader, he thought, lowering his visor into position again. He forced himself to do a slow, detailed scan of the countryside beyond his foxhole—for the present, "the front." He scanned close, then farther out with each additional pass, out to the abbreviated horizon that his foxhole gave him. There was nothing visible moving out there. Nor were there any obvious heat signatures showing up in infrared.

This is crazy, Joe thought. Then, fearing that he might be sliding toward sleep again, he busied himself with little chores. He checked to make sure that his carbine had a full spool of wire in the chamber and a fully charged power pack. He took a mouthful of water, swishing it around in his mouth for a moment before he swallowed. He would make that last until after his hour of sleep. Water discipline. He couldn't be certain when they might get a chance to replenish their supplies.

Should I eat? Joe asked himself after another long look at the horizon. He turned on the microphone pickups in the earpieces of his helmet. That way, he would be certain of hearing anything more than the sound of an insect walking, out to at least forty meters.

Should I eat? He had to admit that he really wasn't hungry. He needed time to recall that it had been twelve hours since his last meal, back behind friendly lines. He needed to eat.

He pulled out a meal pack and stripped the wire that would start heating the food. By the time he got the lid off, the food was as warm as it was likely to get. He ate sluggishly, too tired for either appetite or any reaction to the taste. A single meal pack was designed to provide half a day's nutritional needs, and enough moisture to allow a soldier to get it down without drinking water. Taste had not been high on the list of priorities.

After every couple of bites, Joe would look out over the lip of his foxhole, scanning the horizon while he chewed. Once, he leaned back to look up into the sky. In the trees there was a single gap that he could see through. A few clouds, a few stars. Joe wondered whether there were any Wasps overhead, keeping watch for them, ready to respond if they were attacked. He knew better than to expect to see or hear a fighter, but it was still a way to occupy a few minutes—get through that much more of his hour's watch.

With the dawn, heavier cloud cover moved in from the west. Two hours later, it started to rain. Colonel Stossen and his staff gathered under a tarp that had been erected next to one of the APCs.

"It looks like the rain will be with us most of the day," Bal Kenneck reported. "A steady soaker. The satellite data is pretty solid on this."

"Gives us some cover," Dezo Parks said. "The men need sleep, but still . . ."

"I know," Stossen said. "The general said to hurry. If we moved all day we could get . . . where we're going by midnight, be in position before dawn."

The staff officers waited for Stossen to make his decision. They were all as short of sleep as their men, or more so. After nearly two minutes, the colonel shook his head.

"We've got to have a few more hours. If we start up at noon, we might still reach our destination by dawn, at least get to the head of the valley and get the Havocs and recon platoons in position." He took a deep breath. "And find someplace for the Wasp support vans to take care of our birds." *If we actually get them,* he qualified silently. He was not putting a great deal of hope on that. By the time they got close to Telchuk Mountain, they would be at the extreme edge of a Wasp's range from the LZs back behind Accord lines. And there might be too much action there for the general to actually release them.

"If we set up the Wasp people back about 150 klicks, that would ease things all around," Dezo said. "Of course, we'd have to leave a few mudders to mind their security."

"Setting up that far off might help us deceive the Heggies as to our destination just a bit longer as well," Kenneck said. "Say, here." He pointed at the mapboard. "They might think we're heading for this town, Justice. Even if it only slows the Heggies down for ten minutes, it might make a difference."

"Colonel Stossen!" The call came over the radio. Stossen lowered his helmet to answer.

"Colonel, this is Sergeant Nimz, 3rd recon. We have bogies, a Heggie convoy. Looks like twelve floater trucks loaded with troops and five Novas."

"What's your position?" Stossen asked.

Nimz read off his map coordinates, and Stossen noted the spot on the mapboard. Third recon was on the left flank, a thousand meters off the point of the diamond.

"Hang on a minute." Stossen raised his visor and told the others what the reccers had found. "Can we take a chance on letting them go?"

Kenneck got down on one knee to get closer to the mapboard. He traced the probable line of the Heggie advance.

"Too close, sir. They stay on that heading, they'll come between 1st recon and George Company, too close to both for us to hope that they won't spot us. At that range, the Novas should be able to detect all of the metal we've got with us, heat tarps or not."

The others nodded, and Stossen echoed the gesture before lowering his visor. "Keep contact, Nimz, but try to remain unobserved until we decide how to take them out."

CHAPTER 4

"On your feet!" Joe didn't quite shout into his radio, but it was near enough. He was slow getting to his own feet. He had managed less than thirty minutes of sleep before Lieutenant Keye woke him. It had started to rain. The inside of Joe's foxhole was already starting to get sloppy with mud.

"We're going Heggie hunting," Keye had said.

"We're hunting them?" Joe had managed while he struggled to get his mind fully alert.

"There are Heggies close. Looks like a mounted infantry company and a tank company moving together, not more than twelve hundred meters out from us. Check your mapboard. Their position and course are plotted in red."

Joe ordered his platoon up while he fumbled for his mapboard, switched it on, and adjusted the coordinates to center the 13th's position. He knew he should have done that earlier, as soon as they stopped, but he had forgotten.

As soon as he had the Heggie troops on the board, he linked to the platoon's noncoms and told them what was in the wind.

"We're going on foot, ain't we?" Sauv Degtree of third squad asked.

"Lieutenant didn't say different, so I'd say so," Joe replied. "They're too close. They'd hear the Heyers as soon as they fired up."

"What's the plan?" Ezra asked. "We gonna have any heavy support?"

"I'll let you know as soon as I find out," Joe promised. "Just get everybody ready to move, two minutes ago."

The first sergeant came on the company command channel then. "First platoon on point. Second leads the right flank, third the left. We've got twenty minutes to get into position before the Havocs start firing." He hesitated before he added, "And, if we're lucky, a few Wasps."

"Anything to take care of those Novas," Joe said. He was thinking aloud, forgetting that he was on an open circuit.

"Don't count on them wasting all of them," Walker said. "We've got plenty of Vrerchs. Use them if you have to." The Vrerch was a shoulder-operated video-guided missile, equally adept for surface-to-surface or surface-to-air use. "We may have to stop a few trucks as well. Those Heggie mudders are riding."

"Hope they've been as uncomfortable riding as we have," a soft, anonymous voice said. There were no laughs.

"Let's just see that they walk home, and not many of them," Walker said. "And be careful out there. Third recon is marking the Heggies. George Company will be moving around in front of them as soon as the big guns open up. Now, move 'em out."

Joe had been watching his men form up during the conversation. There was no loose chat among them, not even complaints about the weather. Even though they were dead tired, the men got their weapons ready and assembled by fire team and squad. A word over the platoon channel and a quick point set them on the right course. The rest of Echo started moving as well. Keye, his small headquarters staff, and the heavy weapons platoon would be in the center of the wedge.

Echo didn't have far to travel before they left the cover of the trees they had camped under. Close to the woods, the grass was short, no more than knee-high. Within another fifty meters, though, the grass rose chest-high, or more. In some areas, the men were walking through grass whose flowering heads towered above their helmets.

It provided a deceptive sense of security. Grass tops waving in ways that they shouldn't could pinpoint men as readily as a strobing beacon overhead. And soggy grass wouldn't move back into position as quickly. They would leave a clear trail to any observer in the air.

"Watch your intervals," Joe warned. That was such a routine admonishment that he scarcely thought about it. "Keep those columns narrow. Don't bend any more of this grass than necessary."

For the third time in five minutes, Joe glanced at the power gauge on his rifle. The needle hadn't moved a whisker. Since he hadn't fired the weapon, the needle shouldn't have moved. He dragged a sleeve across his visor to get the water off of it. Working in the rain, that could be a frequent chore.

Lieutenant Keye passed along word for the platoon sergeants to listen in on one of the tactical radio channels. Someone from one of the recon platoons was providing a running commentary of Heggie movements. The reccers were close enough to give head counts on the number of Heggies in some of the trucks.

Almost like they're hanging on the blower skirts, Joe thought. He shook his head, just slightly amazed at how well the reccers did their job.

Echo didn't need the full twenty minutes to get into position. Seventeen minutes after Keye gave the noncoms their orders, the company moved into a skirmish line and started advancing more slowly. Two of the enemy tanks were in sight, less than two hundred meters away. The main Heggie column was just beyond those Novas and moving slowly. It looked as if they were stopping.

"Down!" Joe told his platoon, relaying an order from the lieutenant. "Wait for the Havocs."

Joe took the safety off on his zipper as soon as he had a comfortable prone firing position. At this range, the Armanoc wouldn't be of much use except to suppress accurate enemy small arms fire. When wire was whizzing around your head, you couldn't tell how far away it was coming from, and the Dupuy rocket-assist rifles, the snipers' "cough" gun, could provide enough casualties to keep the enemy from being certain.

The wait for the start of the artillery barrage seemed far longer than three minutes. Joe concentrated on breathing regularly. It was too easy to forget, to hold his breath. Experience did not preclude pre-battle jitters. Joe *knew* what the next minutes might bring.

Finally, he heard the sounds of the Havocs firing. There was no way in the universe to put a silencer on a 200mm cannon. Even at a distance of several kilometers, the sound of thirty-two howitzers firing at once could be heard. Joe suspected that even the Heggies would be able to hear over the noises made by the tanks and trucks they were riding in.

Maybe the big guns'll get all of these Heggies, Joe thought, knowing it was wishful thinking. The Havocs might be accurate and lethal, but the Heggie trucks and tanks were still moving, if slowly, and they were dispersed enough to give them *some* chance. There always seemed to be work left for the mudders. No matter how massive the artillery preparation, some soldiers always survived . . . often, a majority of them.

The prairie in front of Echo erupted in a sudden taste of hell. The Havoc rounds made little noise coming in, and it was only in the last fraction of a second that there was even a chance of getting a fleeting glimpse of one of the shells. Thirty-two suspended plasma rounds went off together, no more than a second separating the first from the last. Several rockets, slower and more easily visible, came in. It looked as if at least two Wasps had come to contribute to the fight. Fiery clouds rose and expanded. Joe ducked just as he saw one of the tanks explode. The turret seemed to rise five meters above the chassis below it. For a few seconds, after the first thunder of the explosions, Joe could hear nothing but a hollow ringing in his ears. As that cleared, he could hear the crackling sound of burning grass. *That* didn't last long. The prairie grass was too damp to burn well.

But not all of the fires went out. There were tanks and trucks burning. Their hydrogen fuel might burn without visible flames, but there was more to the vehicles than fuel.

"Let's go!" Keye ordered over the company all-hands channel. Joe repeated the order on his platoon channel, even though 2nd platoon was already getting to its feet.

Moving forward, Joe could see the damage that had already been inflicted on the Heggies. All five of the Nova tanks were out of action, destroyed or burning. But only two of the twelve trucks appeared to have been hit. Joe could see soldiers pouring out of most of the others, diving into the grass.

"We've still got a fight here," Joe warned his men as he let off a short burst toward the nearest enemy truck. Heggies started firing as well.

"Get some RPGs in there, quick," Joe said. Rocket-propelled grenades. The enemy was in range for those. One man in each fire team carried several of the disposable tubes. Even before any of the men in 2nd platoon managed to comply, there were grenades arcing toward the enemy trucks from some of the other platoons.

"Follow the grenades in," Joe ordered. "By squad and fire team."

Within each squad, one fire team hurried forward a few meters while the other team covered them with enough wire to suppress enemy fire—to at least keep it from being overly accurate. Then the other team moved, leapfrogging. All of the line platoons were operating the same way.

And Echo started to take casualties.

Joe moved with Mort Jaiffer's fire team. The second time they moved forward, Joe saw someone fall in third squad. The man got back up, staggered forward two steps, then went down again. Before Joe, or anyone else, could call, third squad's medic was at the man's side. After a hurried examination, the medic made a thumbs-up gesture: the wound wasn't serious.

Joe had scarcely got back to his feet the next time before he felt wire hitting him. Spent wire. At ranges still well over a hundred meters, it took a lot of concentrated wire, or perfectly placed wire, to do serious damage. Accord net armor could prevent most penetration at that range. But the tiny bits of wire, smaller than staples, could still hurt. They could still leave nasty bruises.

Joe went down again, moving forward another couple of meters on his hands and knees. Around him, the rest of the fire team was doing the same. Some Heggie gunner had them perfectly sighted. Getting down for a moment was the best way to throw off his aim.

The other team went forward. More RPG rounds were sent ahead. A few came back—Heggie grenades. There was nothing to do for that but hug the ground and hope that you were out of the kill zone of the nearest blasts. The closer to the ground you could get, the narrower the kill radius of a Schlinal grenade was. Most of the shrapnel went up and out in a rapidly expanding cone.

Three more enemy trucks had been hit. Joe glanced skyward and saw one of the Wasps climbing toward the clouds, streaking back toward the main Accord lines. It quickly disappeared from sight. *We're on our own again,* he thought. He blinked a couple of times. As long as the enemy tanks were accounted for, it shouldn't matter. Infantry versus infantry, and it looked as if the 13th had the advantage of numbers, with two line companies and two recon platoons closing in on a single company of Heggies.

"Get that heat tarp back in place," Eustace Ponks said as he popped his hatch. The Havocs had moved a couple of kilometers after finishing their part in the attack on the Heggie column. They were under trees again, but not in the same place they had been before. On the other side of the turret, Simon was getting out as quickly as Eustace. In the back, the other two members of the crew were already out, starting to unfold the thermal tarp. The engines had been run, the gun had been fired. For the next hour or more, the Fat Turtle would glow in infrared, bright enough to be spotted from orbit.

The tarp was lightweight, but bulky enough that it took some handling. The men worked as quickly as possible. As soon as they had the tarp spread, they popped pegs into the ground at the corners and hurried off toward a tree twenty-five meters from the gun, as much out of the light rain as possible. The thermal tarps were not quite 100 percent effective, and a Havoc was too tempting a target standing still for its crew to feel comfortable staying in, or close to, it.

The men didn't bother to dig foxholes. They were as far away from the action as anyone in the 13th could be at the moment, with a lot of mudders between them and the enemy. The rest of Basset Battery was spread around them at the edges of the wooded area, no gun *too* close to any of the others.

"This can't be what we came out here for," Simon said over the crew's private radio channel. Even though they were close enough to speak directly to one another, they routinely used their helmet radios, whispering. Gun crews didn't have the same sort of battle helmets that the infantry used. Gun helmets had no visors. In a Havoc, they didn't need night-vision systems or visual overlays.

"Hard telling what we really came out here for," Eustace replied.

"They said more'n a thousand klicks," Jimmy Ysinde protested. "We ain't come half of that."

"Whatever. We'll find out soon enough. We hit those Heggies. The Heggies'll hit back just as fast. You can bet on that." Eustace rarely worried about anything beyond the needs of his own gun or, occasionally, of the entire battery when they were operating together. Mostly, he saw other guns as dangerous companions. The more Havocs that operated close together, the more inviting a target they made.

"Sure was nice while nobody was botherin' us," Simon said. "Now we've waved a red flag for 'em. Even if we took out this whole batch, they'll send more after. Boems, probably." Artillerymen hated enemy aircraft. They had no defense against air power.

"Wouldn't have lasted anyway," Eustace said. "Soon enough, they'd have come after us. That must be what that convoy was out here for." He got up to his knees and looked around. They were too far away from the fighting to hear anything but the occasional soft crump of a grenade or rocket exploding.

Eustace was looking directly at Basset one, Lieutenant Ritchey's gun, when it exploded. Ritchey and his crew weren't in their Havoc, though. Like the other crews, they had put distance between them and their gun as soon as they had covered it.

"Move out," Ritchey ordered over the battery channel. "Forget us. We're going to join the colonel and headquarters. Get the rest of the guns moving. *Now!*"

The crewmen of the Fat Turtle were on their feet with Ritchey's first word, running to their Havoc, looking into the air as if they might see an enemy shell coming in.

"There must be more'n that one batch out here," Eustace shouted at his men. "Recon said we got all of the Novas with that bunch."

"Tell me about it," Simon muttered. He was panting heavily already. "I knew the crap was gonna fly."

"Get the tarp stowed. Simon, you get inside and fire up the engines." Eustace was already ripping one corner of the thermal shield free. He didn't worry about the pegs. If they came with the tarp, fine; if not, they'd make do the next time. There was no time to fold the tarp. It was simply wadded up and crammed into its small storage locker.

"Get us moving," Eustace ordered before he had even climbed into his seat on the right side of the turret. Simon slipped the treads into gear, and Eustace held on for a moment, looking around before sliding into his place. Another shell burst, off near where Basset four had been until ten seconds before. Four had already moved far enough to escape damage from the blast.

"Which way?" Simon asked.

"Straight ahead for now." Eustace clipped his safety harness in place. "Then we'll worry about putting distance between us and the others. Just move this bucket."

They heard several more explosions, close together, back where the battery had been parked.

At least their intelligence is a little *behind the time,* Eustace thought. He swallowed heavily and got on the radio, looking for orders and information. Where to go and what to shoot.

• • •

"Where are they?" Colonel Stossen demanded.

Bal Kenneck was busy on his radio links, looking for the answer. They were under the tarp of the colonel's makeshift command post again. Around them, the rain was starting to get a little heavier, but it was no cloudburst. Reports from the companies farther west, near the point, said that it was getting very heavy there.

Teu Ingels and Dezo Parks were also busy on the radio, Dezo trying to get updated intelligence from CIC, Teu contacting the various companies and recon platoons, trying to determine just where the new Heggie fire was coming from. Even with all three staff officers working, it took nearly five minutes before anyone had an answer.

"The tank fire came from here." Parks pointed to a spot on the mapboard off the right rear quarter of the 13th. "About three klicks out past 4th recon. CIC monitored the muzzle flashes but needed time to get an eye trained on the area. It looks like another column about equal to the one we're engaging on the other side."

"Who's closest to them, Bravo?" Stossen asked.

"Besides 4th recon, yes," Teu said. "And Fox has the point on that side of the diamond. They're not too much farther off."

"Get Digby and Jacobi." Captain Digby commanded Fox. Captain Jacobi, the newest captain in the 13th, had Bravo. "Tell them to move to intercept, pincer these Heggies. And get the Havocs busy."

Ingels got busy on the radio. Stossen turned to the other two.

"If there are two columns that close, there might be a third, the rest of two battalions, infantry and armor. Or more. If so, I want them found before they start hitting us as well. Get patrols out, Dezo. Bal, get back to CIC. Tell them what we're looking for. If there are Novas on the move, CIC should be able to pick them up." The Combat Information Center on the flagship was the only outside help the 13th could count on. With orbiting spyeyes and the long-range sensors on the ships, CIC could provide a lot of information . . . on anything they could see. The problem on Jordan was the limited number of spyeyes the Accord had been able to maintain in orbit.

The seven remaining Wasps of the 13th's Blue Flight headed northwest. They were only halfway to their targets when a half dozen Schlinal Boem fighters intercepted them.

"Straight into them," Slee Reston ordered. "We've got to get past as fast as we can." Most times, he might almost have enjoyed a good mix-up. Like most fighter pilots, Slee was supremely confident of his own ability, and equally confident that his plane was at least on a par with anything the enemy could throw at him. But now they had a vital ground support mission. The rest of the 13th was out in the middle of nowhere, "surrounded" by Heggies. That the 13th still had, apparently, a considerable edge in numbers made no difference to Slee. His flight had a mission to perform, and this fight was just slowing them down.

Blue Flight had the edge in altitude, though that was no longer as major an advantage as it had been before fighters were powered by antigrav engines. The Heggie interceptors rose quickly, aimed directly for the Wasps. At a distance of six kilometers, the two sides exchanged their first missiles . . . then went into violent evasive maneuvers while they launched their spectrum of countermeasures. Both sides used fire-and-forget missiles. Once they had been shown their target, they needed no further guidance from the launching aircraft.

In Blue two, Zel Paitcher dropped decoys and started his Wasp moving up, straight up. After two seconds, he reversed both drives and the Wasp sunk like a stone, the gee-load forcing blood to his head. He held the power dive as long as he could stand the strain, then flipped the Wasp end for end and went back to level flight—toward the Boems. Going into a slight climb, he launched two more missiles toward Boems that were still struggling to evade the first volley.

"Close to cannon range," Slee ordered. "We've got to save missiles for the tanks."

The Wasps converged on the enemy planes as best they could. Almost miraculously, none of the planes on either side had been hit during the exchange of missiles.

Zel picked his target and flipped his weapon selector over to the 25mm cannon in the nose of his plane. The Schlinal fighters also carried cannons, but they were single-barreled and fired solid 40mm rounds, either explosive or armor piercing—somewhat better suited to this kind of fight.

But the Boems did not engage. They turned off and worked to stay just beyond the effective range of the Wasp guns. Their course was perpendicular to the vector the Wasps had been on before interception, taking them away from the 13th on the ground.

"Decoys," Slee said. "They're just here to keep us from helping the mudders. Break off."

When Blue Flight turned, so did the Boems.

"Full throttle," Slee said. "Let's see how far they chase us. Watch out for missiles."

CHAPTER 5

Smoke grenades, white phosphorus grenades, fragmentation grenades . . . and wire by the meter. Since neither side had been dug in, it was a bloody little fight. Once Echo Company closed to within eighty meters of the Heggies infantry, both sides started taking significant casualties.

Forward movement had to be measured in centimeters. One fire team of a squad would cover the other while it crawled forward just a little bit. Then movement slowed even more. One fire team moved while three provided covering fire. More RPGs were shot into the section of tall grass that hid the enemy. The grass itself was being rapidly pruned by all of the metal ripping through it.

Vision was limited. The burning white phosphorus even obscured the infrared sensors of helmet visors. At least the helmets provided better protection against enemy wire than the net armor in fatigues did.

"Keep your fire low," Joe Baerclau warned his platoon. "Third recon is somewhere on the other side of the Heggies, and Delta somewhere to our right."

Joe was in the middle of first squad, where he might have been if he were still only squad leader instead of platoon sergeant. The difference now was that he usually moved with the squad's second fire team rather than the first. The first team was to his left—Ezra Frain, Al Bergon, Pit Tymphe, and Olly Wytten. The second team was to his right—Mort Jaiffer, Wiz

Mackey, and Carl Eames. The new men were spaced between veterans.

There was less room between men than Joe would have liked, but there was no easy remedy for that just now.

"Ez, you got any room on your left to spread us out?" Joe asked over a private channel.

"Negative," Ezra replied. "Second squad's even closer."

"Mort, how about . . . ," Joe started. There was a loud rattle of wire hitting his helmet, and before that ended, he felt a burning pain in his left shoulder. The combined impacts left him too stunned to talk. For an instant, they also left him too stunned to feel the pain of the wound in his shoulder.

The universe closed in on Joe. The sounds of wire impacting on the helmet had produced an almost deafening noise inside the helmet. The almost simultaneous shoulder wound brought a moment of numbness. When the pain followed, Joe gritted his teeth so hard to keep from screaming that he thought several must break. He sucked in a deep, involuntary breath. His eyes teared up and his vision clouded over. All, almost, in the blink of an eye. Then, through still-clenched teeth, Joe said, "Al, I'm hit."

"That you, Sarge?" Al Bergon asked.

"Yes."

"Hang on. I'll get to you as quick as I can."

Joe switched channels. "Sauv, you've got the platoon. I'm hit."

There was a slight pause before Degtree, the next senior sergeant in the platoon, replied, "How bad?"

"Don't know. My shoulder. Tell the lieutenant."

"I heard," Lieutenant Keye said. "Just stay low till the medic gets to you. This is almost over."

Almost over, Joe thought. Then, for several seconds, he hovered near the edge of unconsciousness. But he didn't fall, and he was brought back from the brink by a hand on his right arm and Al Bergon's voice.

"I'm here, Sarge. Hang tough. This doesn't look too bad."

Zel had ceased to have any awareness of his body. He was simply part of his Wasp, a command and control nodule acting and reacting. His hands and feet on the controls were merely cogs in the intricate machinery. They were no more or less part of him than the 25mm cannons, the batteries, or the antigrav drives. Eyes and ears collected data. His brain processed it and produced responses.

Although the controls of a Wasp appeared quite similar to those of a conventional aircraft, there were important differences. The pedals were throttles in a Wasp. The farther they were depressed, the faster the Wasp went. Switches on the control yoke could reverse the direction of thrust. Movements of the wheel, forward and back as well as clockwise or the reverse, controlled climb and dive, and "wing" angle. The proper combination of movements could flip a Wasp end for end, a dangerous maneuver at high speeds because of the gee-load it could subject the pilot to.

The flight of Boems had continued to dog Blue Flight all of the way to the air over the 13th. Only at the end had they closed enough to force another confrontation.

As much as possible, Zel saved his rockets for the ground support mission. He used his cannons to keep the enemy fighters away. The new Wasp tailgun helped immeasurably. The Boems had to stand off and use rockets, and the Wasps' countermeasures had kept any of those from finding Blue two. So far. Not everyone had been so lucky. The numbers in the air were more nearly equal now, six Wasps and five Boems. And both sides were getting low on rockets.

Zel tipped his Wasp over to the right, standing it on edge, then pushed through a quick roll. That gave him a shot at a Nova on the ground while it turned him back toward the Boem that had been dogging him for the past minute. The Boem came almost to a stop before it flipped and dove, away and to the left. Zel thought that the Boem must be out of rockets.

Give me a shot, Zel thought. He glanced at his "remaining munitions" display. Two rockets and twenty seconds of ammo for the forward cannon.

"One rocket for you, one for another tank," Zel whispered. He armed a rocket while his target acquisition system tried to get a lock on the Boem.

"Closer." Zel pushed both throttles to the floor. He *was* closing on the Boem. The Schlinal pilot's braking maneuver before he flipped had cost him precious fractions of a second.

"Closer." Zel heard the twin clicks as his TA system established its lock. He saw the decoy that the Boem launched and heard the "translated" chatter of its electronic countermeasures. "A couple seconds of that and you're finished," Zel said, unaware of the death's-head grin that had taken possession of his face. With enough time to analyze the enemy's ECM, the Wasp's rocket would be able to adjust for them.

"Now!" Zel shouted the word, but it came out after he punched the trigger on his rocket. He eased back on his throttles and made a shallow turn to line up on another tank. He armed his last missile, reminding himself to switch the selector back to cannon as soon as the rocket was away.

By the time the first missile hit the Boem, a solid hit just behind the cockpit, Zel had already locked his last missile onto one of three tanks remaining below.

That tank exploded *before* Zel's rocket reached it, hit by a shell from a Havoc ten kilometers away.

"Damn! I could have saved that." Zel had already forgotten about the Boem, whose pieces were still falling out of the sky.

The skirmish was over less than an hour after the first shots had been fired. The first Heggie column had been hit hardest. Those who had not been killed were captured. Few, if any, managed to escape. In the other two columns, the results were mixed. A few tanks, and perhaps two-thirds of the infantry, were able to disengage, though the infantry was now all on foot.

Lieutenant Keye was still trying to get his breathing back to normal. He could feel that his face was flushed. His lungs were pumping hard. He stood looking at the forty prisoners that Echo had captured.

The Heggies had been herded together, stripped of weapons, ammunition, helmets, uniforms, and boots. The weapons and ammunition were being loaded aboard several of the Heyer APCs. An extra reserve, just in case: that was one lesson the 13th had learned on Porter. The helmets were taken and (except for two that Intelligence wanted) destroyed to keep these Heggies out of communication with their army. The boots and uniforms were also destroyed, to make the Heggie mudders too vulnerable to have any real thoughts of following and making more difficulty. No uniforms meant no body armor. No boots meant a slower, and more uncomfortable, trip back to their lines. The 13th was not equipped to carry enemy prisoners with it.

The Schlinal wounded were treated alongside the 13th's own casualties. There were a couple of Schlinal medics in the group of prisoners. They were able to cope with their own.

"I've got our count, Lieutenant," Sauv Degtree reported.

Keye blinked and sucked in a deep breath before he said, "Let me have it."

"Three dead." He listed the names. Two were from fourth squad, the other from his own, third. Keye closed his eyes while he listened to the roster. "Six wounded, only one bad enough to need time in a trauma tube. Doc Eddles is taking care of him now." Again, Degtree listed the names. Again, Keye closed his eyes.

"Where's the Bear?" Keye asked.

Degtree pointed. "They've already taken him back. He's probably sitting in the Heyer by now."

"His shoulder?"

"Bergon said it wasn't near as bad as it might have been. Bone chips but no fracture. Fair amount of bleeding. Doc may have to dig out the chips if a soaker doesn't work them out." That depended, mostly, on how large the fragments were. If they were too big, the medical nanobots wouldn't be able to transport the fragments to the surface quickly enough and minor surgery would be required.

"The reccers will guard the prisoners until we move out," Keye said, relaying word he was just getting from Major Parks. "Let's get everybody back. Time to hit the trail again."

Al Bergon had tried to get Joe Baerclau to lie still and let himself be carried to the APC, but the Bear had refused. Once there was a soaker on his wounded shoulder and the analgesic had started to work, he insisted on walking.

"Save the litter for someone who needs it," he said.

"You've lost blood, Sarge," Al protested. "There's always shock with this kind of wound. Give the soaker time to do its job."

"I'm not crippled. I've been hurt worse than this before. And don't go trying to hit me with a knockout patch either. That's an order."

Al bit back a reply. The order was not valid. As medic, he could slap the patch on anyway. But he would also have to put up with an angry sergeant after it wore off. Al looked closely at Baerclau's face, checking pupil dilation and how well the Bear's eyes tracked his finger.

"Okay, we'll chance it," he said after stalling for as long as he dared. "But, so help me, Sarge, one hint of swaying or anything else, and down you go, regardless."

Baerclau glowered at Al but didn't speak. He simply put his helmet back on, picked up his rifle, and gestured in the direction of the APCs. Al and the rest of first squad started moving off with him.

I have been hurt worse than this, Joe told himself. But that one time, he hadn't walked away under his own power. It had been thirty-six hours before he had done *any* walking. This was the first time in months that Joe had even thought about that earlier wound. There weren't even any scars to remind him. Medical nanobots left no evidence of wounds or their repair work.

Joe hadn't walked ten steps before he started to question the wisdom of his decision. He was sweating profusely, and he felt light-headed. There was no pain left, though. The soaker had his shoulder so numb that he would scarcely have felt anything if the arm fell off.

He walked slowly, unwilling to give Al the slightest excuse for putting him on a stretcher. Now that he had made his choice, Joe was not about to reverse it. As long as he was conscious and able to stay on his feet, he would walk. After all, it wasn't all *that* far back to the APCs, less than a kilometer.

I could do a klick with both legs blown off at the knee, Joe told himself. He saw nothing ludicrous in the image, didn't recognize that it showed a dangerous loss of alertness. He did stop for a moment. He looked up into the sky. Moving with exaggerated care, he turned twice so that he could see all of the sky around him.

"Those Heggie fighters are gone," he said, still on the channel that Al Bergon was monitoring.

"Yes, Sarge, they're gone. You ready to ride for a bit?"

Baerclau turned to glare at Al again. "I'm getting better every second. I didn't need a ride before. I don't need it now."

It took twenty-five minutes to cover the kilometer. Joe did sit then, in the rear hatch of the APC.

"I'm going to have Doc Eddles look at that shoulder," Al said, lifting the edge of the soaker to look himself. "If the bone chips are too big, he'll have to go in."

Joe didn't reply. After the walk, he was having serious difficulty just staying conscious. Al seemed to swim around in front of him. For a time, Joe felt as if the entire world were spinning around him.

"Even if he doesn't, I'm going to be right next to you in there when we start up again." Al again looked into the sergeant's eyes with a tiny flashlight, then shook his head and threw the light down. "Damn it! I never should have let you walk. I'm going to have to start a drip to replace the fluid you left on the grass."

He didn't wait for the Bear to say anything but got the plastic pouch out and connected it. The bag containing the intravenous solution had separate compartments within it. The largest held a simple saline solution. The other held specialized medical nanobots and the other components they would need to turn the salt water into blood that would match Joe's own perfectly. Al taped the bag in place over Joe's arm. There was no need to put it higher; the nanobots would pump the solution in, even against twice the surface gravity of Jordan.

Joe Baerclau passed out when the needle went into his arm. Al used the opportunity to slap a four-hour sleep patch on his neck.

CHAPTER 6

The 13th buried its dead, marking the location so that the bodies could be retrieved later, if that were possible. The wounded were patched up. Four of the Heyers were used as ambulances. A Heyer could hold only three men on stretchers or in portable trauma tubes. The healthy soldiers displaced from those APCs were crowded into other vehicles.

The rains that had reached the battlefield strengthened and followed the 13th once it started off to the northwest again. The treads on Heyers and Havocs chewed up wet ground and grass, leaving a clear trail for anyone to follow.

Once the 13th was moving, Colonel Stossen and his staff continued conferring over the radio. The communications net was as nearly secure as possible. The various channels were not assigned to specific frequencies. Instead, each channel was switched among as many as a dozen different frequencies according to computer programming. With frequencies being automatically changed as often as three times a second, there was little chance that an eavesdropper would hear enough of any conversation to make sense of it. Even a captured helmet would do little good. Any officer or noncom could disable its communications links by code. Keeping track of helmets was one of the routine duties of squad leaders and their assistants.

"They know we're out here," Stossen said shortly after the 13th started moving again. "It's just luck that our reccers spotted them before they got to us this time. Next time, we might not be so lucky. What can we do to improve our odds?"

"The fleet can't keep enough spyeyes in orbit to do much better," Bal Kenneck said. "Last I heard from CIC, the eyes last an average of six hours before the Heggies shoot them down. That leaves a lot of gaps. When one eye goes out, it takes time to get another into position. Of course," he added, "we're shooting down their spyeyes just as quickly, maybe a little more so."

"How do we make up the slack?" Stossen asked.

"The best way would be to get more Wasp flights out here," Kenneck said. "We can put our recon platoons out a little farther, but there's not a hell of a lot more they can do from inside Heyers, and we're traveling too fast to put them on foot."

"We can't use the Wasps for recon, not on a regular basis," Teu Ingels said. "We're going to have trouble getting them for combat support even. There's simply too much work and too few Wasps. The ones that came out this time were chased all of the way out by Boems. We can't afford the losses for recon."

"You're telling me there's nothing we can do?" Stossen asked.

"Not much," Ingels said. "We're pretty much limited to what we get from CIC."

"And that's what the trouble was before," Dezo Parks said, his first contribution to the conversation.

"Unless and until we get out and walk," Ingels said. "I, uh, presume that's out of the question until we get a lot closer to our objective?"

"Absolutely," Stossen agreed. "All we can do, then, is push on as fast as these mixers will go."

"Unfortunately," Kenneck said.

"Give the order, Dezo," Stossen said. "Full out. Spread the reccers out a little more, and farther out from the main body."

"Too far's no good either," Kenneck interrupted. "Too much chance for the Heggies to slip in between, like they almost did this time."

"Looks like all we can do is go like hell until dark, make our course change, and hope the Heggies don't have anything close enough to pick us up until it's too late for an intercept," Ingels said.

"And we've still got to find time to rest the men for a few hours," Parks added. "Soon as they come down from this fight, they're going to be more beat than ever. They can't go forever on stimtabs."

Stossen closed his eyes for a moment. Sleep . . . what's that?

"If we're going to get any at all," he said finally, "it won't be much. After we make our turn, we'll go to ground, get the thermal tarps spread. Maybe that'll help throw the Heggies off."

But he couldn't help thinking, *Or give them a chance to catch us.*

It was difficult making a proper examination while the APC pounded along at forty-five kilometers per hour, but the sleep patch on Joe Baerclau would run out soon, and Al Bergon wanted to get what he had to do done before the Bear woke. As soon as the sergeant realized that he had been out for four hours, he was going to be mad, no matter how necessary the knockout had been.

Al pulled the soaker off of Baerclau's shoulder. The wound was almost completely healed over. The new skin was an angry pink, but the cuts had healed. What Al was interested in were the three tiny pimples that had formed near the exit wound on the back of the shoulder. He swabbed them with antiseptic, then used a pair of tweezers to pop them and extract the tiny bone chips that the nanobots had deposited there. After another antiseptic swab, he put a small soaker over the area of the exit wound. The entrance wound no longer needed a dressing.

"Well, how is he?" Ezra Frain asked.

"Okay," Al said. "By the time he wakes up, even his blood should be replaced."

"Good as new and mad as hell," Mort Jaiffer observed. "He's not going to like the way you zapped him."

"I didn't zap him, he passed out," Al said.

"If you think he'll buy that, let me sell you my return-trip pass, good for any shuttle up to the fleet," Wiz Mackey said with a sour laugh.

The squad's three new men just sat and listened. None of them felt confident enough around the veterans yet to get into that sort of discussion without an obvious invitation. It didn't matter that all of the new men had already seen combat with the squad, that they were no longer "raw" rookies. In a fight, each of them was paired with one of the veterans, but when they weren't in a fight, they were—mostly—on their own.

"You did the right thing, Bergon," Lieutenant Keye said from his position at the front splat gun. "The Bear gives you any grief, I'll take care of it."

"Thank you, sir."

Al looked at the time line on his visor, then looked at Baerclau again. Al hadn't checked the exact time when he slapped on the sleep patch, but it couldn't be good for more than another five minutes. Of course, there was nothing that said that Baerclau *had* to wake up precisely when the medication expired. He had been tired enough to sleep longer than that without help.

Just then the Heyer took a particularly hard jounce and Bergon grinned through gritted teeth. If the Bear could sleep through *this* ride, he could sleep through anything.

A soft groan did escape Joe's lips, though his eyes didn't open right away. Another two minutes passed before that happened. His gaze was vacant, uncomprehending, not as it would have been if he were waking normally. Joe was a veteran mudder. On campaign, he came awake instantly alert if there were the slightly possibility of enemy activity anywhere near.

After a time, Joe blinked—once slowly and then, after a short pause, several times in quick succession.

"What?" he managed. But his throat was dry. His voice cracked. Al put a canteen to the Bear's lips.

"We're back under way," Al explained while Joe took a short sip of water.

Joe took a deep breath and closed his eyes again for a moment while his mind tried to close the gap between his last memories and the present.

"How long?" he asked finally.

"Four hours, right on the button," Al said. "The bone chips are out of your shoulder, the wounds are almost healed, and you're fit for duty again."

Joe moved his left arm, experimentally at first, then with more vigor. There was no pain or restriction. Then he turned his head to look.

"Sure tore hell out of my fatigues." There was more, but now, with his head clearing, there was little chance that he would complain about being zapped for four hours. That had been the injury speaking.

"Don't sweat it," Ezra said. "I'll slap a weaver patch over it and you'll look good as new in an hour."

Lieutenant Keye turned and pointed at his helmet. Joe put his on to hear what the lieutenant had to say.

"You really feeling fit?"

Joe took time to think it over before he answered. "Yes, sir, especially with the nap. Anyone else have a chance to sleep?"

"Only what little they could get in here."

"Little is right," Joe said. "We're not going to be much good in a fight if the men don't get some downtime first."

"Can't be helped. We're trying to avoid another fight. After dark, we might get a couple of hours."

"What's the situation now, sir?"

"We've got that second river crossing coming up soon. That's likely to be our most vulnerable time until we get near where we're going. Recon's already at the river and beyond. Last word I had was that there's no sign of Heggies."

"We didn't get much advance word the last time," Joe commented. "The Heggies were almost on top of us before we knew they were there."

"I *think* we're getting better dope now. Nobody wants a repeat of this morning."

Joe turned on the bench and opened one of the firing ports in the side wall. It was still raining outside, heavily. The sky was almost dark enough for dusk. Joe checked the time, saw that there were still another four hours before sunset, and shook his head. Then he looked at Al again.

"Maybe you should have hit everybody with sleep patches. That way, maybe we'd all be rested." While he talked, Joe ran his helmet's diagnostics program. The helmet had taken quite a few wire hits. Then he checked his rifle.

"If I was sure we had the time, I'd do it now," Al said, knowing that the Bear wasn't serious. "Leave you on watch while the rest of us catch up."

There were only four Wasps of Blue Flight in the air. Two had been destroyed. Two were being held back to help in the defense of the main Accord foothold on Jordan. The fighting back there had been raging for more than twenty-one hours. A joke so old that its origins could no longer be traced was being repeated with distressing frequency. *"The situation here is quite fluid." "What's that mean?" "It means we're up the creek."*

Zel wasn't certain that he really understood what was going on, but he had spent more than half of the past twenty-one hours in the air. He decided that he was ahead of the game if he even remembered his name. Along much of the Accord perimeter, there was no clearly definable front left. In some places, the Accord had made advances. Elsewhere, they had been forced to retreat. Units were out of contact with their flanking units. Several times, Wasps had been asked to do flybys just to locate friendly units.

Zel yawned, then blinked and took a careful scan of his heads-up display and the two monitors on the panel below it. With a little luck, they'd get out and back this time without any fighting. *Cover the river crossing for the mudders. Look for any sign of another Heggie force moving toward them. Do what you have to do*. Simple, if vague, instructions. But recon work was something of a break.

As long as no Boems showed up to contest the operation.

"There's the river," Slee said. "To the right, angled about ten degrees right of your centerline."

Zel looked at the mapboard monitor rather than out the canopy. The monitor gave a clearer view.

"How far are we from the ford?" Zel asked.

"Shouldn't be more than twenty klicks."

"How far out do we stooge around?" was Zel's next question.

"We'll do a grid search out to thirty klicks around the ford," Slee said. He and Zel would take the near side of the river, the other two Wasps the far side.

"We've already got a few Heyers across," Slee reminded the others. "Reccers there to guard the crossing point."

"How many Heyers?" Zel asked.

There was a pause before Slee had the answer. "Eleven. Two full recon platoons, spread out in a semicircle."

"There," Zel said. "Picking up those blips now." He counted carefully. Eleven—no more, and no less. *Now let's see if they've got any company,* he thought as he turned Blue two onto the next leg of its search pattern.

Colonel Stossen made certain that his APC crossed the river early, with the infantry companies that followed the first two Havoc batteries. The word from the Wasps overhead was encouraging. They hadn't spotted anything anywhere near.

"Get across as fast as possible," Stossen told the commanders of the remaining companies and support units. "Every minute we're sitting here, the more danger we're in."

The first men across were out of their Heyers now, in a two-tiered defensive line. There might not be Heggies close . . . or again, there might be.

On another channel, Stossen told his exec. "I want to know the instant we've got half of the Team across."

Switching channels again, Stossen talked with the leader of Blue Flight. "You're sure there's no enemy activity around us?"

"As sure as we can be, Colonel," Slee Reston replied. "They haven't even sent Boems to challenge us, and we've been drawing them the way a rotting carcass draws maggots."

Stossen wrinkled his nose at the image. "How far out have you searched?"

"A fifty-klick radius around your position, Colonel. Not a glimmer of Heggies. Of course, there could be a regiment of infantry and we might miss them, but there are sure as hell no tanks or trucks. Even with heat tarps, we've been low enough to pick up a magnetic signature."

"How much time over us do you have left?" Stossen asked.

"Twenty minutes unless you're set up to replace our batteries here."

"Hold on a second. Let me see if your vans are across yet."

They were, only just.

Slee and Zel flew broad figure-eight patterns over the 13th while the other Wasps landed for fresh batteries. As soon as the others were back in the air, Blue one and Blue two landed.

"Slummin', are you, sir?" Roo Vernon, crew chief for the first two Wasps of Blue Flight asked as soon as Slee was on the ground. The ground crew was already moving toward the two fighters.

"Somebody's got to keep you out of trouble," Slee replied. As usual during land-and-lift maneuvers, neither Slee nor Zel bothered to get out of his cockpit or open his canopy. They spoke with Vernon over the radio.

"You got any idea what this is all about?" Roo asked. The depleted batteries were out of both Wasps. The new ones were being inserted and connected.

"Not a glimmer, Chief," Slee admitted. "Thought maybe you'd picked up the dirt by now."

"Hell, they don't tell us nothin'," Roo complained. "Didn't even know you were around till they told us to unbutton to service four Wasps."

"See you later, maybe," Slee said. The battery hatches were sealed. Slee and Zel restarted their engines, and they were off, back up into the rain.

• • •

"Half the Team's across, sir," Dezo reported. It was a little more than half, actually, since all of the headquarters and support personnel were across. But half of the recon platoons, line companies, and artillery were now on the northwest bank. And the four Wasps were all back in the air.

"Move the lead recon units out," Stossen ordered. "I'll have the Wasps check the course we're taking."

It was only ten minutes later that Slee Reston reported a strong enemy presence eighty kilometers away, blocking the route that the 13th was on.

CHAPTER 7

Everything that the sensors of Blue Flight saw was relayed directly to Bal Kenneck. Stossen gave the Wasps orders to do whatever they could to hurt the Heggies. "All out. They've got to think that we're heading straight for them with everything we've got."

The last elements of the 13th were crossing the river. Stossen sent 1st and 3rd recon ahead with orders similar to those he had given the Wasps. Afghan Battery went with them.

"Hold them down," Stossen told the unit commanders. "Make them think you're half the 13th and that the rest of us are right behind you."

Stossen's staff members came to his APC for a face-to-face. The colonel had his mapboard open before they arrived.

"This could be it," Stossen said. The others had been linked in for his orders to the Wasps and the lead ground units. "We've got to hold those Heggies where they are."

"It looks like a reinforced regiment," Bal Kenneck said. "Two thousand men, minimum, perhaps twenty-five hundred. Two battalions of armor. I don't know where they came from. With that many assets, they must have air ready to come in when they're needed."

Stossen shrugged.

"There's not much chance that 120 mudders, 5 Havocs, and 4 Wasps can keep a regiment bottled up for long," Teu Ingels said. "What we need to worry about is that regiment swinging around behind us after we make the turn up into that valley. They could bottle us up without much trouble. If that happens, we'll play hell getting out. It certainly doesn't look as if there are any other routes, not that we can take vehicles over."

"And any other routes would take us that much farther from the rest of our people," Dezo said. "The Heggies won't have to do much more than keep us occupied. We would be irrelevant to the fight."

"As long as we do what we've been ordered to do, the rest doesn't matter," Stossen said.

The four men did little but stare at one another for nearly a minute. *The rest doesn't matter*. That could only mean one thing. General Dacik had already counted them out of any further part in his plans for Jordan.

"I think it's time I give you the rest of it," Stossen said.

"They must be involved in something truly revolutionary," Kenneck commented when the colonel had finished.

"There's no point in guessing," Stossen said. "Whatever it is, it won't do the Accord any good unless we can get them out, and back to our people. Off-world. Failing that . . ." He had already told them of the stop-loss option.

"No chance for a pickup, even for them?" Ingels asked.

Stossen shook his head. "Not according to the general. We're completely on our own. If we can't get them out, they don't get out." He paused before he added, "And neither do we."

Blue Flight stayed near the bottom of the cloud bank until the last instant. Barring the appearance of enemy fighters, their only worry was mudders with surface-to-air missiles, and as long as those mudders couldn't *see* the Wasps, there was little chance they could point a missile near enough to get a target lock.

The four Wasps chose their targets and nosed over, presenting the smallest possible profile to the enemy. Zel was just behind and to the right of Slee. He showed two tanks to his first two missiles. As soon as he had the double click of target lock for the second missile, he fired both, then flipped his weapons selector to cannon. There was a lot of infantry down there with the tanks, and Blue Flight had chosen its attack vectors to allow the pilots to go directly from missile launch to strafing.

Zel didn't bother to watch his missiles running in. His heads-up display would tell him when they hit. With ground targets, there was little chance that either missile would miss. Instead, he turned his attention to the strafing.

Six seconds was all that his strafing run lasted. Then Zel hit full power on a vertical ascent that took him to the edge of blackout before he eased off and zigged left in level flight, back in the clouds. He heard the whistles to signal missile strikes. There were no other alarms going off in the cockpit. No return missiles had been detected, and nothing else on the ground could pose any threat to a Wasp as it climbed through eight thousand meters.

Deep in the heart of a thunderhead.

Zel had zero visibility through the canopy. There might as well have been a coat of slate-gray paint over it. Except when a bolt of lightning flashed. But Zel rarely bothered to fly by eye in any case. The instruments were more accurate, and quicker. He could pick out the other three Wasps on his display, now spread over an area of more than ten kilometers horizontally and three vertically. They came back together, somewhat, as they prepared to stage their next attack.

This one went the same as the first, and so did the third. There were enemy missiles coming up after them now, but none came close enough to be particularly dangerous. The Wasps could boost at the same speed as the best Schlinal antiaircraft missiles, and hold that acceleration much longer.

Altogether, the four Wasps each made five passes. That expended all but two of the missiles that each plane carried, and more than 90 percent of the ammunition for their forward cannons.

"Head for home," Slee said. "Yellow Flight is sending four birds to replace us." He had just received that news. He didn't mention that it would be fifteen minutes before those planes arrived. There was nothing to be done about that.

If the ride had been rough before, it was murder now. Joe Baerclau braced himself and tried to roll with the bouncing of the Heyer. He had his helmet on, and only the padding in that kept him from getting knocked senseless every time his head slammed against the side of the APC. The driver had the throttle cranked to the stop. Orders had come from the colonel to shift course by five degrees. Apparently, that would add a few kilometers to the distance they had to travel, and the extra speed was to keep them from losing time.

At some point, the seal around the splat gun turret had started to leak. Water dripped into the troop compartment. It wasn't enough to do any damage, but it was another annoyance. The men closest to the leak moved as far apart as they could, but there wasn't enough room to let them get completely clear of it.

Talk was too difficult to be worth the effort. Each of the men was effectively alone, isolated with his own thoughts.

Few men had the gift of being able to escape from thought.

It was hardest on the new men, the almost-rookies. None of them had ever been on a ride like this, and their experience of combat was too short to have taught them the mental games that might have minimized it.

Fear and pain. And, above all, uncertainty.

Of the three new men, Olly Wytten was best at hiding his emotions. Even in garrison, he had been noted for never showing anything. There was no way that any of the others in the squad could tell what he was feeling by the look on his face or the way he acted. If he was upset, or angry, no one knew it until he reached the breaking point. He was a fighter, but not quick to resort to violence.

Pit Tymphe was almost as much a blank. He was quick to laugh, and just as quick to respond with an angry word when it was called for. The surprise of training had been when Tymphe had put Wytten down in a very short fight. After that, the two had become close friends—which, as often as not, meant that they were silent together.

In the second fire team, Carl Eames was more open. His usual expression was a grin. He was quick with a joke or a song. If his jokes were seldom particularly funny, his delivery was. And he *could* carry a tune. Though he usually disclaimed any real musical ability, his songs were generally composed as he sang them.

There was nothing to sing about in a Heyer APC careening cross-country at fifty kilometers per hour.

Even Eames was grim-faced, simply holding on as best he could, and still being bounced around. After being beaned severely earlier, he kept his helmet on now. He was the largest man in the squad. At less stressful times, the rest of the squad might carp that he took up more than his fair share of room. But no one was joking now.

It's still better than fighting, Joe Baerclau thought. A ride like this might leave some livid bruises—or even a concussion—but it was unlikely to kill anyone. Still, fighting was almost certain to come, and when it did, the odds would be stacked heavily against the 13th.

"This could be worse than Porter," Lieutenant Keye had said during the last stop. He and Joe had been talking privately.

"Porter. First squad had two men killed," Joe had replied. Two out of seven. And two other men wounded badly enough to need time in a trauma tube. The 13th had suffered like that across the board. They had come within minutes of being wiped out completely, down to the last rounds of ammunition before their relief arrived.

The colonel had made it clear that there would be no last-minute relief this time. The 13th had to get in and out entirely on its own. Stand or fall.

What in the universe can be that important? Joe wondered. No one had told the rank-and-file mudders anything about their mission yet. Not one word.

"Fifteen minutes," Joe told the platoon when the APCs stopped. "Try to get a meal down your necks while you can." They had traveled two hundred kilometers since the last break, at the river—four hours of constant bouncing. Joe wasn't the only man who was unsteady on his feet when he got out of the Heyer. Joe covered his stumble by moving a step to the side and leaning against the open hatch of the APC. While the rest of the squad piled out, he flexed his knees several times.

"One more stretch in the mixer, then we walk," Joe added. That had come as news to him. "A *long* walk." Just how long hadn't been part of the forty-five-second briefing he had just received from Lieutenant Keye, who had just received the same information from Major Ingels.

"I wouldn't care if we had to walk all the way back to the lines," Mort Jaiffer said. He stopped as soon as he was out of the Heyer, on the other side of the wide rear hatch.

"Don't say that too loud," Joe cautioned. "I've got a feeling we might have to." Back to the lines, or even farther. "The Heggies haven't forgotten us. We've got one Havoc battery and two recon platoons facing down a regiment or more of them, out ahead, not quite on the route we're taking."

"Then they'll be on us soon enough," Mort said.

"That's what it looks like. My guess is that we're heading into the mountains. If we can find some decent high ground . . ." He didn't have to finish the thought. Jaiffer, the one-time college professor, could do that for himself. A fight could still come down to high ground and cover.

Lieutenant Keye was the last man out of the Heyer.

"Joe, come over here for a minute."

Mort took the hint and walked off in the other direction, pulling a meal pack from his backpack.

Keye was very unsteady walking.

"You okay, sir?" Joe asked.

"Just stiff. My bones are too old for this kind of ride."

"You and me both, sir," Joe said. Keye was, perhaps, the oldest lieutenant in the ADF. In the 13th, there were only a couple of senior officers in headquarters who were older than Hilo Keye. If the 13th got off of Jordan, he would almost certainly find that he was a captain, but there would be no promotions until the end of this campaign.

"I just got a little more information about our mission," Keye said after lifting his visor to get the microphone away from his mouth so that nothing he said would be broadcast. "For now, this is just between you and me, company commanders and platoon leaders." Second platoon didn't have a platoon leader, a lieutenant, so the platoon sergeant had to do.

"Yes, sir," Joe said, lifting his own visor. "You and me."

Keye hesitated before he told Joe everything that he had heard from the colonel and from Major Ingels—basically, everything but the names and descriptions of the people the 13th was supposed to collect. Even Keye hadn't been given that information.

After Keye finished, Joe was silent for a moment. He looked down, then back up at the lieutenant. "What's so important that they're willing to throw away two thousand trained soldiers to make sure that three civilians aren't grabbed by the Heggies, sir?"

"I haven't the faintest idea, Joe. I can't even *imagine* what might be that important. Something that would tilt the war decisively in our favor, obviously. But what? I'm no skull jockey, Joe. I don't even have any idea what field they might be working in."

"If it's that important, I guess we'd best do our damnedest to get them back to the Accord in one piece."

Keye chuckled. "Not to mention getting ourselves back the same way."

"Yes, sir."

"Remember, not a hint of this to anyone until I say it's okay."

"Yes, sir."

Joe watched Keye walk away. He was so busy thinking about what the lieutenant had said that he almost forgot to pull a ration pack and eat.

It didn't take long for Ezra Frain to come over to Joe. "What was the big powwow about?"

Joe shook his head. "Nothing." He stared at Ezra hard enough that the squad leader got the message that further questions would be unwelcome. Ezra shrugged.

"That's official, Ez," Joe added. "Not even a guess."

Sergeant Dem Nimz thrived on cat-and-mouse games. Usually. But this time there were just too many cats and not enough mice. The Havocs could stand back seventeen or eighteen kilometers from the enemy and hit with agreeable regularity, but reccers had to get a lot closer to do any good. Even with Dupuy RA rifles, a marksman still needed to be within five hundred meters to have any realistic hope of scoring hits, even though the rifle was accurate at several times that distance. People just didn't remain motionless long enough for a slug to travel three or four kilometers, if they could even be *seen* at that distance.

Dem had started the Jordan campaign as leader of one of the five 12-man squads in 3rd recon. Now he was acting platoon sergeant. The hard way. His predecessor hadn't made it through the first hour of the landings. Third recon was down to forty-seven men. Ten had been killed and three wounded seriously enough to be out of action. The pessimist in Dem kept telling him that they would require a miracle to get out of this fight without taking even heavier losses.

"Fredo, down on your left," Nimz said, his voice an urgent whisper over the radio. "Watch that gully. I saw something moving in there." Fredo was Corporal Fredo Gariston, who had taken over Dem's squad when he became platoon sergeant.

"Tito and Jonny," Fredo replied. "I sent them down there to set up."

"Don't let them get too far out," Dem said. "We're not gonna be here long enough to set up housekeeping."

"Just planting a coupla H and Gs," Fredo said. H and G: hello and good-bye—reccer slang for their small anti-personnel mines.

"Get 'em back as quick as you can. We're gonna be moving. We've been here too long already."

Third recon hadn't yet gotten really close to the Heggie lines. All they had managed to do was ambush three patrols and plant a few dozen mines and booby traps. None of that would slow the enemy for long, and 3rd recon's job was to hold the enemy in place as long as possible.

They *were* close enough to hear the explosions of Havoc munitions hitting Schlinal targets, mostly tanks. Dem had counted a dozen explosions in the last twenty minutes, and he assumed—hoped—that there had been more, farther off, that he hadn't heard. A battalion of tanks, perhaps two. That was a lot of firepower. If thirty or fifty tanks got close to the 13th, the Heyer APCs would be sitting ducks, unable to defend themselves against the 135mm main guns of the Novas.

"It's gonna take us another hour to get around the Heggies even if we don't run into any more patrols," Dem said. "We gotta get in back and give 'em something to think about." They had abandoned their APCs more than an hour before. There was no way that they could creep up on the enemy in Heyers. Going on foot might slow them down, but it did give them a chance to actually get close enough to *do* something behind enemy lines.

Behind enemy lines. This was the work that reccers really trained for, commando-style operations. That was much more important than their nominal role as pathfinders for the line companies of an SAT.

"Okay, we're ready," Fredo said as his men came out of the gully.

"Move 'em out," Dem said. "You've got the point."

Ten minutes later, 3rd recon walked into an ambush. Automatic weapons fire came at them from three sides, followed by a half dozen RPGs. The platoon was spread out enough that no single grenade or burst of wire could catch many men, but the volume of fire was intense. Before they could get down and mount any organized return fire, there were four men dead and two more injured.

"Fredo, you there?" Dem demanded. Nimz was in a thicket off the side of the trail, so snared by prickly vines that he could scarcely move. There was a long pause before Gariston answered.

"I'm here." The voice was weak. Dem knew what was coming next. "I'm hit. Pretty bad, I think."

"Can you see anything?"

"Just an occasional flash. They musta been under heat tarps or we'd have seen them. Half my squad's down. The rest can't move without gettin' their butts shot off."

"Hang on. We'll move out around them, get you some slack."

He hoped. Dem passed word to the other squad leaders, gave them their orders. Then he started working to extricate himself from the brambles. Escaping from chains and shackles might almost have been simpler.

Kleffer Dacik had left his headquarters building for the first time in three days. The fighting around the Accord perimeter had been virtually nonstop since the 13th's breakout, and all of the intelligence available couldn't replace a firsthand look at what was going on.

"Twenty-six hours now, General," his aide said. They were making their fourth stop of the tour, watching from a hillside bunker some two hundred meters behind where the front was now—in this sector. The 6th SAT had actually managed to advance a little more than a hundred meters, and hold their gains.

Dacik stared at his aide without speaking. The aide didn't need long to look away and wish that he had kept his own mouth shut.

I never dreamed they'd keep it up this long, Dacik thought. *The Schlinal commander* had *to respond to the Accord attacks, of course, but this? There's no logic to it.* Dacik blinked several times, wishing he at least knew the name of his opposite number. *This marathon has to be as hard on them as it is on us.* That was the only saving grace. The last twenty-six hours had taken a lot out of the Accord soldiers, but it had to work the same on the enemy, perhaps even more so. They were doing most of the attacking now. The Accord force had switched entirely to the defensive, content to hold their lines, where they could, and keep the enemy from overrunning them.

"At least they can't pull too many troops to hunt the 13th," Dacik mumbled. His helmet visor was up, so only his aide heard, and that lieutenant was not about to say anything else, not unless his boss said something that absolutely demanded a reply. The aide rather preferred his current assignment to any of the obvious alternatives.

For another ten minutes, Dacik stared toward the front. He pulled his visor back down so he could read the overlays, but even that didn't tell him anything new.

"Let's get back to headquarters," he said eventually. "I've got to get some sleep before I drop."

And hope there's something left of my command when I wake up.

CHAPTER 8

Five Wasps of Blue Flight raced through the clouds again. The last five. Another had been shot down and one had been lost to mechanical failure. Night had fallen. All of the pilots were exhausted. They had been scheduled to get four hours off, but then the call for help had come from Afghan Battery. They were under attack by Boems and Novas.

We'll never make it in time was a thought common to all five pilots. Even at maximum speed Blue Flight would need twelve minutes to reach Afghan Battery, and it had taken a couple of minutes from the time of the call before they got in the air. A Havoc had no defenses against air attack, and if the enemy tanks got within range, that would make them no more than an even match. It depended on which side was getting the better targeting data.

Three minutes away from the fighting, Slee got a call from Afghan four. "We're the last one. The rest have all bought it."

"You still have Boems around?" Slee asked.

There was an agonizing delay before Afghan four's gun commander replied. "It looks as if they've gone. At least they're not shooting at us. But there are a half dozen Novas on our trail. We're haulin' ass." He gave Slee the course. "Don't count on us staying on that. I'm not about to give the Heggies a line to hit."

"We'll find you," Slee promised. "Just hang on."

"I saw two get it," Afghan four said. "Two rockets. Blew the gun all to hell. The others are shot too. I don't think anyone survived from any of the other guns. They hit us with too much."

"Two minutes," Slee said. "I've got the tank positions on screen now. I think you're out of range of them, but not by much. We'll get them off your back in a hurry."

"If it's okay with you, we're not gonna hang around to watch."

It was a turkey shoot. Almost. The five Wasps made their runs on the six Novas they had spotted. There were three more, a little behind the first group, but that just meant another run. But there was infantry with the armor. And the infantry had antiair missiles. Blue three and Blue five went down almost simultaneously, coming out of their first run.

"Get those mudders," Slee ordered after the last of the tanks was in flames. "Burn those bastards."

He led the way in on the next run—rockets for the Schlinal trucks, cannon fire for the infantry. Zel and Irv Albans—Blue six—followed him in, one on either side. The Wasps were at the bottom of their strafing run when the next missile came up.

Slee had no chance to evade the rocket. It was launched less than a hundred meters from him. Blue one exploded. The debris was scattered over a square kilometer of grassland. Slee didn't even have time to eject.

Zel and Irv continued to attack the Schlinal infantry until they had neither rockets nor cannon shells left to fire. The flight back seemed to last for hours.

Three hours past sunset, the 13th abandoned most of their APCs. The Heyers moved on without them, on a course near that which they had been following for the last five hours. The APCs carried only their drivers now. The infantry watched them go with mixed emotions. Everyone was relieved that the bone-jarring ride was over, but those Heyers did represent the only easy (or at least quick) way back to Accord lines.

"Decoys," Joe Baerclau muttered. Give the Heggies something to shoot at. There was a hollow feeling in his stomach. The drivers had to know full well what they might be in for, but they had gone on without protest. No more than a half dozen of the APCs had been held back with the 13th and the support vehicles for Havocs and Wasps. The colonel was using one for a headquarters. The rest were for casualties who were hurt too badly to walk.

Joe switched to his noncoms' channel to give the squad leaders the routine. "Half and half. Ninety minutes downtime for each fire team. Then we walk." At least the rain had finally eased off. There was only a light sprinkle falling at the moment.

An hour and a half to try to get *some* sleep. That was only marginally better than no sleep at all. With a little luck, they might get one more break before the night was over, but that—according to Lieutenant Keye—was very iffy. "Don't bet on it unless you get damn good odds" was how Keye had put it.

Echo was in a particularly rough stretch of trees and narrow gullies. Joe invested five minutes in improving his own position before he settled in to get his own ninety minutes of sleep. Keye had told him to take the first shift. Joe hadn't argued very hard against it. Despite the four hours the sleep patch had given him earlier, he was still not feeling 100 percent.

We do get out of this, I'm gonna put in for a month's leave and spend twenty hours a day in bed, Joe promised himself as he dozed off. Sleep came almost instantly when he shut his eyes.

Beautiful, oblivious sleep.

Colonel Stossen's APC, his command post, had been driven into a space too small for it, under and among the branches of three densely intertwined evergreens. A thermal tarp had been stretched over the Heyer first. Between that and the natural cover of the trees, the APC should be invisible from above. Only a magnetic signature *might* give it away to a low-flying plane. If there were significant ore deposits in the ground, even then it might escape. They were close to the mountains, and ore deposits had been behind the settlement at Justice, little more than eighty kilometers away. There were extensive iron and aluminum ore deposits throughout the mountains, and smaller amounts of just about everything else, according to prewar accounts.

A second tarp had been hung over the back of the Heyer, to make a covered pavilion. Stossen and his staff were there. The colonel was sitting in the APC's hatch. The others were kneeling in a semicircle around him. Stossen had his mapboard open on his lap.

"We've lost all but one gun from Afghan. Three Wasps left in Blue Flight, if they can get the one fixed that blew an engine. First and third recon are both taking heavy casualties." Bal Kenneck recited the losses. The diversionary effort was proving as costly as they had feared, much sooner than they had hoped.

"That's why we had to send the APCs on," Stossen said. His eyes were closed. He really didn't want to look at the faces around him. That was too depressing, and he didn't need any help getting depressed.

"It was the only way," Dezo said. "This buys us the time to get into position."

"As long as the Heggies don't tumble to what we've done," Kenneck said.

"We've got at least until they hit the decoys and take a look inside a few of them," Parks said. "They won't have any way to know that they're decoys unless they look inside and don't find enough bodies."

"Enough already," Stossen said. "We've got a lot of tired men and twenty klicks to walk. I want to be at Telchuk Mountain by dawn, ready to make contact, but there's just no way. Maybe 4th recon can get a squad to the lab, get those people out and coming back down the valley to meet us."

"I don't know," Parks said. "Fourth has done more than the rest already. Even reccers need sleep."

Stossen shook his head. "Fourth rec has the Special Intelligence team with them. *Those* people seem to do the impossible with great regularity."

"Abru and his men did some amazing things on Porter," Teu Ingels offered.

"Just the SI team. I'll talk to Abru myself." Stossen pulled down his visor and made the call.

Gene Abru was something of a legend to those who knew even a little of his past. Even within Special Intelligence—a service that could boast more than a few extremely "special" individuals—there was an almost mythical quality to his reputation. Stocky and just a trifle below average height, Abru was certainly not prepossessing in appearance, but he made a fetish out of physical fitness. With more than twenty-five years of military service, he had qualified for minimal retirement from the planetary defense force on his home world of Ceej. But when he retired from that service, he had joined the ADF and was quickly routed to the Spaceborne Assault Teams and Special Intelligence. The fact that he was only listed as a platoon sergeant made very little difference—to anyone, least of all to Abru. His relationship to the highest brass in the ADF was that of an equal.

Accord SI might be called on to perform almost any sort of task, from assassinating an enemy commander to setting up and training a guerrilla force on a planetary scale. Or anything in between. Gene Abru, like most of the people who gravitated toward SI, was willing and able to tackle anything, confident that he would find a way to accomplish even the impossible. He was one of the very few people in the Accord military who had actually been on one of the core worlds of the Schlinal Hegemony since the start of hostilities . . . and returned to tell the tale. His mission there remained a closely guarded secret. There were, most likely, no more than two people in the galaxy, apart from Abru himself, who knew just what his orders had been.

Abru listened closely to what Colonel Stossen told him. His only reply was a simple "Yes, sir."

"I hope you don't need any special equipment," Stossen continued. "I really can't get you anything you don't already have."

"We'll manage," Abru said. "I've got four men here. We're, ah, fairly well equipped."

"You need more men, you can have as many reccers as you want."

"I think we'll make do. Nothin' against the reccers, but my men and I will most likely do better alone."

Probably, the colonel thought. "Whatever. As long as you get to those people. And one more thing."

"Yes, sir?" Abru prompted when the colonel hesitated.

"I don't want to leave the least doubt about this. No matter what happens, the Heggies aren't to get them. But, please remember, if it's that important that the enemy doesn't get them, they have to be absolutely vital for us."

"Don't worry," Abru said. "If we have to take that option, there absolutely won't be any other way out. Besides, if they don't get out, neither do we, and I firmly plan to retire from the ADF."

That was not bravado, at least not *conscious* bravado. Abru meant it very sincerely.

After taking a quick look at a mapboard to get his bearings, Gene touched each of his men on the shoulder and pointed. The others got up, adjusted their packs, and followed him into the night, away from the recon squad they had been with. All Abru told the squad leader was that they had orders and were leaving. The reccer sergeant knew better than to ask for anything more.

The four men of Abru's team had been with him for more than a year, in training and in action. They were all considerably younger than him, all taller, all at least as heavy and fit as he was. None of them had any difficulty keeping up with the pace he set for the night march, but none would have been willing to try to set a faster pace. They worked together very well. After Porter, they had decided not to replace the one man of the team who had been killed. It would take too long to bring any replacement along to the point where he would not be a liability to the rest of them.

In an hour, the team covered just slightly less than ten kilometers. While they took a five-minute break, Abru outlined the mission, precisely, with less wasted verbiage than he had received. He spoke face-to-face, visor up, microphones switched off. Abru made a conscious point of distrusting the almost foolproof security of the radio net. He used the radio only when there was no other possible way to communicate in a timely fashion. It was a chance he simply preferred to avoid whenever possible.

After the briefing, the team reverted to silence. All of these men were comfortable with that. On Porter, they had spent ten days together, lying in wait, after jumping in a week ahead of the main invasion force. In all of those ten days, not one of them had spoken a single word.

When the team reached the narrow valley leading toward Telchuk Mountain, they climbed to the southwest slope and moved along that, hidden by evergreen trees. The wooded slope was not very dense. The trees tended to be scrawny, and few of them were more than five or six meters in height—most were barely half that. But the SI team moved easily, from tree to tree in broken formation. From habit, the men avoided showing even the simplest patterns to their movement. They moved closer together, or farther apart, climbed higher on the slope or lower, they zigged and zagged, stopped and started. Even if an enemy spyeye should happen to note the movement—a very remote possibility under *any* circumstances—computer analysis would not tag it as human.

When the team stopped for its second break, they had traveled twenty-three kilometers in two hours and forty minutes. Abru's power binoculars showed him where the entrance to the secret lab was concealed. He couldn't see the entrance directly, but there were vague signs of a pathway, visible even through the night-vision systems of his helmet optics.

He pointed, then lifted his helmet. The others lifted theirs as well, an automatic response.

"We'll get some rest. Two hours. Then we make contact and get those people out of there no later than sunrise." There would be no time for extended chitchat inside, certainly no time for the researchers to waste gathering things to take along. In and out, and back under cover as quickly as possible. Gene considered forgoing the rest, but decided that this might prove to be a foolish economy. It would be more difficult to get civilians out and moving in the dark, especially if they didn't have night-vision gear, and he doubted that they would.

The SI men did not post a sentry. None of these men would sleep so heavily that they wouldn't wake at the slightest untoward sound, even after a long march on little sleep. The men each found a good position, well separated from the others, and rolled himself in a thermal blanket. Two hours. That was enough of an alarm clock.

About the time that the SI team bedded down, the rest of the 13th was nearing the entrance to the valley, fifteen kilometers from the hidden laboratory. The remaining Havocs had been deployed. They would be able to provide at least some covering fire for the infantry through most of the valley. Only the last six kilometers would be out of range for all of the big guns. The support vans for Havocs and Wasps were deployed, away from the valley. The remaining recon platoons moved up onto the slopes on either side. Fox and George companies took up defensive positions at the end of the valley. They would stay put while the rest went in, rear guard.

Echo Company had the point.

"I don't like it," Mort Jaiffer said as 2nd platoon started along the lower slope. First platoon was a hundred meters ahead of them. On the other side of the valley, Bravo Company started out just minutes after Echo.

"What don't you like?" Joe asked. It was poor sound discipline, but the Bear was too tired to be strict. Twenty minutes before, he had been wakened from his second too-short nap of the night. Usually, Joe was quick to come fully alert. If there had been guns firing, or some obvious threat, he would have this time too, but with only another march ahead, and no enemy anywhere near (as far as he knew), his mind remained sluggish.

"Like cattle being steered into the chute at a slaughterhouse," Jaiffer said, a thoroughly cryptic comment, the sort of thing the others expected from their professor. There were few Accord worlds where such things as slaughterhouses might still be found.

"You ever see a cow pack an Armanoc?" Joe asked. "Don't bother answering. And let's forget the chatter." He was finally beginning to wake up fully.

Within 2nd platoon, first squad had the point. Joe followed them. First Sergeant Walker was somewhere ahead, with 1st platoon. Lieutenant Keye was farther back in the column, somewhere near the middle of Echo.

Joe had taken a long look at this valley on his mapboard. He didn't much like it either, but no one had asked him to. It could be a narrow killing zone, with the 13th on the wrong end of it. There was nothing Joe could do about that but wish: *I hope they don't know we're here.* There had been no reports of the Heyers being hit. That, Joe thought, might be the only way—except blind luck—that the Heggies would learn about the deception. *If they don't know we're here, if they don't see us, it wouldn't matter if we all had bull's-eyes painted on our butts,* he reasoned.

The pace that 1st platoon set would have been trying for such tired men even on the flat. On a 20-degree side slope, it required concentration just to keep from falling behind, or falling. There were no recognizable paths, just rocks and moss and overhanging branches. At least there was little real underbrush. In the rocky soil of the slope, trees managed to hog most of the soil and nutrients. They permitted little competition.

"Ez, make sure you don't lose sight of 1st platoon," Joe warned after twenty minutes.

"Just at the edge," Ezra replied. "We don't want to get too close to them either. They might pick up the pace."

In and out, Joe thought. *Just let us get in and out in one piece.* That was about as close as he came to prayer. He wasn't overly religious, though he did not *dis*believe in a God. As long as he was a soldier, in a war, he would not rule out any possibility of help. Even divine.

It's gone too easy so far, he worried. *For us.* If the platoon had been rushing from one firefight to the next, dodging enemies right on their heels the whole time, he wouldn't have had time for such thoughts. In a way, he would have been more comfortable avoiding them. A long march gave him too much time. Think or fall asleep on your feet. The latter was unthinkable, so the former had to be endured.

Memories came. Joe remembered playing soldiers as a child on Bancroft. As often as not, his gun had been a tree limb scavenged from the woods near his home. There was little in the way of a toy industry on Bancroft. Back then, at least, he qualified with a smile. And his war games had often been anachronistic by thousands of years. Mankind might have spread far from Earth, but he carried old histories, old legends and myths, along with him. As often as not, the war games on Bancroft had been Cowboys and Indians, and Joe had been Sitting Bull directing the attack on Custer at Little Big Horn.

The alternative had been Space Jockeys, running around pretending he had a compact space fighter under his control, laser guns blasting alien creatures out of the universe—bug-eyed monsters with mouths large enough to eat a small human in two bites.

But there were no intelligent aliens, or any alien races that might qualify as BEMs. At least, none had ever been found, in all of the hundreds of star systems that humans had explored. No intelligent aliens, no artifacts of defunct alien civilizations. Life was found in abundance, plant and animal, but none of it smart enough to rival man.

That had always made Joe sad, when he was young, to think that humans were all alone in the galaxy. When he was young, and now—but only at times like this, when he had too much time to think.

One foot in front of the other.

Van Stossen walked with his men. He was, he knew, far too close to the front of the column, trailing along behind Echo Company with his headquarters security detachment. Dezo Parks was across the valley. The rest of the staff was divided between the two columns.

The colonel had more than enough to keep his mind occupied, off of the slogging along. He was on the radio more than he was off of it, checking with company commanders, and trying to get some idea of what that Heggie reinforced regiment was up to. First and third recon were only in occasional contact with them. After Afghan Battery was cut up, the reccers had had little choice but to play their mission as coyly as possible, darting in and out, moving quickly and in what they hoped would be unexpected directions.

The Heggies *were* on the move. They knew where the convoy of APCs was. Twice, flights of Boems had attacked the empty

Heyers, destroying a few more each time. But there had been no ground combat. No Heggies had been able to look inside the wreckage of a Heyer and discover that it wasn't loaded with troops.

A few more hours, Stossen thought, his own wish for the night. *Give us a chance to at least get those people.* He didn't want to think too hard on what might have to come then. He would carry out the extreme option if he had to—even if he had to kill the researchers personally. But he hoped for a way to avoid that. That occupied more than half of his radio time, as he talked with Bal, Dezo, and Teu. Even on the move, he had them working on their mapboards and on the radio with CIC, plotting possible escape routes. Get in and out—*away* from this valley. Find some way to avoid interception. Worry about getting back to the lines later. Much later if necessary. And possible.

This mountain range continued almost forever, it seemed. The chain went on for nearly two thousand kilometers, with a few breaks. At one point, the chain was eight-hundred kilometers wide. Much of that land was completely unsettled, unexplored. The Accord settlers hadn't found it necessary to go traipsing through much of that, and the Schlinal occupying force certainly hadn't bothered. They were only interested in what had already been found and exploited. The 13th could move into areas that were out of reach of Schlinal air power, to terrain far too rugged for tracked vehicles to approach. That might mean abandoning the Havocs and all of the support vans, but it could be done. It would preserve most of the 13th. But that would only work, in the long run, if the Accord somehow held on and won the campaign for Jordan. If the rest of the invasion force were destroyed or forced to evacuate, all the 13th would be able to do was postpone their own capture or destruction. For months, perhaps, but certainly not long enough for the Accord to mount another, even more powerful, invasion force.

And that would mean the loss of whatever research those people had been doing inside Telchuk Mountain.

CHAPTER 9

Zel Paitcher *had* slept, for nearly five hours. The sleep patch might not have been necessary, but the wing medtech had insisted. Zel hadn't been in very good shape when he and Irv Albans returned from their last mission of the evening.

Slee was dead. Zel had battered himself with that throughout the remainder of the flight. His mind had replayed Slee's last seconds over and over. They had been wingmen for nearly a year, but more than that, they had been friends, closer than brothers. Zel had brothers, and he knew that he had never been as tight with them as he had been with Slee.

An explosion. There wouldn't be enough of Slee left to make a pickup, if pickup ever proved possible on Jordan. Zel had, of course, logged the exact position. When the time for such things came, if it ever did, people would go out there to retrieve whatever remains they might find. It probably would not be much, but Slee Reston would be brought "home"—back to some common burial ground for fallen soldiers on Jordan if not back to his own homeworld.

A sleep patch with its four hours of guaranteed oblivion. Almost another hour of natural sleep. But even that had ended.

Zel woke lying on his back under his Wasp. Camouflaged thermal tarps covered everything. What remained of Blue Flight—three Wasps of the original eight—was down, at least for the remainder of the night. After that . . .

For just an instant after he woke, Zel's mind remained blissfully blank of memory. He was staring up at the underside of his Wasp. In the dark, the contours of the black fighter were invisible. Black on black, almost impossible to see even from no more than eighty centimeters away. The Wasp hid the sky and sheltered Zel from the continuing rain, now no more than a persistent drizzle.

The smell of wet earth, rich and sweet, caught Zel's attention. The novelty brought just an instant's amusement. Zel had been born and raised in the largest town on his homeworld. "Wild" smells had never touched him before as this one did. It was a welcome distraction until Zel realized that that was all it was—a distraction, something to keep his thoughts from returning immediately to his loss.

"Slee." He whispered the name so softly that no one could possibly have heard, but it was a whisper, more than a thought. This wasn't the first time that he had lost comrades in combat. It had happened before even here on Jordan. It had happened on Porter . . . and even back in training. But those losses could not compare to this one.

Memory brought back the emptiness, the ache. Tears rose in Zel's eyes. He brushed at them, slowly, then took a deep breath and rolled toward the front of his plane. There was no time for a proper period of mourning. There was still a war to be fought, and what remained of Blue Flight would soon be sent back up to take its part in the battle.

Zel didn't roll completely out from under his Wasp right away. It was still dark, and raining. He took a moment to orient himself. Then he scooted out, stood up, and made a quick dash over to where the support van was parked. Its outline was just barely visible at twenty meters.

Irv Albans and Jase Wilmer, the other two remaining pilots of Blue Flight, were standing together under an awning—a thermal tarp—draped off the side of the van. Jase's Wasp had been the one grounded by mechanical failure. It had been, somehow, repaired in the field, and was ready to go again.

"Get some coffee into you, Zel," Irv said. "Then call Major Tarkel." Goz Tarkel was the commander of the 13th's air wing, the only senior officer who had remained behind.

"What's the Goose want with me?" Zel asked as Jase handed him a mug of steaming coffee—prepared right there in the support van.

Irv hesitated before he said, "You're Blue one now," very softly.

That brought Zel to a full stop for a moment. The knot in his stomach seemed to double in size. Finally, he took a too-long drink of the hot coffee. It scalded his mouth but did serve to get him thinking again.

"Sorry, Zel," Irv said. "I know how close you were." Irv had been with Blue Flight since before Porter. Jase had joined the 13th after that campaign—replacing another dead pilot.

"Yeah." Zel couldn't think of anything else to say. He took a more cautious sip of coffee. Somehow, the crew chiefs always managed to find real coffee to brew when the rest of the 13th had to make do with the reproductions that molecular replicators came up with. Nanofactured food and drink was *supposed* to be identical to its "natural" prototypes, but, somehow, that never worked with coffee. Zel could always tell the difference.

He took time to enjoy at least the first half of his coffee before he put on his helmet and called the major. Pilots' helmets weren't as heavily equipped with radio channels as mudder helmets—the Wasps carried the bulk of their communications gear—but there were a few channels available.

"You got that sleep patch worked out of your system?" Major Tarkel asked. The Goose sounded as if he were still more than half-asleep.

"Yes, sir."

"Good. You're Blue Flight commander now. You've got . . . twenty-seven minutes. Blue Flight is going out to the 13th. You'll operate from there for the time being. Major Parks will be your immediate boss while you're out there. He'll tell you what they need."

"Yes, sir."

"Good luck, Zel."

Good luck. *We'll need it,* Zel thought as he took his helmet back off. He glanced at his watch, as he had when the major gave him twenty-seven minutes. Twenty-six now. He told the others what they had to look forward to.

"Sounds hairy," Jase said.

"You can bet on it," Zel said, draining his mug. Irv took the mug and refilled it. "Slee and I talked about it before . . ." That brought an awkward pause. To cover it, Zel waited for the second cup of coffee and his first sip from it. "When we heard that some of the support crews would be out there. We'll play hell getting even fifteen minutes to sleep if we've got to keep hopping around with the mudders. The only time we'll be able to count on staying down longer than it takes to service the Wasps is when—if—they settle down, and even then only if there's no immediate threat that needs us in the air. I hope both of you managed to get some sleep tonight."

"We did," Irv said. "After you were out, the major told us to sack out as long as we could, that we wouldn't be going up before morning." He looked at the sky. "I guess this is as close to morning as we get." Dawn was still nearly an hour away.

Zel moved to the edge of the awning. The rain was slackening off even more. It was hardly more than a heavy dew now. At least the sky was heavy enough to keep any sounds of war at a distance. The pilots were far enough from the front lines that they couldn't hear any small arms fire, and even after listening closely for a couple of minutes, Zel didn't hear anything heavier than that.

"Heard anything about the fighting here?" he asked.

"Nothing close," Irv said. "For the rest . . ." He shook his head. There was just barely enough illumination in the night sky for Zel to see the gesture. "All we get is rumors, confusing and contradictory."

"Nothing very good," Jase said. "The big talk is that we might have to evacuate Jordan."

"Give up?" Zel asked.

"Give up," Irv confirmed. All of the pilots knew that the invasion had not gone according to plan. By now, there was supposed to be nothing left to do but finish mopping up any last pockets of enemy resistance. It was a sour joke, when there was time for jokes.

"If you haven't eaten, now's the time," Zel said after a minute. It was hard for him to start thinking like a flight leader. Ever since joining the 13th, he had been Slee Reston's wingman. Slee had made the decisions for both of them, back when they were Blue three and Blue four, and then Slee had gained the entire wing when he became Blue one and Zel became Blue two.

Zel didn't want to be Blue one. It wasn't just that he didn't want to be succeeding his best friend; he simply didn't want to be responsible for other pilots.

"We ate once," Irv said. "We were waiting for you to get up before we had another breakfast. You'd better get a couple of meals in you while you've got the chance. Mealtimes might be few and far between once we're out hopping around with the mudders."

Zel nodded, absently. He moved around to the rear of the van. There was a case of meal packs there. He picked two and pulled the self-heating strip on one of them. Appetite or not, he had to eat.

Although he did not check the time immediately, Gene Abru had no doubt that he had awakened precisely at the end of the two hours he had allotted for sleep. He was alert even before he opened his eyes, listening to the sounds of the late night. Then he lifted his head just enough to look to either side. The other members of his team were also waking, and going through much the same routine as Gene—almost totally silent. There were no loud yawns, no creaking of bones as men stretched.

There was nothing to be seen around them but the scattered trees. Not even a single animal seemed to be moving anywhere near them. If there were any birds on the wing, they were silent and could not be seen. The ridge line above the SI team was clearly silhouetted now. On the far side of the mountain, morning dusk would already be well advanced. Dawn would not be far off.

"Eat fast," Gene said, just loud enough to be certain that the others would hear. He was already pulling a meal pack out for himself. It took ten seconds to warm up after he pulled the strip. He wouldn't have bothered except that the strip also served to open the pack. By the time those ten seconds had elapsed, Gene was already chewing his second mouthful. He sat hunched over, trying to keep as much of the drizzle as possible from finding its way into his food. With his visor tipped up and the meal pack held close to his face, he was mostly successful.

He was the first finished. Using his knife, he scooped out a small hole and buried his trash. The others did the same. The covered-over holes were camouflaged as best they could be in the waning dark. There was little chance that anyone would stumble over the buried refuse.

Gene took time to check his rifle and pistol, then got to his feet. The rifle was an Armanoc zipper, the same carbine that most of the infantry carried. The pistol used the same sort of rocket-assisted projectile as the Dupuy cough gun. Each of the men had the same pair of weapons, plus knives and an assortment of grenades and "special" explosives.

Once they were all on their feet, Abru simply nodded to the others, then started walking. He figured that they would need about twenty minutes to get into place. He had a special channel available on his helmet radio. That was reserved for one purpose . . . and one-time use. When they got close, he would use it to tell the people inside the lab that they were there, that it was time to go. That notice was mostly to keep anyone inside from shooting when the SI team appeared.

Nine people, Gene reminded himself. They had been told that there were nine people waiting for pickup, the three primary researchers and their six assistants. If they found more than nine, something was wrong—*dangerously* wrong. It might not be wise to shoot first and ask questions later, but the temptation would be there. And if there were fewer than nine people waiting, Gene would want to know what had happened, see a body if there was a body to be seen. Being suspicious came naturally to Gene Abru. He had been that way long before his assignment to Special Intelligence had made it a matter of survival.

The team walked single file now, each man stepping, as far as possible, exactly where the man in front of him had stepped. That was standard drill. If an enemy should happen to find their trail, it would be impossible to guess exactly how many men had passed.

It took no more than ten minutes to reach the shoulder of the mountain. Gene stopped and went prone, bringing up his binoculars to get a better look at the narrow break in the side of the mountain that concealed the entrance to the secret lab . . . and to get a long look at all of the approaches. From this vantage, he could see a lot of the valley. There were no signs of any *large* force lying in wait. Gene still did not discount the possibility of ambush, or treachery. He took as long as he dared to scout out the terrain. This close, he thought he could even see the doorway to the lab, but he wasn't 100 percent certain. It was concealed well, back under an overhang, in what was almost a cave.

Damn good planning, he thought, with grudging respect for the forethought that had gone into the planning and construction of the lab. Remarkable for a world that had been at peace at the time. Before the Schlinal Hegemony had started its military push into Accord space.

And, once more, the thought intruded: *Just what the hell are they working on that took so much secrecy?* If there were time, even thirty seconds, Gene knew that he would look around for any obvious clues. He didn't really expect to see much. If the lab itself were likely to give away the secrets of the researchers, he would have had orders to blow it up, not just to get the people out. Or dispose of them.

Maybe the researchers had already prepared explosives. With all of the care that had gone into selecting the location, Gene had to admit that some provision might well have been made for its destruction, but he couldn't really make himself believe it. That was too much to expect on a world that had *never* known war.

Gene let out a slow breath and slid away from where he had made his observations. It was time to go over the final details of the plan with the others.

"Asa, you'll come with me. We'll make the contact and go in." Asa Gooding. "Ben, you and Vel stake out good positions to cover that nook, two different angles." Ben Howard and Vel Zimmer. "Mac, you get up and back, cover our tails." Robert "Mac" MacDonald.

The others nodded. Ben and Vel got up just enough to start looking for their covering positions. Mac moved away from the others, toward the ridge line behind then.

Gene and Asa started moving forward, cautiously on the slope, but not slowly. Mountain climbing was part of the ordinary training for Special Intelligence teams. The two men picked out their path, deciding in advance just where each step would take them. The slope wasn't steep, nor the rock rotten enough to pose any great threat. There was no need for a line between them, or any climbing gear. They were able to keep a rifle in one hand and use the other hand, occasionally, for balance, or to guide them past a minor obstruction.

The entrance to the secret lab was two-hundred meters—direct line—from where Gene had done his last visual search. On the ground, Gene and Asa covered three times that distance. Gene waited until the two of them were just outside the hollow before he switched to the special radio channel and made his call.

"Gopher, this is Hedgehog," he said after two sharp clicks on the channel.

It took nearly a minute before there was any response. Gene had watched the seconds tick off closely. If there were no answer to his first call, he was to wait ninety seconds before calling again.

"Hedgehog, this is Mole." The change in call sign was a gimmick, part of the recognition process.

"Amanda Pays sends her regards." Gene wasn't bothered at all by the ridiculous-sounding code sequence. It was one that would be impossible for any enemy to stumble on. To the best of Gene's incomplete knowledge, only four people—besides himself—had been aware of it—the three senior researchers inside the lab and Colonel Stossen.

"We got her roses" came from inside, the code that all was well. Anything else would have been a danger signal.

"Coming in," Gene announced. He ran the last twenty meters, with Asa right behind him. Both men had their rifles at the ready, safeties off. Despite everything, it seemed wise to be ready for anything once the door opened.

There were no signs of footprints, no evidence that people had ever been in the cul-de-sac that held the door to the lab, except for the door itself, and that had been camouflaged, by a false rock facade over the actual door and frame. Although he had been given no instructions on the door, Gene thought that he saw the obvious handle, a place where you would have to reach up under a small overhang.

Gene used his left hand. The right held his rifle. There was a bar under the overhang. He pulled back on it, then tugged on the door. It came open with surprising ease, silently.

Asa was off to the side, the muzzle of his zipper pointed directly into the opening.

There was no light inside, and at first, the two SI men had difficulty seeing. Had it not been for the infrared sensors in their night-vision gear, they would have been unable to see at all.

Asa went in first. Gene covered him, then followed.

They *were* in a cave then, a large chamber that had been left natural but for the door they had entered through, and another door at the back, near the left wall, about eight meters from the first.

That door opened, slowly. One figure, dressed in loose coveralls, stepped through the opening, moving with exaggerated slowness, hands held high and out to the sides.

Very obviously a female figure.

CHAPTER 10

Dawn brought a professional paranoia to Joe Baerclau. Light was more an enemy than a friend, particularly a thousand kilometers behind enemy lines. Echo Company had covered nearly two-thirds of the length of the narrow valley. If Heggies appeared now, there would—literally—be no place for the 13th to run, and little solid cover. They would be caught on the slopes flanking the valley, easy targets for enemy aircraft or artillery. Enemy mudders on the ridge lines could mow them down. A force back at the entrance to the valley, strong enough to hold down the two companies left to guard it, could pin them in place and allow their leisurely destruction.

Joe felt his mouth getting dry, but he didn't waste time wishing that he had less imagination. The best way to avoid getting caught in an untenable position was to work out all of the possible traps in advance, and do whatever could be done to counter them.

Unfortunately, the only way Joe could see to avoid all of the potential hazards in this valley was to avoid the valley itself, and it was far too late for that, even if their orders had permitted it.

Joe spent most of his time scanning the ridge lines on either side. Those were the most likely places for any threat to appear. Reccers were, supposedly, in place up there, watching the reverse slopes and the air approaches. But only half of the 13th's recon platoons remained with the Team, too few men to adequately cover so many kilometers. The rest of the reccers . . . Joe swallowed hard and shook his head. There were rumors that one battery of Havocs and both of the recon platoons that had been sent to harass the enemy had been wiped out. Even on the march, scuttlebutt like that could not be totally suppressed.

"Joe, we're going on up to the ridge line," Izzy Walker said. "Start your platoon up first."

Joe acknowledged the order, then switched channels to get the men turned. Climbing three hundred meters of slope was work, but it was easier on bodies than walking along the slope. Near the top, there were a couple of spots where it was almost real mountain climbing, but most of the path was relatively mild. There were trees all along the way, extra handholds and footrests when needed. Near the top of the mountain, the trees were puny little things, scarcely man-high, with trunks no thicker than Joe's ankles. Many looked as if they could be pulled out with very little effort.

Joe found a place for himself where he could look through a notch between two high, jagged rocks, to survey the reverse slope of the mountain. That far side was far more rugged than the one that Echo had been traversing. Rocky and steeper—but it might still allow enemy mudders access, if they were coming that way. The rocky slope would even provide decent cover for an attacking force.

I'd rather be attacking up that slope than trying to stop that attack, Joe concluded. An enemy might close to within forty meters of the ridge before they would be exposed to much wire.

He scanned the slope as carefully as he could but found little relief in the fact that he didn't see any enemy soldiers climbing toward him. He pulled back from the ridge line and spent a couple of minutes making sure that each squad was just where he wanted it, the men in the best positions available.

Then he called the first sergeant.

"We're all set. How long do we have to wait?"

"Until the SI team gets back. That's all I know," Walker said. "Shouldn't be too long. But however long it takes, keep your eyes open. I think we're going to get some air cover in."

Joe signed off, already looking into the sky. Air cover was handy, but it carried its own danger. Wasps circling overhead would be a beacon for any enemy close enough to see them, and in daylight, the Wasps *could* be seen. Especially now. The rain had finally stopped and the clouds were thinning out rapidly.

• • •

Zel could not recall ever being as nervous as he was in the few minutes that Blue Flight was on the ground. They had made the flight out from the main Accord lines without incident, then they had landed for fresh batteries. Out in the middle of hostile country, with fewer than two hundred mudders to protect them from whatever the Heggies might throw their way, Zel felt as edgy as if he had just been thrown into a pit of hungry lions.

Roo Vernon was unnaturally quiet while the Wasps were on the ground. For a moment, he stood by Zel's canopy, looking in. Over the radio, he said, "Sorry about Captain Reston, sir." His face was drawn. It was all he said.

All Zel could do was nod, and swallow hard. Roo's words had brought back the sting of his loss. Again.

With only batteries to replenish and separate crews to do the work on each of the three planes, the Wasps were back off the ground in record time. The support vans and their defending troops got ready to move. When Blue Flight returned, they would land in a new place, as far away as the ground crews could get.

"We're going to stage a few klicks away from the 13th," Zel told his wingmen. "I don't want to be right overhead unless they need us there." His heads-up display showed several locators for the bulk of the 13th.

"How about a chance to get some payback for . . . the others?" Irv said.

"The 13th gets in and out and completes its mission, that's payback enough. For now," Zel said. *Whatever the hell they're doing in that valley.* "Forget the chat. Keep your eyes open. Let's not have any more losses." It wouldn't really be payback enough to satisfy Zel, but there was no way that he could bring back Slee or any of the others. The only true payback would be to chase the Heggies all of the way back to their core worlds.

And then some, he thought as his eyes swept the horizon. In daylight, there was a good chance that a pilot might spot a Boem before his electronics did.

"We'll do a wide circle, ten klicks out from the blue-on-white blinker," Zel said, referring to the locator for Colonel Stossen's headquarters. "And we stay together. Jase, you'll take high cover, four thousand meters above Irv and me."

Zel banked his Wasp left. There was some rugged country up ahead, the worst that Zel had ever flown over. If one of them had to eject, the ride down would be touchy. The escape pod of a Wasp might be well padded, but there seemed to be some nasty drops. Once a parachute was fouled, there would be nothing left but a fall. And even if a pilot reached the ground in one piece, he might have the Devil's own time getting out on foot.

"Good thing they don't have to go in any farther than they do," Zel mumbled. The valley the 13th was following was near the edge of the mountain chain. The easy part.

Blue Flight had been back in the air for twenty minutes before Zel had a call from CIC.

"We have a report from the one gun left in Afghan Battery," the voice on the radio said. "He says there's a flight of six Boem fighters that just passed over him. Their course is straight toward you. About six minutes off."

Zel acknowledged that and passed the word to Irv and Jase. "We might as well go out to meet them. Try to keep them away from the mudders." *If we can.* Three against six. "Irv, I think you and I had better put a little more sky below us."

"I'm Dr. Philippa Corey," the woman said, still keeping her hands away from her body.

Gene Abru blinked once and nodded. Then he identified himself. No one had mentioned that there were women here. *Or said that there weren't,* he reminded himself.

"I hope you have your people ready to leave right this instant, Doctor," Gene said. "We're short of time."

"We've been packed and ready since we learned of the landing, Sergeant. The others are in the next room."

"How many of you, altogether?" Gene asked.

"Nine. That's all there's been since before the Schlinal invasion."

Gene nodded again. "Call your people out, Doc. I was serious about leaving immediately."

Dr. Corey lowered her arms, then turned and looked back into the room. She passed along Gene's instructions and nothing else. He had the exterior microphones cranked up on his helmet to make certain that there were no extraneous asides.

Eight others filed out. Three of them were also women. All eight were dressed much as Dr. Corey was, in nondescript coveralls. They weren't camouflage, but other than that the garb looked about perfect for a long walk. One of the others handed Corey a pack. She slipped the straps over her shoulders.

"I hope that there are more than just the two of you," she said when she finally crossed over to where Gene stood, still near the exit.

"A lot more, Doc, but it didn't seem wise to bring them all in here."

"I take it that introductions can wait?" she asked.

Gene nodded. "Is this place set up so you can destroy it after we're out?"

"Destroy it, no. But the overhang outside the entrance is mined. So is this chamber. We can bury the entrance under several thousand tons of rock."

"Good enough. I'll lead the way out. You and your people stay behind me. For now, Asa will bring up the rear. Either of us says to do something, you people do it, at once. Save the questions for later." It was much too long a speech for Gene, and his clipped tones made that obvious even to a stranger.

"As you say," Dr. Corey replied. "We're in your hands."

Gene blinked again. Dr. Corey was an attractive woman of indeterminate age. She might still be in her late twenties from her looks, but from the way she spoke, Gene guessed that she might even be sixty or more. With the techniques available for stalling, or reversing, the aging process well past the century mark, there was simply no way to be certain.

He turned and headed out of the stone foyer.

At the edge of the shadows in the hollow outside, Gene stopped for a moment, both to let his eyes adjust to the higher light levels and to give his men across the way time to identify him.

"How close do you have to be to bury this entrance?" he asked Dr. Corey.

"I would suggest that we get at least a hundred meters away, and behind cover," she replied.

"Cross the way and up the slope?"

Corey looked where he pointed. "It'll do. The transmitter has a range of five hundred meters, but closer is better."

Gene simply started walking again, back over the route that he and Asa had followed on their way in. They had covered no more than half of the hundred meters when there was a radio call from Major Kenneck.

"Ab, there are enemy Boems heading our way. They'll be overhead in less than three minutes unless our Blue Flight can stall them."

"Odds?" Gene asked.

"Six to three, the wrong way. You have those people?"

"We're on our way out. We'll be blowing the entrance to the lab in less than two minutes."

"That'll give the Boems a target," Kenneck cautioned.

"We'll do what we can. A few Vrerchs headed toward those Boems from your location would help."

"Any that come close enough."

Gene hadn't slowed his pace while he talked. As soon as he signed off, he turned his head toward Dr. Corey.

"Enemy fighters on the way in. Three minutes. They see the explosion, they'll be on us in a hurry."

"If they've got any idea where the lab is, that it even exists, it's essential that we deny them access," Corey said. "No matter what."

I wonder if she knows the rest of our orders, Gene thought as he picked up the pace. Then: *I bet she does. She might even have given them.*

It had taken Teu Ingels less than thirty seconds to convey the tactic to Zel Paitcher, and Zel had needed even less time to tell his wingmen. "Hit and run," Zel said. "We dive in at them, shoot off a pair of missiles each, then run like hell. Clear those two ridges with less than fifty meters below us. Get them to chase."

If the major's plan worked, it wouldn't even matter if any of the Wasps' missiles hit a target on the first pass. Hits would be a bonus.

"There they are," Zel said, not ten seconds later. "Tally ho!"

The six Boems were flying in two three-plane formations, one a thousand meters above the other, and somewhat to the right. All six of the Schlinal planes were below Blue Flight, though. Zel nosed his fighter over on an intercept course. The weapons selector was already on rockets, and Zel got lock clicks almost as soon as he showed the missiles their targets. He didn't bother waiting to close the range. He was willing to give these pilots plenty of time to take their countermeasures.

As long as they pursued.

Zel did hesitate for a couple of seconds after launching his rockets. There was no sign that the Boems had locked on to his Wasp, or even that they had seen the six missiles streaking toward them. That didn't last long, of course. The Schlinal pilots scattered, as if they were part of an air show, going in six different directions as they launched decoys and other countermeasures, and worked to get into position to launch their own rockets.

Zel flipped his Wasp and headed back toward the ridges where the 13th's mudders were waiting.

I hope they remember we're coming through first, he thought.

Irv and Jase made their turns, both taking wide outside loops, putting more distance between Wasps for this part of the maneuver. All three Wasp pilots pushed their throttles to the stops. They wanted the Boems to follow, but they didn't want them to get close enough for accurate missile fire.

Eighteen seconds after Zel flipped, his Wasp crossed the first ridge. He was too low and moving too fast to have a chance to actually *see* any of the men on the ridge, but there were no surface-to-air missiles coming up at him, and that was all that really mattered. He kept going, past the second ridge, still losing altitude. The six Boems—none had been hit—kept coming, gaining very slightly on the Wasps, concentrating entirely on the pursuit.

"Just hold off for a few more seconds before you look down," Zel whispered. A rear-looking camera gave him a partial view of what was happening. He saw dozens—scores—of Vrerch missiles jump up from the first ridge, almost equal numbers from the second. The firing was so nearly simultaneous that it looked as if all of the rockets might have been fired on a single order.

Zel put his Wasp through a tight, climbing turn, just barely in time to see the culmination.

The six Boems had no chance to escape. There were too many rockets coming at them, all at once. Anywhere they might deke to get away from one would put them in the path of two or three others.

Three of the Boems actually were hit by more than one Vrerch. It looked as if one of them was struck by four within the space of a few hundredths of a second. Only one Schlinal pilot managed to eject, and his escape module was hit by a missile before it got ten meters from his plane.

Jase Wilmer screamed in delight. "Six down!" he shouted.

"Can it," Zel said sourly.

Just then, there was an explosion on the ground, on the mountain at the head of the valley.

"Somebody did good work," Gene Abru said as he watched the dust clear across the way. The blast had not been excessive, but it had certainly done the job. An entire section of mountain had crumbled and slid down to cover the only entrance to the laboratory.

"Thank you," Dr. Corey said without looking at him. She was still staring at the new mound of rubble. "I wish it hadn't been necessary."

"Yeah. Let's get moving. I'm supposed to deliver you and your people to the colonel." *And then we've got to get out of this death trap,* he thought.

CHAPTER 11

Sergeant Dem Nimz wrapped a second soaker around his left elbow, with help from Fredo Gariston. The painkiller in the first soaker had worn off, and there was still enough pain to bring a grimace to Dem's face. There were no broken bones in the elbow, but short of that there had to be considerable damage—torn muscles or cartilage, something. Anything that a soaker couldn't heal in four hours was major. There wasn't a single medic left from the ten that the two recon platoons had started out with. Medics always had high casualty rates, but this went beyond the normal attrition. The two platoons had been chopped apart. Together, they could only muster thirty-two men, little more than a quarter of their usual complement. And nearly half of them were wounded, a couple worse than Dem.

The two platoons had, in effect, merged. Dem was in command of the survivors. That they were cut off from any other Accord units by as much as three hundred kilometers rarely entered his mind. They still had a mission, to harass and delay a Heggie force that outnumbered them by approximately seventy to one.

Not that there was much they could do any longer.

"They're moving again," Fredo reported. He had recovered from his own, earlier, wound. He knelt at Dem's side and watched the pain fade from Nimz's face as the painkillers in the new soaker took effect. Dem let out a long, slow breath of relief, more emotion than he normally showed in a year.

"The new ambush?" Dem asked.

"They'll hit it in five or six minutes," Fredo said. All of the reccers who were still fit enough to move had gone off to set that trap. No one was short on ammunition. The reccers had been religious about reclaiming ammo from fallen comrades. Even after several hard skirmishes, the survivors had more ammunition than they had each started out with—wire for zippers, rocket-assisted cartridges for the Dupuys, Vrerchs, and hand grenades. The only munitions they were running short on were the RPGs. In this kind of work, that was often the preferred weapon.

"Then we'd better get moving too," Dem said. It was awkward getting to his feet. He couldn't use the left arm for anything, not even to extend it to the side to help balance himself. "Move around and get ready to hit them again."

"Dem, we're gonna have to contact headquarters, find out where we should go," Fredo said.

Dem shook his head. "Not yet. Even if the Heggies can't read our calls, they might be able to DF them. We're far enough up against it without that. As long as we follow these bastards, we're gonna get closer to our people."

The two men stared at each other for a time, then Dem turned and started walking. "On your feet," he said, speaking conversationally. Their Heyers were no longer available. They had been smashed by the Heggies several hours before.

The eight others who were near got up and followed. Fredo Gariston brought up the rear. They would rendezvous with anyone who made it back from the latest ambush up ahead.

The 13th was on the move again even before Abru's SI team brought the researchers to Colonel Stossen. Those elements of the 13th that were in the valley headed toward a high pass at the far end, north, and farther into the mountain range. Those that had been waiting outside, including the artillery and support vehicles, were to circle around to the right, keeping as close to the rest as they could—with only a mountain between them.

"We'll try to get as far as here," Stossen told his staff, pointing out the location on his mapboard. "If we can stay just one or two valleys in from where the artillery can go, we might be able to keep some sort of cover from them. We'll try to rendezvous at this point." He indicated the spot on the map again. Then he looked around at the others. "If we can."

"What about the APCs?" Dezo asked. "They're still out there. They've taken a loop around Justice and still haven't had any enemy contact on the ground."

"The Heggies are chasing them," Bal said. "They know that *we're* here after losing six Boems, but they still seem more interested in the vehicles."

"That's almost the only good news we have," Stossen said. "That and the fact that we got the people we came for." He looked up again. He could see the column coming—the researchers and the SI team.

Gene Abru didn't wait for the colonel to beckon him closer. He lifted his helmet visor and went right up to Stossen. "Colonel, this is Dr. Philippa Corey, head of . . . these people. Dr. Corey, Colonel Stossen."

Stossen had had his own visor up for his staff conference. "Dr. Corey, I'm glad to see you made it."

"So far. I'd be grateful for anything you can tell me of the current situation. We've been pretty much in the dark."

"I'm afraid it will have to be on the march, Doctor. We can't hang around here. I hope you and your people are up to some hard walking. It may well be several days before I can offer you a ride."

"It's hard to stay fit cooped up in a hole in the ground," Dr. Corey said, "but we'll make do. We don't have much choice, do we?"

"No, I'm afraid not. You might have been safer where you were."

"That wouldn't have lasted much longer," Corey said. "Another six months and even our food replicators wouldn't have been sufficient, even if the Schlinal army hadn't found us."

"Sergeant Abru. Your team will stay with the doctor and her people. From now until this mission is over, they are your only concern. You understand me?"

Gene did, completely. "Yes, sir." If worse came to worst, it would still be up to the SI team to make sure that the researchers didn't fall into enemy hands. "I understand."

Stossen stared at him for perhaps a half minute before he nodded and turned his attention back to Dr. Corey. "We're starting out immediately, over the pass at your end of the valley, into the next reach."

"Difficult country, Colonel," Corey said. "We'll try not to slow you down too much."

• • •

"I hear half of those people are women," Wiz Mackey told Mort Jaiffer. "They gonna put you on a leash to keep you away from 'em?"

"More slander?" Mort asked, as tired as his voice sounded. Mort hadn't been able to escape rumors that he was a womanizer, that he had left his university post because of some scandal involving the dean's daughter. Or wife. Both versions remained current. "Anyway, there are only four women, and they're probably all too old anyway."

"That's not what I heard," Wiz said. Word had quickly floated through the 13th of the women, and the men, who had been brought in by SI. No one seemed to know just who they were, or why they were so important, but the general consensus—even among those who had no real information—was that those nine people were the entire reason why the 13th had been sent on this mission. "I heard that at least two of 'em are real lookers, including the boss lady. Anyhow, they're brainy types, like you."

Mort shook his head. "I swore off brainy types when I enlisted. Now, get your mind back where it's supposed to be."

Mort pulled his visor down to emphasize the end of the conversation and moved farther ahead of Wiz. Like many others, Mort was still trying to puzzle out *why* those people were important enough to risk more than two thousand highly trained elite soldiers on what looked as if it might easily turn into a suicide mission. *With my background, I* should *be able to figure it out,* Mort thought, but beyond the obvious *It must be* really *big,* he didn't have a clue.

The climb at the end of the valley was relatively easy, but the way was too narrow for comfort. All of the 13th had to funnel together, up a narrowing slope leading to a pass that was no more than fifteen meters wide along much of its length. Colonel Stossen called for speed, trying to get everyone through the bottleneck as quickly as possible. Intervals were cut to almost nothing, bunching up several hundred soldiers at a time. They were far too vulnerable to an air attack like that.

"Maybe the Heggies won't be so quick to send Boems the next time," Joe Baerclau muttered as he led his platoon through the narrowest part of the pass. "Not after what we did to that last batch." It would be impossible to sucker another flight the way they had the first. But seeing six enemy fighters blown out of the sky simultaneously had been a major morale boost for the men of the 13th. There had actually been cheers along the ridge line. *As if we'd just won the whole damn campaign,* Joe thought, somewhat sourly. He had shouted at his men when they started cheering with the rest. Maybe it *was* a time for them to feel good, but in moderation. There was still a long way to go, and no better than an even chance to make it to the end.

If that.

Everyone who carried Vrerchs had one loaded. Anxious eyes watched the sky. The three Wasps had gone, off to find their ground support to rearm and get fresh batteries. It might take some time with the rest of the 13th on the move again.

Near the end of the pass, First Sergeant Walker was standing to the side, watching Echo Company move through. Joe got out of line and went over to him.

"Any ideas where we're going now?" Joe asked.

Walker shook his head. "Not beyond this next stretch. Colonel hasn't passed the word yet except that we're going the length of this next valley. My guess is that we're going to rendezvous with the Havocs and the rest somewhere up ahead. After that, your guess is as good as mine."

"Anything on the civilians?"

"Just the same scuttlebutt I'm sure you've heard. Your lads keeping up?"

"We're in pretty good shape, I guess," Joe said.

"And you?"

"Fit as ever."

"We get around to taking a break, you'd better have your squad leaders do a quick inventory—munitions, food, and water. All our reserves are with the support vans."

Joe grinned. He couldn't help himself. "We are getting a bit tight on Vrerchs."

"With any luck, we won't need them for a while." Izzy Walker shook his head to keep from grinning back. He had enjoyed the show himself. "Now, you'd better get going or you'll have to run to catch up with your men." Second platoon was already past the two men, as was half of third platoon.

Joe took a moment to scan the sky through a complete circle before he moved after his platoon. There were no planes visible, from either side.

The descent on the far side of the pass was somewhat more gentle than the climb, and the way widened out as well. The 13th didn't have to remain bunched up for long, and most of the men got at least a few minutes to rest waiting for those wider intervals to develop.

The new valley was wide open. There were virtually no trees in it, merely grass and extensive patches of wildflowers. Little cover. Only along the lower slopes of the hills on either side was there any place for a man to hide. On both sides there were rather extensive scree fields—loose rock and a fair number of larger boulders. The slopes just above those fields were rocky and broken. The 13th could make decent time down the center of the valley and, with just a little warning, disperse to the rocks at either side if trouble approached.

One line company and one recon platoon were set to follow the high ground on either side, as close to the crests as they could reasonably get. Patrols were sent all of the way to the top to provide what security they could.

Joe whispered a short prayer of thanks that Echo didn't draw one of the flanking assignments. The going had to be a lot rougher up high.

Three Nova tanks were coming along the riverbank, in line, not twenty meters from the water. Dem Nimz raised his head just enough to look over the lip of the slit trench he had excavated for himself. A camouflaged thermal tarp was stretched over the top of the hole, the edges weighted down with rocks. Three tanks. Dem pulled his head back down. At least none of the Novas were headed *directly* at his hole, or at any of the others scattered along this stretch.

We'd better get all three of them the first time, Dem thought. Once the reccers showed themselves, they would be in for it—again—unless all three tanks went at once.

Where's their infantry? he wondered next. It was unlikely that tanks would have been sent without mudders. Armor and infantry depended on each other. Without mudders, tanks were juicy targets. Without tanks to back them up, infantry was also especially vulnerable.

Dem gave himself thirty seconds before he lifted his head again. His hole wasn't the closest one to the oncoming tanks, but he didn't want to risk radio communications yet. All of his people knew what to do, and he had no doubts about their talents. Or determination.

The first tank was less than forty meters from Dem, between him and the river. The interval between the Novas was about fifteen meters, as near as Dem could estimate from his hole. Mudders? . . .

There. A skirmish line just behind the third Nova, a second line twenty-five meters behind them. Dem glanced at the time line on his visor display. Then he looked at the lead tank again. *Any second now.*

He slid his Armanoc forward a little. Once the tanks were hit, they would have to deal with the enemy mudders. It looked as if there were at least a full company of them, perhaps even as many as two hundred men.

Before the first Vrerchs streaked out toward the tanks, Dem discovered that he was holding his breath. He had to force himself to start up again. The rockets flashed out from concealed holes. None of them had more than sixty meters to travel, and even if the tankers had spotted the rockets the instant they were launched, they would not have had time to maneuver to try to escape them. Everything depended on the aim of the shooters, and the working of the Vrerchs' video guidance systems. There wasn't room for error.

The Novas went within a second of one another. The Schlinal infantry started shooting even before the rockets hit. Vrerchs did leave a thin trail in some circumstances. The reccers who had fired them were slammed with heavy return fire, first from wire rifles, and then also with grenades.

Dem pulled his head back down for an instant. They had all known the risks. But he did need a second to swallow the lump in his throat.

Let them get closer, Dem thought. Hold off until the last possible second, until wire would rip through Heggie body armor without difficulty and there were too many targets too close to miss. It might prove to be a last stand for the reccers, and Dem wanted to make it memorable.

One more quick look—just up a few centimeters, then back down. Anything longer or higher was too dangerous. The Heggie skirmish lines were still advancing. Several groups were coming together, moving toward the holes from which the Vrerchs had been fired.

Good, good! Dem told himself. The closer together they were, the easier it would be to mow them down.

All together now: Dem silently counted to ten, then said one word over his helmet radio. There was no longer any need to worry about the enemy intercepting it.

"Now!"

Dem came up to his knees, pushing the tarp back. His finger went down on the trigger of his zipper as soon as the muzzle was above ground level. He moved the stream of wire back and forth over a narrow front, scarcely aware that all of the men left to his command were doing the same.

The Armanoc Mark VI could fire continuously for twenty seconds before it emptied a full spool of wire. When Dem's gun went dry, he already had the next spool in his left hand. His right thumb ejected the old spool, the new one went in, and within three seconds he was back in business.

Firing one-handed was no problem. The Heggies were close enough that there was no significant loss of accuracy. Dem started tossing hand grenades, scarcely letting off on the rifle's trigger each time he hurled one of the one-kilo bombs. The Heggies had, naturally enough, gone to ground as soon as the rifle fire started, but they had no real cover, not even the minimal protection of a slit trench.

It almost made up for the wide disparity in numbers.

Dem used every grenade he had. There was no sense trying to save anything for "later." There was too little chance that there would be another opportunity to use any of his weapons. A third spool of wire.

The volume of fire, from both sides, faded quickly. Dem went back down into his hole as he emptied the third spool. Little more than a minute had passed since he had started shooting. Perhaps another twenty-five seconds had elapsed since the Vrerchs were fired.

"Down!" Dem ordered. The volume of fire dropped again, but not by much. There weren't many reccers left.

"Everybody get fresh spool in," Dem said. He might as well get talkative now. There was no use in leaving anything to chance.

How much time do we have? he wondered. The most likely scenario for the Heggies would be a sudden barrage of grenades, to save on people—not that the Schlinal military was known for that sort of consideration.

Twenty seconds. Most of the Heggies had also stopped firing, waiting to see what happened next, or waiting for new orders.

Not much longer, Dem decided. Whoever was in charge of the Heggie company would have to do something, even if it was only to send a single squad out to root out any remaining Freebies (as the Heggie soldiers called Accord troops). One squad to draw fire and expose the enemy.

"On my order, up and break for those trees over to the left," Dem said, uncertain how many of his comrades might be left to hear the call, or how many might be alive but too badly wounded to make it out of their trenches.

"Go!" It was not a mad, heedless run. Twelve reccers got up shooting. The trees were off at an angle to the line of Heggies. It might be difficult for the reccers to run and fire to the side at the same time, but they did it, trying more to suppress enemy fire than score hits now. They ran hunched over, zigging and zagging, doing everything they could to increase their slim chances. This time, Dem didn't keep his finger on the trigger continuously. He squeezed off very short bursts, no more than a second at a time, trying to extend this spool until he hit the next cover. Reloading on the run would take too much time.

The return fire was lighter than Dem had expected—feared. It seemed as if there were few more Heggies shooting than reccers. For just an instant, Dem wondered if he had made a mistake ordering this retreat. If they had stayed put, they might have been able to save wounded comrades.

Or not. There were too few of them left to be able to carry many seriously wounded. That would just make them all easy pickings for the enemy. To be able to continue the fight, they had to be able to keep moving, and moving fast. If they escaped this fight.

Dem saw one of his men go down but couldn't be certain who it was. He didn't even know who was left. *Eleven of us now,* he thought, but he kept shooting and running.

Once they reached the trees, it was a little easier. The temptation was simply to stop, to lean against the first tree of sufficient size, to rest for a second and do a little more-accurate shooting, but Dem resisted, and without orders to the contrary, the rest of the reccers kept running as well. They stopped shooting. By this time, they were far enough from the Heggies that there was little incoming wire, and little chance that it would do serious damage.

The Heggies didn't get up and start in immediate pursuit either. For a second, that surprised Dem, then he realized that, by now, they must suspect that even this mad dash was no more than a ruse to pull them into yet another trap. The reccers had done that before . . . when there were enough of them.

"Grab cover," Dem said over the radio, barely able to find the wind for even two words. He flopped to the ground, careful to have a tree between him and where—he thought—the Heggies were now.

For nearly two minutes, Dem could do nothing but suck in air convulsively. There was a muscle spasm in his neck, trying to jerk his head around to one side a little. He fought that, and fought to control his breathing. Finally, he was able to scuttle around on his belly so that he was looking back toward where they had left the Heggies—and far too many of their own comrades. He saw no sign of pursuit yet. There was no shooting going on either.

"Dem?" Just the name over the radio.

"Yeah. Who's that?"

"Fredo."

"What?"

There was a noticeable pause before Fredo said, "That was my question. What now?"

And Dem hesitated before he answered. "Two more minutes, then we'll put more distance between us and them. We'll worry about later later."

At least there was going to be a later, even if it proved to be very short-lived.

CHAPTER 12

Dr. Corey had merely flopped on her back in the nearest patch of shade when Colonel Stossen finally gave the word for a break. For the first several minutes, she managed to keep her mind almost a blank. Her aching legs gave her plenty to think about.

"A little water, Doctor?" Stossen asked. She opened her eyes.

"Thank you." She sat up and took the canteen he offered. After a long pull at the tepid water, she said, "I knew I was out of shape after two years cooped up inside that mountain, but I didn't realize just how much out of shape. You people set a wicked pace."

"Unfortunately, it's necessary," Stossen said, sitting on his haunches. "Things haven't gone very well for the Accord on Jordan."

Corey looked down. "We had guessed that when so long passed without people coming to get us. Just how bad is it?"

"We may have to evacuate what troops we can. If that happens, it will be very bad. Withdrawing from a planet under fire . . ." He shook his head. A rear guard, probably all of the Wasps left, maybe a few companies—even a complete regiment—of infantry to provide some cover. "Very bad," he repeated.

"Will it be possible to get a secure data-link to one of your ships?"

"Yes. That much we can arrange, once we rendezvous with our vehicles. All we have here is voice and the telemetry signals for mapboards and helmet displays."

"A cube reader?" Corey asked.

Stossen hesitated. "That I'm not sure of. Probably not."

"We have six gigabyte cubes of data that needs to get back to the Accord even if we don't," Corey said. "The results of a lot of work. If we had anything secure enough to use at the lab, we would have done it from there, but we simply weren't set up for that contingency."

"Don't even hint at what your work is all about, not even to me," Stossen said.

"I won't, but I must say that getting our work out so that others can finish it is absolutely vital. Just as vital as making sure that Schline doesn't get it or us."

"I'll have my people find out if we have cube readers on any of the vehicles. If not, then—maybe—we can have one of our Havocs fly the cubes back to General Dacik's headquarters. I know for certain that they have the equipment there."

Dr. Corey nodded slowly. "I'd prefer something less . . . chancy, if possible. A Havoc can be shot down, and I'd hate to lose all that data that way. Besides, if Schlinal people got to the wreckage, they might be able to salvage the data from the cubes, and *that* is unthinkable."

"There might not be any other way. I'll find out."

"Of course, the most preferred way would be for us to get out with the data. The time that would be lost if a new team had to get up to speed on what we've already done, before they could push it forward . . ." She let that hang in the air. It really didn't need to be finished.

The three Wasps flew scant meters off of the ground. The formation was very loose. There was simply no room for maneuver otherwise, not even with the sophisticated anti-collision and terrain-hugging navigation systems the Wasps boasted. Zel was at the apex of the triangle. Irv was on his left, and Jase on the right, each keeping at least fifty meters to the side and thirty behind the new Blue one. The planes had found their support vans and had even stayed on the ground for some twenty minutes before receiving new mission orders.

They were going back to harass the same Heggie force they had attacked the day before. That force had been weakened by its clashes with the 13th's reccers and Afghan Battery, but they had also exacted a murderous price. The lone Havoc left from Afghan had finally rejoined the rest of the 13th's artillery, but there was no trace of the two recon platoons that had also been sent out to slow down the Heggie regiment.

Stay low to avoid premature discovery. In daylight, the matte black coloring of the Wasps could be seen visually if not by radar or laser tracking devices. And there was no rain, no low, heavy clouds to provide cover today either. Stay down so that the Heggies won't see the Wasps coming until they are right on top of the formation, making their first rocket and cannon runs. Take on whatever targets of opportunity appear in front of you. Tanks were choice, but they weren't to go out of their way—or spend excessive time over the enemy—just to get tanks. Strafing enemy infantry was almost as valuable, and knocking out trucks was even better. Take whatever presents itself first. Make one quick run through the enemy and then get out. Keep moving. Time a return for at least twenty minutes later, from a different direction, and then make just one more quick pass, the same way, before returning to base for new batteries and ammunition.

Most importantly, do everything possible to avoid air battles. If enemy Boems are detected, run, even if that means aborting the ground attack mission.

Zel had mixed feeling about the orders. Part of his mind was glad to see the low-risk plan, but another part rebelled. It didn't seem right to cut and run. A Wasp could inflict a lot of damage on an enemy. To do anything less seemed almost indecent.

He watched all of his displays, wishing that he had an extra set of eyes so that he could keep a constant watch over everything. It was downright dangerous flying a Wasp at nearly the speed of sound this close to the ground, following every contour, cutting through forest clearings below treetop level, hopping up only to clear obstacles before dropping back. Quite often the digital readout on the altimeter flashed red with the collision warning—Zel had switched off the audible alert siren—when the numbers dropped below five meters. That was the farthest down the alert system could be set for. The default was thirty meters.

"Less than thirty seconds," Zel warned his wingmen. "If the tracking data is right," he added. The Heggies couldn't be *too* far from where the spyeyes had last located them, even though that data had to be at least five minutes old—and probably twice that. Most of the Heggie force was on foot now, and their armored support had been marking time to stay relatively close to the mudders.

Zel took a last look at his readouts, then adjusted his grip on the control yoke so that his left thumb was a little closer to the weapon selector switch. He wouldn't know whether he needed rockets or cannon until the last instant, until he saw whatever was in front of him when the enemy appeared.

Once he saw the Heggie force, Zel had no time to really notice the full disposition of their men—the three columns of infantry marching some scores of meters apart, the few trucks that were still with them, the flanking lines of tanks and scouts. There simply was not enough time over the target for observation of that sort, not for a human brain and senses. The cameras and other observation gear that the Wasps carried did record everything and transmit it to CIC, but Zel was not aware of most of it.

What he did see was a Schlinal Nova tank right in front of him—less than one degree off his initial heading. He made that adjustment, armed two rockets, and showed them the target. As soon as they had been launched, he switched to the forward cannons and started his strafing run, cutting across all three infantry columns. At the end, he switched back to rockets and launched another two at a Nova on the far side of the formation.

Then he was gone, before the Heggies could get even a single surface-to-air missile up after him.

A restrained whoop from Irv showed that he too had made it clear of the enemy. That was followed almost immediately by a quick call from Jase.

"They didn't know what hit 'em."

"Don't get carried away," Zel warned. "They may have Boems on call. Keep your eyes open. We'll do a large clockwise loop to come back at them. Twenty minutes, they'll still be nervous. We'll see SAMs next time."

It *was* a good skirmish, though. The three of them had accounted for at least four Novas, several of their remaining trucks, plus uncountable infantry—without even taking enemy fire. The number crunchers in analysis liked numbers like those.

The 13th's remaining Havocs had gone to ground. They were no more than eight kilometers from the rendezvous point, close enough to get there—or send in covering fire—in a hurry, but far enough away that they wouldn't tip the location to the enemy if they were discovered. In any case, they had better cover where they were than they would have had closer to the rendezvous point. They were in tall timber, engines off, thermal tarps spread over the gun carriages. The crews were out of their Havocs, away from them, trying to get a little rest.

The crew of Afghan four, the one gun that survived from that battery, was sitting with the crew of Basset two. The Afghan men had already told their horror story. Empty meal packs were scattered around the gunners, not yet collected and buried.

"Apt to happen to all of us," Simon Kilgore said. "That's what 'expendable' means. They don't figure any of us are likely to make it back from this one."

"Don't get off on that again," Eustace Ponks snapped. "Afghan just got the bad break. Rest of us haven't even had a taste yet. Just been a long ride."

"Won't be a free ride, though," Simon said, looking at his boss. "Those Heggies that hit Afghan and the reccers are still coming. With a gaggle of Novas."

"Novas, bah." Eustace hawked noisily and spat to the side. "We kin knock Novas out ten klicks before they get close enough to even shoot at us."

"If we know where they are," Simon reminded him. "This mess, that ain't likely."

"Colonel'll find some way to give us targets," Eustace said. "Wasps or reccers if we can't count on spyeyes and CIC." *Just as long as he doesn't block us in deep in these mountains,* Eustace thought, looking up at the range that was already right on their flank. The rendezvous point was *in* there, past that first thousand-meter ridge. But Eustace was trying to sound positive, to counter Simon's pessimism. It wouldn't do to mention his own considerable worries.

"Hell, we've got almost a full load of ammo yet," Karl Mennem, the gunner, said. "We'll give a good showing. Ain't we always?"

"Course we have," Eustace said. Then he met the gaze of Afghan four's commander, and he had to look away. There was terror in those eyes.

Dem Nimz couldn't remember just when he had started limping. There had been too much else happening for him to think about that. The limp had started and grown gradually worse before he was even aware of it. His right knee was sore and slightly swollen. The muscles in the back of the leg had tightened up, cramping. At first, Dem had simply tried to favor that leg—as much as he could—but that effort had just brought stiffness to the other leg as well, and to his hips and back.

"We'd better take a break and give you time to put on a couple of soakers," Fredo said.

"Not yet."

"Yes," Fredo said, his voice getting firmer. "You might be in charge here, but unless you do something fast, you're not going to be able to walk at all before long, and we've got enough problems without carrying you."

Dem looked at him for a moment—still walking—then he nodded and stopped. Fredo passed the order to the others. Altogether, there were only ten of them left, out of the hundred who had begun the mission.

When Dem fell trying to ease himself to the ground, he had to concede (to himself at least) that Fredo had been right.

"Let me take a look," Fredo said.

Dem didn't protest. When Fredo asked, he described just what hurt. Fredo took nearly ten minutes making his examination and wrapping soakers.

"We're going to have to take a little more time," he said when he had the last in place. "You won't be able to navigate decently for at least thirty minutes. An hour's rest would be a lot better."

"Thirty minutes," Dem said. "That gives us all time to eat and get a little rest."

They had been moving hard for more than two hours since escaping the last firefight. Dem wasn't certain, but he thought that they must have covered at least sixteen kilometers of broken country in that time. That had included one touchy river ford, in water up to their necks. Cold water. It had been after that when Dem's leg had started to bother him enough to matter—something he recalled only sprawled out on his back with the analgesic in the soakers starting to relieve the pain.

"You keepin' track of our course?" Dem asked after a couple more minutes.

"I've had an eye on it," Fredo said. "By now, we must be at least a dozen klicks northeast of that Heggie force. And we're getting farther away from our own people as well."

"We'll angle back toward the southeast when we get started again," Dem said.

"You're not thinking of another ambush, are you?"

Dem hesitated before he shook his head. "No, I guess not." He *had* considered the possibility, but he had quickly dismissed the idea. Even if he were willing to attack a full regiment with ten men—and he was—they simply did not have the ammunition to sustain an attack, to do enough damage to make the almost certain cost worthwhile.

"If we can, we'll rejoin the Team," he said. "If we can find them."

"We can find them," Fredo said. "We might have to turn mountain goat to get to them, but we can find them." Even the climbing wouldn't bother Fredo Gariston. Or any of the other reccers.

His voice little more than a whisper, Dem asked, "Where did we go wrong, Fredo? How did we manage to screw up so badly?"

"Who said we screwed up? Considering the odds we faced, we did damn good, us and the Havocs and the Wasps."

"With ninety percent casualties?"

"We still hurt the Heggies bad," Fredo said. "Their losses must be more'n twice ours. They just started out with twenty times as many men."

"We've taken hits before," Dem said. "Never this bad. Never. No reccer unit ever has." The soakers were starting to take effect. The relief was limited to the areas where they had been applied, but Dem seemed to feel a more general analgesic effect, almost as if his brain were growing numb as well. He let his head sag back against the ground. Within seconds, he was asleep.

Fredo stared at his friend for a moment. *Just as well if he gets twenty minutes,* he decided. Then he got up. While he was playing medic, he might as well make the rounds, see if anyone else needed help.

But he couldn't help thinking how welcome a little sleep of his own would be.

Echo Company had been cycled into the center of the formation, providing additional security for Colonel Stossen's headquarters detachment and the civilians that had been pulled from the mountain. This sort of rotation of duty was fairly common, when there was a chance. It gave a company time away from the greater stress of perimeter duty. Echo had been on point for one column for much of the night. They were due a little relief.

The new position gave everyone in 2nd platoon a chance to see the research team at relatively close quarters. Second platoon was right behind them on the march. Joe Baerclau had difficulty keeping down the extraneous chatter among the men in his platoon. He had to act the part of the Bear to do any good at all.

They're sure not cut out for this kind of hike, Joe thought as he watched the civilians trying to keep up. Several of them had gone limp, necessitating short stops while medics applied soakers and gave advice on how to minimize walking injuries. The 13th wasn't making anywhere near the time it could have made without the civilians. Rest stops were more frequent, and longer, than they would have been without the amateurs, and the pace on the march seemed to be off by about 10 percent.

Guess we can't expect more, Joe conceded. Nine civilians, four of them women, the youngest probably past thirty-five and none of them used to this kind of trek. They'll be better off once we can get them a ride.

Trucks, APCs. There would be rides for the civilians, at least, once they rejoined the rest of the Team. But where were the APCs that had been sent out as decoys? Joe hadn't heard any news of them. Even Lieutenant Keye claimed to have no word of their fate, or location. Nothing had come from headquarters.

Bal Kenneck was the one who got the first message from the APCs. They were coming under fire from enemy tanks. Several times during the past day, Boem fighters had made quick passes, but this was the first time that the Heyers had been attacked by Schlinal ground forces.

"Okay, they've done their job," Colonel Stossen said when Kenneck gave him the news. "Tell them to break off and run for it as far and as fast as they can. We'll worry about rendezvous later. If they have a later. Don't tell them that last part," he added, unnecessarily.

Kenneck switched channels to pass the orders. Stossen stared at him, his teeth clamped so tightly together that it seemed they must splinter. Sacrificial lambs. Stossen had known that when he sent them out. Heyer APCs had no defense against tanks or artillery, or air attack. Their splat guns might do some good against infantry, for a while, but their armor wasn't thick enough to stand up to the 135mm munitions that Novas could throw at them.

If half of them escaped, it would be a victory, but Stossen held little hope of that. He didn't allow himself to dream of that sort of miracle. All the APCs could do now was—perhaps—buy a few more minutes of time for the rest of the 13th . . . the way 1st and 3rd recon and Afghan Battery had.

"They're running due south," Kenneck said when he had finished talking to the leader of the Heyer formation. "They have about a ninety-minute straight run that way. The Heggies will have to decide whether or not to risk pursuing them with just their armor or letting them get away."

"They've sent armor off without infantry support before."

"But this force has already walked into several traps. They might be hesitant to risk it again," Kenneck said.

"I hope you're right. It's about the only chance those poor bastards in the mixers have."

Kenneck didn't try to counter that. "Assuming that at least a fair number of them escape, Colonel, what sort of routing should we give them? After they've made that ninety-minute run, they're going to face a couple of options."

"Dig out your mapboard. Let's take a look." Stossen shook his head, almost angrily. "I guess I'm going to have to decide what *we're* going to do before I know where to send them."

It was a decision he had been putting off. There didn't seem to be any particularly *good* choices. Two long conferences with General Dacik hadn't helped much. The general had left it up to him. "We'd like to have you back here to help," Dacik said, "but you are stirring up the enemy nicely the way you're going. Bottom line is, you still have to remember your primary mission. Do whatever seems to offer the best hope of getting your charges to safety."

Where in the name of all that's holy is there any *safety on Jordan?* Stossen asked himself. Not out here, more than a thousand kilometers from the rest of the Accord forces and support. Not back with them. The Accord was still outnumbered by at least three to two on Jordan, and the enemy seemed to have greater stores of munitions.

Bal adjusted the field of view on the mapboard to include all three elements of the 13th—the infantry, the armor and support vehicles, and the convoy of APCs. The first two groups were now no more than a dozen kilometers apart. The APCs were more than three-hundred kilometers away, and extending that distance slightly on their southward run.

"If we break due east, toward the coast," Kenneck suggested, moving his finger over the screen from their present position to the edge, "then south. That might give us the best chance of getting back to our lines. Eventually."

"Expand the view," Stossen said, and Kenneck did. At the new scale, there was little detail to be seen. "That's got to be, what, fifteen hundred klicks or more to the coast?"

Kenneck worked the controls. "Closer to seventeen hundred," he said. "One major river crossing. We'd have to make that here." He pointed. "It's the only place along that last eight hundred klicks of river that we could be sure of getting the Havocs and the other vehicles across."

"And if the Heggies see that that's where we're going?"

"They could catch us there and pretty much do what they want," Kenneck admitted. "But it's so obvious that maybe we can get away with it. Especially if General Dacik can arrange some sort of diversion at the same time. Maybe the same sort of effort he staged to let us break out at the start of this chase."

"On the other hand," Stossen said. "If we break east, then turn *north*." He showed Kenneck what he was thinking of on the board. "We could get so far from any Schlinal base that we'd be almost in the clear. That might make it possible for us to get landers in, at least to evacuate our guests."

Kenneck nodded. "That would put us well out of Boem range, at least any base we know of. But it would put us completely out of everything else here, Colonel. As far as either side was concerned, we'd be effectively out of existence. Total displacement. The Heggies could ignore us, and we wouldn't be helping our people. If that made the difference, they could come after us later, whenever they felt like it, *after* they'd wiped out the rest of our forces. Maybe we can get off-world, but that won't help General Dacik, or the Accord."

"It would accomplish our primary mission," Stossen said softly.

"But?" Kenneck prompted, noting the hesitation in the colonel's voice.

"We *might* make the difference here. You've been through the same command schools I have. Tactical displacement. I'd hate to see the 13th rendered irrelevant." He stared at the mapboard. He knew what choice he had to make, but still he hesitated. Once he gave the orders, the 13th would be committed.

Finally, he nodded. "We'll go your way. Figure out the best place to bring us all back together and get the orders out to the APCs. I'm going to talk to Dr. Corey, let her know what we're going to try."

And then I'll have to convince the general that I know what I'm doing, Stossen thought. Despite the way that Dacik had left the decision to him, he still thought his orders might be overruled.

CHAPTER 13

Blue Flight made three runs against the tank column that started chasing the Heyers. The first time, the Wasps were unopposed in the air and had only a few surface-to-air missiles to worry about. On that trip, the three Wasps accounted for six tanks without taking any losses themselves. The second time, they had only made their first run when a flight of six Boems appeared. The Wasps had turned and run, leading the Boems away from the APCs, playing cat and mouse with them until the planes on both sides had no choice but to return to base for fresh batteries. But that mission did give the Heyers a chance to put a little more distance between themselves and the Novas. The Schlinal tanks continued their pursuit of the Heyers, but—for the moment at least—they were too far away to do any damage to the APCs that had made it that far.

It was late afternoon before Blue Flight made their third sorties to provide cover for the Heyers.

If I were the Schlinal air commander, I'd have an entire squadron of Boems waiting to jump us, Zel thought as he led his flight toward the enemy Novas. *I'd have them low, maybe even on the ground, close enough to get to us in seconds, maybe from two or three directions.*

"Keep your eyes open for enemy fighters," he warned Irv and Jase—for perhaps the third time since their last takeoff. "This time, they *have* to be expecting us."

But not only were there no Boems waiting, not even the Novas were where Zel expected to find them.

"Get some altitude," he told the others. "Let's see if they've broken off the pursuit or just changed course to throw us off."

Unless the Novas were shielded, they would be able to spot them from a long way off, by heat signature if not visually. A tank put out a lot of heat if its engine was running. The stealth technology put into aircraft wasn't wasted on ground vehicles, by either side.

Blue Flight climbed to twenty-five hundred meters and started a wide loop. It only took a few seconds for the tank formation to show on their screens, moving slightly north of east, roughly perpendicular to the course that the APCs—who had not completed their own turn to the east—had been following.

"Must be rendezvousing with their mudders," Irv suggested. "Heading east, they must still figure on coming after our people."

Zel radioed back to Colonel Stossen's headquarters for instruction. There was a delay while the ops officer conferred with the colonel.

"One more pass at the tanks," Zel told Irv and Jase. "Then we move south to provide direct cover for the Heyers. They're turning east themselves."

It wasn't until the Wasps were in their attack dives that any of the pilots noticed that there were other vehicles with the tanks now, several trucks of the sort that the Heggies used for infantry transport. While the Novas started maneuvering to try to escape the attack as soon as they spotted the Wasps, the trucks just stopped. Men started jumping out of them.

"Watch out for SAMs," Zel warned. It was too late to do much more. He had his first pair of missiles armed and targeted. As soon as they were clear of the launch rack, he flipped his Wasp over on its side so that it presented its narrowest profile to the infantrymen. At the same time, he pushed the throttles full forward. If the men on the ground couldn't get a target lock, their missiles were almost useless.

The Wasps broke in three different directions, circling and climbing. The shoulder-launched infantry SAMs the Schlinal army used had an effective ceiling of no more than six-thousand meters. Above that, they lost power and fell away.

"Let's give those mudders something to think about," Zel said as soon as he saw that his wingmen were out of immediate danger.

"Out and down, then back low. Don't give them a look at us until it's too late."

Coming in the next time with cannon instead of missiles, Zel was right at ground level. To the Schlinal troops he was aimed at, it had to appear as if he had come out from behind a stand of trees, no more than a hundred meters from the nearest truck and less than five meters off the ground. While his 25mm cannons were firing, with the needle-like projectiles spreading out, there was nothing any mudder could do but hug dirt and hope that he wasn't in the direct path of any of those splinters. Two trucks erupted as fuel tanks were sieved.

Zel would have jumped, had he been able to, when he saw the muzzle flash on a Nova almost directly in front of him.

"Too low!" he said, unaware that he was screaming. The Wasps had evaded any enemy missiles with the tactic, but that had put them low enough for the enemy tankers to take a few shots.

Zel flipped his Wasp to the left, going through three complete rolls no more than ten meters off of the ground, before he turned and fled.

"I counted five shots," Jase called over the radio. He was shouting too.

"Let's get out of here before they start up again," Zel said. I don't want to try that again.

Basset and Dingo batteries were heading west, traveling back over ground they had traversed only hours before. For what little good it might do them, the Havocs were all running with thermal tarps tied in place over them.

"It's nuts," Simon Kilgore said in Basset two. "We're putting out an exhaust plume fifty meters long in infrared. What possible good can that tarp do except partially blind *us*?"

"It saves us the trouble of putting it up every time we stop," Eustace replied. He wasn't happy with the tarp either, but as long as Simon was complaining, he wouldn't. "And we can see just fine. I made sure none of the lenses were covered when we strapped it on. Don't use that as an excuse for your driving."

That shut Simon up, for a time at least. A slur against his driving ability was almost guaranteed to provide at least fifteen minutes of silence from him—save for the demands of the work.

An ambush. Eustace was rather intrigued by the possibilities. Havocs weren't normally used that way, stuck in camouflaged positions to wait for an enemy to come within certain killing range. It was dangerous, but it would also give them a chance to inflict heavy damage. Once the shooting started, the Havocs would be moving again, no doubt about that. And then it would be the same old chase. But the initial ambush might give them a decent advantage, even if the Heggies still had the numbers, and the tanks.

Eustace paid more attention than usual to the map console in front of him. It was scaled back to show a two-hundred kilometer square now. In most actions, Eustace kept the scale much tighter, worrying only about the twenty to thirty kilometers right around the Fat Turtle. The danger zone. But now he was watching two other groups—the Heggie column and the retreating Heyer APCs. If either of them changed course, the Havocs might also have to make adjustments.

Haul 'em right past us, Eustace thought, a silent message to the Heyers. *We'll be waiting.* He grinned. Basset and Dingo could get in a little payback for what these Heggies and their air support had done to Afghan Battery.

"When we make our final turn to the right, we'll drag down on the throttles, do what we can to minimize the exhaust," Eustace said. That was as far as he would go toward soothing Simon's hurt feelings. They *were* part of the same team. The men of a gun crew lived and, all too often, died together. They were cooped up with each other all of the time in the Fat Turtle. It wouldn't do to let conditions get *too* strained.

Simon didn't respond. As long as the engines were running, it wouldn't make much difference if they rode along at an idle. There would still be that plume of heat behind them.

"I want good holes," Joe Baerclau told his squad leaders. "It looks as if we'll be here at least eight hours, maybe longer. Colonel said we're waiting for the APCs. If they can't shake the Heggies chasing them before they get here, we could have our hands full."

"They're *leading* the Heggies to us?" Ezra asked.

"No, they're leading their tanks, maybe all of 'em, into an ambush, a good 250 klicks or more from here. Air and artillery both gonna blast the Heggies. Colonel says maximum effort."

"Three Wasps?" Sauv Degtree said; it wasn't really a question. The third squad's leader was blunt under the best of circumstances, and these weren't the best.

"Red Flight's coming out to get in on this one," Joe said. "That's another five or six Wasps. I don't know how many they've got left. That still works out to about half the entire wing. And two batteries of Havocs."

"We'd still better get our sleep while we can," Degtree said. "Heggies'll be on us soon enough."

"We'll do our job," Joe said. "Now, see to your men. One man from each squad on watch. Rotate them enough so's everybody gets as much sleep as possible. We all need that after the last couple of days. And one squad leader up at all times. I'll share that round with the four of you, and take the first watch. I hear anything more, I'll let you know."

Joe had to work to keep from snapping. Thanks to that sleep patch he'd been hit with—yesterday?—he was still several hours ahead of the other noncoms in the platoon on sleep. Even he was edgy. They had more excuse.

To use the energy his edginess gave him, Joe worked at improving his foxhole. It was just large enough for two men, side by side. Even though Joe was alone in the hole, he made it large enough for two, just in case. But no larger. That would just make the hole a better target for anyone trying to toss a grenade in. With the extra time, he put a grenade sump hole in at the bottom, a cavity slanting off to the side. With a little luck, a grenade would roll all of the way down there before it exploded, shielding Joe from the shrapnel. Lacking a grenade, the sump would also take care of water should it start raining again.

It was an extra touch there wasn't often time to incorporate.

Joe had built up a low dirt berm around the hole and packed it. He prepared firing positions on every side. Even though Echo was facing one side of the elliptical area the 13th was camped in, Joe wanted to be ready no matter which direction the enemy might attack from.

When the hole was finally done to his satisfaction, Joe sat down and pulled out a meal pack. He had a narrow ledge to sit on that kept his eyes above ground level, just enough. In any case, any threat was still—*almost certainly*—hours away. They hadn't seen any evidence all day that anyone had ever been over the ground they were marching across.

"How could the general issue an order like that?" Teu Ingels asked. The colonel and his staff were inside the APC that served as the 13th's command post. "I mean, we're supposed to kill *women* to keep them from the Heggies?"

The women in question, all of the researchers and their assistants, were camped at some distance from the command post, still under the watchful eyes of Sergeant Abru's SI team and the 13th's headquarters security detail.

"Maybe the general didn't know there were women," Dezo Parks suggested.

"Men or women, what's the difference?" Bal Kenneck asked. "It's too important that they don't fall into enemy hands with what they know. If we can't prevent capture, we have no alternative."

"*That,* gentlemen, is the bottom line," Stossen said. He had been listening to the debate with growing impatience for ten minutes. He didn't like the possibility any more than Ingels or the others, but he also knew that, somehow, the order had to be obeyed. "Dr. Corey herself emphasized the importance of making certain that she and her people are not taken by the Hegemony. If you have no stomach for the one option, find a way to make sure that it never comes down to that and quit this pointless arguing."

Stossen took a deep breath and leaned back when he realized that he had started shouting. When he resumed, he was doing little more than whispering.

"I don't like the idea either, but the 13th *will* obey its orders. If I have to carry them out personally." He let his gaze travel around the circle of officers. Because of the limited room available in a Heyer, they were *close*. "It's a rotten position to be in, but we have no choice."

"The 13th gets stuck with the crapola again," Kenneck said.

"We get the tough assignments because the brass knows that the 13th does what it has to. We get results. We do the job. That's not going to change simply because we've been given an order we . . . don't . . . like." The last three words were widely spaced and spoken through clenched teeth.

"We're a long way from final options," Dezo said. "Bal, what's the latest from CIC?"

Kenneck shrugged. "That reinforced regiment, what's left of it, is still chasing our Heyers, but they're too far back to pose any immediate threat. Another ten or fifteen minutes and our two Havoc batteries will be in position for the ambush. Red Flight's due in for fresh power cells at about the same time. Blue Flight is up to cover that operation. Then they'll land and take on fresh batteries of their own. Unless something unforeseen happens, the ambush should be sprung about twenty minutes past midnight."

The others all looked at either their watches or at the time line on their helmet visor displays.

"Less than a half hour from now," Ingels noted.

"What happens after that depends on what happens then," Kenneck said. "We can't hope to take out much of the Heggie infantry in the dark. Not if they play it smart. What we hope to do is destroy the rest of their armor and the trucks they have left now. It might be dawn before we know whether or not they're still coming after us." He let a smile slide briefly across his face. "At least they'll be on foot, and without much armor by then."

"Don't count on that until we can see it," Stossen said. "The last thing we can afford is overconfidence. We've already had their trucks reported destroyed once only to find out that they were still traveling forty klicks every hour."

"Even if we do take out this regiment as an effective fighting force, there's no way to say that's the end of it for us," Teu said, speaking as softly as the colonel had earlier. "It just might make the Heggies decide that we're worth an even greater effort. And we're a long way from any kind of safety."

The eight Wasps staged at twenty thousand meters over the Heggie column. Climbing that far was a drain on their batteries. It would cut their air time considerably. In the dark, they were invisible to any enemy detection gear. With the Wasps' stealth technology and with the antigrav engines running at low throttle, they were less than ghosts. They could cruise unheard, unseen, at two hundred meters in the night. But the fighters were waiting, high enough that they wouldn't even be stumbled on by enemy Boems. Until the Havocs opened the attack, and the Heggies had identified the incoming fire as artillery, the planes would stay out of the fight, completely. Once the Schlinal force was concentrating on countering a ground attack, the Wasps would dive in, aiming for tanks and trucks. And if Boems arrived, the Wasps would be there to keep them occupied, away from the Havocs.

"Just stay cool," Zel told Irv and Jase. "Remember, at night, mudders have about as much chance of hitting us as I do of becoming Prime Minister of the Accord."

"Unless they've got Boems to back 'em up," Jase said.

"There could be a hundred Boems right here with us and we wouldn't know it until they turned on their TA systems,"

Irv added. TA: target acquisition. The Wasps' sensors would pick up any enemy TA radar as soon as it brushed them. And vice versa.

"If there were even half that many, one of us would have stumbled onto them, the hard way, by now," Zel said. He wasn't trying to be funny, and no one laughed. "Just watch for the shooting to start down below."

They would see the flashes of shells being fired as clearly as they might see lightning streaking across the sky. Once they were alerted by those flashes, they would be watching for the explosions at the other end. The navigation monitors in all of the Wasp cockpits showed the positions of the Havocs as blue crosses. Transponders in the guns would keep the aircraft apprised of their locations no matter how wildly guns or planes moved once the fighting started. And the targeting systems would not allow a Wasp pilot to mistakenly lock on to a Havoc. That would take a specific override, with two fallback safeties.

Zel thumbed off his microphone just long enough to whisper, "Slee, this time's for you. We'll do what we're supposed to do."

Then he saw the first flashes as the howitzers opened up. Silently, he counted the seconds until the first explosions appeared on the other end of their ballistic trajectories.

"Get ready," he warned the other pilots of his own flight. "Red is going in first, from in front of the column. We'll come in from the far side." The side away from the Havocs.

Less than thirty seconds passed before he saw muzzle flashes from the Heggie column as Novas started to return fire. A quick glance at the scale on his navigating monitor assured Zel that the Novas were too far away to hit the Havocs. They were firing blind.

Wait, he told himself. Then he opened his link to the commander of Red Flight to make sure that he knew that the Heggies didn't have any certain targets yet.

"I know, Zel. We'll wait . . . a few seconds, at least."

The tanks were moving, racing, using the vector of the incoming rounds to guide them. It wouldn't take them long to get close enough to make their return fire count.

The blue crosses were moving, jumping to new firing positions.

"Okay, Zel," the Red Flight leader said. "Here we go. See you later."

"Yeah, later," Zel replied absently. He switched channels to pass the word to the other pilots of his own flight.

"Time to go. Give 'em hell." He pushed his control yoke forward and advanced the throttles.

CHAPTER 14

There were many differences between the Accord Havoc and the Schlinal Nova. The most basic was that the Havoc was a self-propelled howitzer and the Nova was a tank. Though they might look similar to an observer, their basic missions were quite different. Artillery stood off and lobbed its shells in from as far as twenty kilometers from the target. The maximum range of the 135mm main gun on a Nova was slightly under ten kilometers, and even with that it was used primarily for line-of-sight attack as a direct infantry support vehicle or to attack enemy strong points and armor or artillery. The Havoc was lightly armored and depended exclusively on speed and mobility for defense. Its armor was only thick enough to stop small arms fire. The Nova was much more heavily armored. The Havoc carried a crew of four. The Nova relied on two men and more extensive automation. In the Nova, the gun commander minded everything but the driving. The main gun was loaded automatically. The two splat guns could also be operated remotely by the gun commander. In the Havoc, three men did the work that one did in a Nova. A loader ran the machinery that moved the heavy shells from magazine to breech and locked the barrel when it was loaded. The shell casing was, however, ejected automatically through a port that sent the spent brass out of the turret. A gunner oversaw the computerized targeting and could, at need, override the automatics. In a Nova, the gun commander had no choice but to accept what the TA system told him, except on line-of-sight shots.

Not surprisingly, perhaps, the Havoc could maintain a higher rate of accurate fire for much longer than the Nova. And as long as the Havoc could maintain its distance, it was out of reach of those tanks.

It wasn't always possible to keep away. But this was one time when the gunners of Basset and Dingo batteries certainly intended to stay more than ten kilometers from the enemy.

Karl Mennem and Jimmy Ysinde were one of the best loader-gunner combinations in the 13th, fast and accurate. Their positions low in the rear of the gun's long turret kept them well separated from the others, at the front of the turret. The howitzer's breech was between Karl and Jimmy. Karl's seat at the targeting controls was a little higher than Jimmy's. They did their work without talking. When the Fat Turtle was speaking, they couldn't have heard each other—not even over helmet radios—anyway.

In the front compartment, Eustace took care of navigation. He gave Simon a course and gave Karl his target priorities. All four men kept busy. Eustace also kept track of the number of shots that went out, a silent roll call, a habit he had never been able—(or really tried)—to break.

This wasn't a perfect mission. There weren't enough Accord spyeyes available to give them pinpoint targeting data for each shot. With adequate data, it would have been one target, one round, with a high degree of certainty that each target would be destroyed in turn. Now all they knew was the location of the enemy column, along with rough corrections from the Wasps that were also hitting it. The data was good, but not precise enough to give the guns their best accuracy.

"We'll make do," Eustace muttered, not really caring whether or not any of the others managed to hear.

Shoot and move. The Havoc commanders were netted in with the two Wasp flight leaders. That gave the howitzers some data, voice and telemetry, but not nearly enough. When one of the flyers reported a hit, there was no way to be certain which of the guns on the ground had scored. Everyone was firing almost as quickly as their guns could be loaded and targeted.

"It's like we've gone back three thousand years," Karl Mennem complained. "More than that. We might as well be firing scrap metal from muzzle-loaders."

"You want we should go nose to nose with Novas?" Eustace asked. "You want that, we *could* do it . . . for about eight seconds."

"You want that," Simon said before Karl could answer, "you can find yourself another driver. I'll get out and walk back."

All of them had the amplifiers in their headsets cranked to maximum. Even with that, they shouted into their microphones. Artillerymen always suffered hearing damage. That was a given. Once they were out of the guns, the damage could be repaired, given time. Short of that, treatment was reserved for cases where the damage was severe enough to interfere with job performance.

"Okay, you've both made your points," Eustace said. "Let's concentrate on doing what we can with what we've got." There was no mistaking the annoyance in his voice. With more than a year of working together as a team, the others knew that it was indeed time to shut up.

Rockets and cannon. Blue Flight expended everything but the rounds in their rear-facing 25mm cannons, then hurried back to the temporary bases their support vans had established. They were only on the ground long enough to get new munitions and fresh batteries, then they hurried back to the fight at full throttle so that part of Red Flight could replenish. Once the rotation was established, the eight Wasps could keep up the attack as long as their pilots could remain alert enough to fly. Or until they were shot out of the air.

Once more, Zel fell into the illusion of being part of his Wasp. Eyes, hands, brain—all became nearly automatic subsystems of the fighter. He took absolutely no thought for the death and destruction he was bringing to the enemy. This was game playing at its most intense, with little more thought given to the possible outcome for himself and his companions. As long as the gameboard was lit up, he would play.

Reflex. Training. Deadly carnage.

The Schlinal tanks continued to maneuver, both in an attempt to evade Accord fire and in a continuing hunt for the Havoc howitzers that were bombarding their regiment with continuing effect. Most of the trucks that had been carrying the infantry had been abandoned in the first seconds. The squads in the backs jumped to get clear of the larger targets. Drivers dove for cover as well. A lone human being presented a much smaller target to any enemy. In the night, he could almost hope to achieve effective invisibility from any long-range attack. And even if he were visible in infrared, he would be just one man among many hundreds. The more distance between him and his companions, the better his odds were.

Although Zel paid no attention to the figures, his targeting system recorded the number of vehicles hit, even though it could not always distinguish between tank and truck. By the time Blue Flight was ready to go back to rearm for the second time, that number stood at twenty-seven total for the eight Wasps. Slightly more than half of those hits were trucks, but the tank battalion had been hit hard throughout the series of engagements. No more than a half dozen, the equivalent of a single tank company, were still operational.

Blue Flight was on the ground when the first enemy Boems reached the battle. Red Flight had no warning until the Heggie squadron was right in the middle of them. The initial numbers were, as close as anyone in Red Flight could tell, sixteen to five.

Two Wasps went down before their pilots could react to the sudden attack. A few seconds later, a Wasp and a Boem took each other out in a head-on collision at speeds too high for their collision-avoidance systems to overcome.

"Hurry it, Chief," Zel told Roo Vernon. "They need us back there right now."

There were just two Wasps there to face fifteen—then thirteen—Boems. Zel bit at his lower lip. They'd never make it back in time to help. The ground crews were just buttoning up the panels over the battery wells when the next call came from Red Flight.

"We're getting out of here, just plain running, out of ammo, low on juice as well."

"Blue Flight, this is Major Parks. You're to go back just far enough to cover Red Flight's withdrawal and landing. Repeat, just far enough to cover Red Flight."

Zel hesitated, for just a second, before he acknowledged the order. *If the Boems give chase, maybe we can turn the tables yet,* he thought.

The Havoc 200mm self-propelled howitzer was a well-designed machine. The planners had accounted for every cubic centimeter of space. The allowances for the four crewmen had been carefully evaluated to give a man exactly the amount of room he needed, and not a bit extra. As a result, the spaces actually fit very few men, most not conforming strictly to the average data that had been used to compute the allocation. The composite bucket seats were a particular source of complaints. Any type of padding eased the situation, but only men who were rather below average size could find space to install such a comfort. Small containers near each station held other essential personal equipment, such as meal packs and water. The one "extravagance" that the planners had designed into the Havoc was provision for cool water. Cool, not cold. The argument was that gun crews needed the water because of the temperatures that could occur inside the gun turrets—routinely in excess of 40 degrees Celsius in even moderately warm weather if the gun were being fired with any regularity. Two coolers, each large enough to hold four 1-liter canteens, would keep the contents at a modest 12 degrees Celsius.

The Havocs of Basset and Dingo batteries had gone silent. The crews had all parked their guns and draped their thermal tarps more effectively. Many of the crews, like that of Basset two, had chosen their havens earlier, marked locations, and then carefully avoided using them as firing positions. Not one Havoc of the two batteries had been hit by the enemy counterfire. The Novas hadn't come close enough to be effective, and the Boems had concentrated on the Wasps.

It was the arrival of enemy fighters that had brought the Havocs' part in the ambush to an end, just as the Boems had chased the Wasps from overhead.

The crew of Basset two was hiding in bushes twenty meters from the Fat Turtle. With tree branches overhead and thick underbrush around them, they felt as safe as they could possibly feel under the circumstances. They weren't crowded together, but they were closer than infantrymen would have been in similar circumstances. And the gunners hadn't bothered to excavate foxholes or slit trenches. It was something they weren't apt to consider unless they came under direct fire . . . or had reason to believe that they were likely to in the immediate future—say, within the next five minutes.

Each man did have a canteen of water with him. He also had night-vision goggles. Those weren't built into gunners' helmets the way they were in the infantry version, but numerous complaints from gunners who had been forced out into the night, away from the optics of their Havocs, had led the quartermaster corps to issue the extra equipment. Finding room for the gear in a Havoc had been rather more difficult.

Eustace was enjoying the new goggles more than the cool water at the moment. He could actually *see*. In the Porter campaign, the lack of portable night-vision gear had been very nearly disastrous for him and his crew. If the army hadn't provided the goggles, he had been ready to purchase his own before going into combat again. "I don't want to end up blind in the wrong circumstances again," he had told the 13th's chief gunner after Porter. "A man could get killed that way, an' there's more'n enough ways for a gunner to get dead now."

With night goggles over his eyes and his pistol in hand, Eustace felt ready to take on anything that the Heggies might throw at them. He spent more than twenty minutes just scanning the limited horizon he could see after he and his crew went to ground.

"We might as well try to get a little sleep," he said then. "Two and two. Simon, Jimmy, you take the first hour." Eustace couldn't have slept yet in any case. After the action of the last hour, he would need time to come down from his battle high, to let the adrenaline—and two stimtabs—work their way out of his system. Although he was as short of sleep as any of the Accord soldiers on Jordan, just now he couldn't have felt more wide awake if he had just slept for a week straight.

Eustace smiled, enjoying a private memory. *Sleep for a week.* He had tried that once, taken a furlough to do nothing but sleep after a long field exercise. He had checked into the Galaxy, the best hotel on Albion, the world where the 13th was based. He had spent the first afternoon and evening eating and drinking, but only in the hotel. For a change, he hadn't made the rounds of the bars that hosted most military traffic, and he didn't associate with any other soldiers. After that first eight hours, he had returned to his room ready to spend the next seven days there, eating, sleeping, and—in between—relaxing.

Two days of that had been all he was able to stand. He couldn't sleep and got far too nervous to relax. After several hours of pacing around his room—Eustace Ponks was a very stubborn man—he had given up. He had taken a taxi across town and started making the rounds of bars and theaters on what was known as the Strip, looking for people he knew from the 13th. He had broken a lot of personal rules during the binge that followed, mostly by buying drinks for people he didn't owe favors to. There had been two brawls, that he could remember afterward, and several brief encounters with the other sort of professional who frequented the Strip.

I could use a little action of that sort now, Eustace thought, grinning widely. He had been married once. That had proven less satisfactory than simply renting companionship when he felt the need. And when he was somewhere where the urge could be satisfied.

There was a little chatter on the radio now. The battery commanders kept in touch with all of their guns. In the field like this, each crew operated semi-autonomously. The men's primary sense of identification was with their own guns, not with the battery as a whole. Guns moved independently, if usually within well-defined areas. Each gun commander was responsible for movement and concealment. But there was always the battery channel on the radio, and always *some* contact. At the moment, Lieutenant Ritchey, the Basset Battery C.O., was trying to provide a running account of the air action. Ritchey had taken over Basset five after losing his own gun. The trouble was, his information always seemed to be several minutes out of date. Ponks paid little attention to it. His private thoughts were more . . . entertaining.

"Sarge, how long you figure they'll leave us sitting here?" Karl asked, breaking into Eustace's reverie.

"Either too long or not long enough," he replied, blinking several times to get his mind back to the business at hand. *It's not like fairy tales; they never get it "just right,"* he thought.

"The Wasps are really taking a licking again, ain't they?"

Eustace didn't answer. He had heard about the three planes of Red Flight going down, and that Blue Flight was back getting more rockets. That was the latest information he had.

The two remaining Wasps of Red Flight were low, hugging the terrain as they tried to escape from the pursuing Boems. Blue Flight waited, higher, across the course that the other planes were taking, but a thousand meters above the Boems. Waiting, idling, running silent. Blue Flight's Wasps didn't even have their TA systems running. They used a radio relay of data from Red Flight. That added a couple of seconds to the process of acquiring a target, but it did maintain the element of surprise for Blue Flight—until their missiles were armed and pointed at the targets.

Six missiles went out. Four of them found targets. There was a moment of confusion for the Boem flight, time enough for Zel and his wingmen to put out six more rockets. Only one of those found a target.

"Into them," Zel said, nosing his Wasp directly toward the heaviest concentration of Boems. "Give Red time to get away."

In the dark, it was a duel of ghosts. The fighters on both sides used their TA systems sparingly, switching them off as soon as targets were acquired and locked into missiles, trying for that essential invisibility. No pilot on either side ever actually *saw* the enemy, only electronic signatures on cockpit monitors or on the heads-up display.

It was a brief battle, no more than three minutes for Blue Flight. "We're clear," the new Red one told Zel.

"Break contact," Zel told his own pilots.

That was much easier at night than during the day. The pilots simply switched off everything that might put out a visible signature. They swung out on diverging courses and went low, reversing course once they were below fifty meters, and cutting back their speed. Zel went so far as to hover for nearly a full minute, his Wasp almost completely silent. The only audible noise in the cockpit was his own breathing.

That hover might have saved him. At least some of the Boem pilots were also crafty. One of them flashed by Zel's Havoc, not more than twenty meters away. Even then, Zel didn't actually *see* the other plane, but it did register on the Wasp's instruments. It came close enough that even a passive scan detected the magnetic field generated by the Boem's antigrav drives.

The Boem didn't have a chance to turn to get its missiles aimed at Zel. Zel armed two rockets and got them off while the Boem was still within a hundred meters of him. There wasn't enough time for the Schlinal pilot to do anything but die.

CHAPTER 15

For a moment, Dem Nimz had mistaken the flashes on the horizon for lightning, even though the sky was clear. There had certainly been enough rain in the time that the Accord had been on Jordan for that to come to mind. But Dem was exhausted. Had his mind been functioning normally, he would have known instantly that what he was seeing was the flash of artillery strikes.

"The fight's still going on," Fredo whispered at Dem's side.

Dem nodded slowly. "At least it gives us a marker," he said, taking a fix on the direction. "They've shifted course a little, I think."

The few men remaining from the 1st and 3rd recon platoons were no longer even thinking about engaging the Heggies. Following the enemy was simply a convenience now, a way to make sure that they were on the best route back to their own people. Unless the Heggies turned around and followed their own path back.

Dem and his rump command had made use of the enemy's leavings. Coming on one of the places where the Schlinal regiment had been hit, each of the men had appropriated a Schlinal rifle, all of the wire for it he could carry, and a few grenades, either hand or rocket propelled. Schlinal wire spools would not fit in Accord weapons, so rifles and ammunition both had to be taken. And the reccers had also taken what food they could find. They had eaten well a couple of hours back, each man forcing down two or three of the Schlinal field ration packs.

"Almost makes you appreciate our stuff," Fredo had commented at the time.

Most of them ate again now, while they rested and watched the distant duel. It was too far off for them to hear anything of it, and they weren't even seeing all of the flashes over the horizon. But it was enough to know that *someone* was still carrying on the fight, now that the reccers were out of it.

"When you gonna call the colonel, Dem?" Fredo asked. "By now, they must figure none of us made it."

Dem didn't answer right away. He was always reluctant to use the radio when he was exposed, but this time he had to admit that there was more to it than that. He didn't want to confirm the bad news.

"Soon," he said. "Soon."

"We don't let 'em know there's still a few of us kickin', they might take off just about anywhere and really leave us stranded," Fredo pressed. Earlier, while Dem had been sleeping, Fredo had been sorely tempted to make the call himself. Only his strong sense of discipline had stopped him. He still wasn't certain that he had made the right choice.

There is that, Dem admitted to himself. He sucked in a deep breath, held it, then let it out slowly. "Okay, I'll call the CP now."

The exec, Dezo Parks, took the call. "We'd just about written all of you off."

"Close enough, sir," Dem replied. "Only ten of us left, and we're too far away from the Heggies to do any more good."

"Just get back to us the best you can, Nimz," Parks said. "Avoid all contact with the enemy. That should be easy for a bunch of reccers."

"We'll try," Dem said. "Where do we head?"

"It's going to be a long chase for you." Parks laid out the current plans for the 13th. "Figure out what you can do and decide on your own rendezvous."

"Like to take us a few days, sir," Dem said after a quick look at his mapboard. "Sure wish there was one of those Heyers still around."

"We'd heard from you even six hours ago, we might have been able to fix that. But it's too late now."

Fredo had been listening in on the call, but he knew better than to say "I told you so" to Dem Nimz. "I think we'd best take the rest of the night to get some sleep," he said instead. "Start off fresh in the morning. We'll make better time that way."

Eleven hours in one location. That gave the men of the 13th plenty of time to catch up on at least some of the sleep they were behind, and it gave the research team from the lab inside Telchuk Mountain time to recover from their first day's hike, but it was a dangerous respite. In that much time, they were certain to have been spotted by the Schlinal spyeyes. A concentration of eighteen hundred men was almost impossible to hide if the enemy were looking hard enough.

"It's a chance we have to take," Colonel Stossen told his staff when they met two hours before dawn. "We're here until the APCs arrive and we can all ride."

"Those drivers are going to be too beat to do anything," Dezo pointed out. "Most of them have been on the go constantly for thirty-six hours or more. They can't keep going."

"Then we'll have to improvise," Stossen said. "There are more than enough others who know how to pilot a Heyer. The regular drivers will have to get their rest however they can, even if the medics have to sleep patch the lot of them."

"They will," Teu said. "If you expect anyone to get any real sleep in a Heyer on the move, it will take sleep patches."

Stossen nodded. "I wasn't making a joke. Pass the word to the companies. We'll get those drivers at least four hours of sleep whether they want it or not."

"We've had one break," Bal said. "Those drivers did their job. The Heggies never got a chance to see that the APCs were a diversion until it was too late."

"By now, they must have found out their mistake," Parks said, "but it doesn't matter any longer. We got in and out of that valley with the . . . cargo we were sent for."

"At a price," Stossen said. "Twenty percent of our air wing, nearly a quarter of our artillery, almost *half* our reccers. Plus the Heyers and drivers we lost. I don't even have any idea how many of them were tagged. And we're not out of this yet. We're not half *into* it if we're going to have any shot of getting back to friendly lines."

"There's one more decision we have to face before long," Teu said. "What do we do with the Wasps we still have? Do we keep them with us or send them back? We're going to have to choose before we get much farther from our people."

"What do you mean?" Kenneck asked.

"Right now, we can stick new batteries in the Wasps and they'll have the juice to get all the way back. Depending on what kind of speed we make heading east, they'll be out of range of our lines either late today or early tomorrow. If we keep them with us, they'll be stuck with us until we get close enough to our lines again for them to fly back. If we do."

"And if we turn them loose," Parks said, "once we get past that line we won't be able to get them back."

"How are we on support for them?" Stossen asked.

"Fine," Ingels said. "We brought along enough to keep half the wing flying, and we've never had two full flights out here. We have good stores of munitions, and there's no problem with batteries or anything else. We have enough ground crews to give each Wasp its own and still have a couple of spares."

"The problem with keeping the planes with us is that we have to be able to stop to put new batteries in them every seventy-five or eighty minutes," Kenneck said.

"Not really a problem, unless we're under attack at the time," Ingels replied. "And if we are under attack, we want the support over us. The problem is that if a Wasp is actually running dry and we can't provide cover for it to land. That's always a possibility, here or anywhere else."

"We'll keep them with us if we can," Stossen said. "At least, we'll plan on it. Five Wasps could make a big difference. Dezo, bring it up again when we get close to the limit for sending them back."

Olly Wytten stared at the meal pack in front of him. He ate slowly, chewing each mouthful as if the food were resisting being eaten. The rest of the squad was nearby, each man in his own foxhole, relatively close. The 13th was occupying a fairly small area. There was no need to stretch out the lines. Most of the men were eating. A couple of them were on their second breakfast. Food wasn't in short supply. Even the most conservative estimates indicated that they had a solid fifteen days of full rations left. Fifteen days. Few of the men in the 13th could think that far ahead on any campaign.

"Damn it! We're not doing any good out here."

Those who were close enough to hear Olly's vehement exclamation turned to look. It was the longest speech anyone in the squad had ever heard him make. And no one could recall ever hearing him sound so intense about anything. They waited to see if more would follow.

Wytten looked around, as if he had just realized that he had spoken aloud. But there was no embarrassment on his face. "We're wasted out here. Back in the lines, we'd at least be killing a few Heggies."

"We're not wasted," Mort said. Though the two were in different fire teams, their foxholes were next to each other.

"How do you see that?" Olly demanded.

"I can't give you hard proof, but we might be doing far more good sitting out here than if we were back there killing off Heggies by the regiment. Those people we picked up. Whatever they were doing is so important to the Accord that the general figured that it was worth the entire 13th to save them, or even just to keep the Heggies from getting them. Whatever they were doing in that mountain, it was *big*. It had to be."

"But what?" Olly asked.

Mort shrugged. "My fields are history and political science, not military technology. I can't even guess beyond suggesting that it might be a new weapons system, something so radically beyond anything either side has now as to spell victory or defeat for the side that manages to get it through development into production. And even that might be wrong. It could be communications, or even an improvement to jump space technology." He hesitated before he added, "Or something I haven't even got the background to imagine."

Olly looked down at his meal pack. "Maybe it's a food replicator light enough for a mudder to carry along. Drop in a shovel of dirt and get lunch."

Mort stared at Wytten, amazed that he had put so many words together. Then he shook his head. "That's as good a guess as anything I could come up with."

Joe Baerclau came over to first squad then. "You've got about forty-five minutes left. The Heyers will be here then, and we're gonna shove off as soon as they get here."

"Where to, Sarge?" Mort asked.

Joe shook his head. "Beats me. East, I think, and don't ask me what's there 'cause I don't know."

"Just another fancy run?" Ezra asked, getting out of his foxhole and walking over to meet Joe.

"Could be. Maybe the colonel's figured a way to get us back, or up to the ships. We go far enough off, the Heggies won't be able to get planes in to intercept the shuttles. But don't go banking on that," he added quickly. "That's just my own wild guess. Nobody's said anything about that." *I shouldn't even have mentioned it,* Joe thought, almost angry at himself. It was too good a way to start wild rumors. "Far as I know, we're just playing keepaway, getting those civilians as far from the Heggies as we can."

"And we can go farther and faster in the mixers," Mort said.

"So the Heyers aren't comfy," Joe said. "They do the job."

"What's east of here?" Al Bergon asked. "More mountains?"

Joe's smile was brief and restrained. He had taken a long look at his mapboard while Lieutenant Keye was briefing the platoon leaders and platoon sergeants. "Not so much. We head due east, there's foothills, then rolling countryside. Broad valleys framing rivers. Some rocky terrain for about three-hundred klicks, something like the rift valley on Porter but not so extreme. Good country to hide in."

"And no Heggies?" Pit Tymphe asked.

"Not as we know of. Not much of anybody."

"Why not?" Mort asked.

"Guess there's nothing there anybody wants. Nothing special in the way of farmland or minerals. Not enough people on Jordan to make it worthwhile." A lot of worlds were like that. Even though some of them, like Jordan, had been settled for a thousand years or more, their populations were still small enough that there was no mad scramble for every hectare of usable land. The population of Jordan had reached nearly three million before the Schlinal invasion. Even so, less than 20 percent of the "good" land was occupied, or used for anything more than casual hiking and camping. The ecological horror stories that had left Earth with the earliest colonists continued to haunt people wherever they went.

"Anyway, get anything done that needs doing and be ready to load up when the Heyers get here," Joe said. "Colonel's anxious to get moving. We've been in one place too long."

When the squad turned to gathering their gear, Joe beckoned Al away from the others.

"What is it?" Al asked when they were several meters away from the rest.

"Special instructions for the medics. The drivers of those Heyers have been on the go for close to two days without sleep. They get here and we load up, the first thing you do is hit the driver with a four-hour sleep patch. Get him settled in the back."

"We're gonna knock out *all* those drivers? That's . . . bizarre."

Joe nodded. Bizarre was a good word for what he thought might be the strangest order he had received in all his years as a soldier. "All of them. That comes direct from the colonel. Guess he figures it's the only way anyone can sleep in a Heyer."

"I can believe that," Al said.

"Just be ready, and get one of the others to help you move the driver. I've got to tell the other medics."

Kleffer Dacik stared at his haggard reflection in the mirror. His face was lathered up and he had a razor in his hand, but he wasn't moving, not his hand, not even his eyes. A chance thought had started him idly fantasizing on the pleasures of cutting his throat. He was not suicidal. The idea wasn't one that he could ever *seriously* entertain, but he was short enough of sleep that he didn't simply dismiss the errant thought and get on with the business of shaving.

Part of his mind was amused at the nonsense of standing as rigid as a statue and picturing himself lying on the bathroom floor with a new grin across his neck, while blood and shaving lather spread in a puddle around him. Foamy icebergs on a red sea. No more worries or trouble. Let somebody else drive himself mad with the situation.

His fantasy extended to imagining his aide coming in and finding him. "There he goes again, taking off without me," he imagined hearing Captain Lorenz say.

"General?" There was a banging at the bathroom door.

Dacik blinked several times, having difficulty bringing his mind out of the reverie. That was Captain Lorenz at the door.

"What is it, Hof?" he asked finally.

"News."

"Come in. Talk to me while I shave." Dacik hurriedly started shaving so that his aide wouldn't guess how long he had been standing there. The lather was already starting to dry on his face.

"The Heggies are up to something, General," Lorenz said as he entered. "You'll want to check out what we have on your mapboard, but I can give you the basics."

"Well, go ahead," Dacik said when the captain hesitated. Lorenz always looked, and often acted like a parade-ground soldier. Tall, slender, with a rigidly military carriage, Lorenz always looked as if he were waiting to pose for a recruiting holograph. Although he *had* seen duty with a line company through one campaign, most of his career had been spent in a series of staff assignments. It wasn't a matter of special privilege or connections. Lorenz simply had a talent for the work, a talent that more than one commander had decided it would be a shame to waste.

"They're pulling troops out of the lines. We can't get exact numbers, but intelligence estimates that they've pulled two mechanized infantry regiments and either two or three battalions of armor."

"Where are they headed?" Dacik asked, staring at Lorenz in the mirror.

The captain shook his head. "No word on that yet, but Colonel Lafferty's guess is that they're going after the 13th." Lafferty was Dacik's intelligence chief.

"What about that regiment that's *been* chasing them?"

"No change that we've seen. They're still in pursuit, but they're on foot now, what's left of them, and the 13th should be back in its APCs by now."

"Any sign that the Heggies are bringing in air transport for any of the units they've pulled?"

"Nothing was said about that, General. I'll call Colonel Lafferty and ask."

"Just get him to my office. I'll be there in two minutes. Get the rest of my staff as well. Maybe we can do something positive for a change."

Dacik had forgotten all about his earlier fantasy.

CHAPTER 16

"Tell me what you know and how you know it," Dacik said as he entered his office still buttoning his shirt. Colonel Lafferty was standing by the large mapboard. The rest of the staff hadn't arrived yet.

Lafferty didn't waste time with pleasantries either. "Information's still coming in, sir. What we have so far is less than one-hundred percent solid, but promising." He waited until Dacik joined him in front of the mapboard.

"Two places, here, and here." He pointed. "On the left, we're relying on data from bugs we planted before we drew the perimeter back. On the right, we got a patrol out during the night without them being spotted. It looks as if the Heggies are pulling units out of the line, spreading the units on either side to cover the gaps. It's all been coordinated too precisely to give us much chance to poke through quickly during the changeover."

"What makes you think that they're going after the 13th?" Dacik asked. "I can think of at least two other solid reasons for pulling units back like that without stretching to conclude that they're going to run them twelve hundred klicks. They might simply be resting troops, or they might be massing a strike force to try and break through our lines somewhere."

"Either of those is possible," Lafferty conceded, "and we're watching as closely as we can. But I don't think that either is particularly likely right now."

"Why?"

"As far as resting troops, it's just not something a Schlinal warlord is likely to do until the men are so far gone that he doesn't have any choice, and even then, he's as apt to order them forward into an attack where they're at. The other . . . Well, I'm going a little farther out on the limb with that. It might even come down to a toss of the coin which is more likely, but I think my estimate is right. As soon as we know where the units are rendezvousing, if they do, I'll be able to say with more certainty, but it looks as if they're pulling back too far to be simply massing for a strike against us. And, if that *was* the case, I think they'd have done it several hours earlier, so they'd be in position before dawn, not still moving in daylight. Finally, the direction they're moving is consistent with preparations to move toward the 13th."

"Any sign that they're going to bring in air transport for them?"

Lafferty shook his head with considerable vigor. "Absolutely out of the question. They can't manage that any more than we could. We're still too near parity. They'd have to move out of range of our Wasps before they could try. In the time that would take, they could just as easily be going after them by land—be damn near where the 13th is now. They should have enough vehicles to move the mudders, and their tanks are mobile enough."

"How many men are they pulling?"

"I can't give you a good number on that, General, not now, maybe not ever. Infantry, I'd guess—and I do mean *guess*—close to four thousand, at a minimum. Maybe half again that number. That we've spotted so far. Plus two full battalions of armor, maybe a little more."

"Any unit identifications?"

"None that mean anything."

"Now the big question. Are they weakening their lines enough that we can exploit it?"

"The scattered reports I have so far suggest that the Schlinal troops still facing us have moved to a strictly defensive posture, digging in."

"That's not what I asked. Are we going to be able to use this to break the stalemate here?"

"I don't know, General. Not too soon, in any case. As long as those troops are close enough that they can be brought back in time to effect the outcome, no. Once they're nearly to the 13th, maybe. *If* we can find an edge, somehow. If we take too big a chance, it might give the Heggies what they need to end it."

"Let's get the rest of the staff in on this," Dacik said. "I need more information."

Dem Nimz and his remaining men had started hiking again just before sunrise. Dem pushed the pace as hard as he could. Within an hour, the legs of every man were aching from the strain, but they had covered nearly nine kilometers in that hour. After a ten-minute break, Dem stood. He didn't have to say anything. The others got up when he did. They moved on in two columns of five, keeping about five meters between the columns and three or four meters between men in each column.

They had only been on the move for ten minutes when the last man whistled over the radio, one sharp blast. It was the only signal reccers needed. They dove for cover, facing outward, guns at the ready, waiting for more information.

"Engines," the man said. By that time, the rest also could hear the sounds of truck engines, coming on strong.

"Can you see them?" Dem asked. He turned his head to look toward his left, back the way they had come.

There was a pause before the reply, "Yes. Parallel to our course, about forty meters out."

"Keep way down," Dem said. "Don't let them see us."

The noise grew steadily. Even before Dem spotted the first Schlinal truck, he could tell that there was a considerable convoy moving east at high speed. The trucks were the standard Schlinal type, half-tracks, and Dem guessed that they were going full out, near sixty kilometers per hour. Over this kind of terrain, it had to be a bumpy ride.

Carefully, Dem raised his head. He wanted a count of the trucks, and some estimate of the number of men they might be carrying.

After ten minutes, he gave up trying to count the trucks. There were several columns of them that he could see, and he had no way to be certain that he was seeing all the way to the far side of the formation.

Must be another whole regiment, he thought, his spirits sinking.

Then one of the trucks lurched to the left after hitting some obstruction, and Dem had a clear peek into the back of the vehicle. It was empty.

"I know where they're going," Dem whispered. He nearly held his breath until the last of them was past. As soon as the convoy was out of sight, he got on the radio. Colonel Stossen had to know about this right away. Those Heggies up ahead weren't going to stay on foot much longer.

The "cockpit" of a Heyer APC was quite similar to the layout of a Wasp cockpit. A Heyer's driver had two monitors on the panel in front of him, and a heads-up display directly above that, between the two periscopes that gave him a direct view of what was immediately around the vehicle. Each tread was controlled by a separate pedal, similar to the throttles in a Wasp. The difference was that in a Heyer, the throttle, for a single engine, was at the driver's left, a lever protruding from the side of the compartment. There was no steering wheel or control yoke. The combination of throttles and individual tread transmissions took care of steering. The Heyer driver's hands were occupied with other controls. He could even, at need, aim and fire both splat guns remotely, with separate targeting monitors high on the front wall of his compartment.

Every infantryman in the Accord's SATs took a basic driver's course—four hours of instruction, four hours of simulator sessions, and one hour actually driving a Heyer. Generally, one man from each squad received the "advanced" course—an additional four hours of simulator training and another two hours of actual driving. There was no extra pay to be had for the extra training, only the rather dubious prospect of someday being called upon to drive a mixer in combat.

Carl Eames drew the extra duty in first squad—volunteered for it. There was more room in the cockpit of the Heyer than there was cramped up in the rear compartment. The Heyer's regular driver was propped up in a corner back there, wedged between two other men, sleeping off his patch. Because of the APCs lost on their decoy mission, the overcrowding in all that remained was severe. One fire team from the platoon's second squad was crammed in with first.

The formation of Heyers didn't move with the precision that their regular drivers might have achieved, but the 13th did manage to stay together. What they couldn't do was move unobserved. A hundred and forty Heyers, added to the artillery and all of the support vehicles, meant that the formation was vast. The good news was that the ground was too damp for the 13th to raise massive clouds of dust. Those would have been easily visible to any of the Schlinal spyeyes in orbit, blatant enough to draw the attention of probes that weren't looking for them.

The formation had to be obvious enough as it was, if anyone was looking.

Joe Baerclau was at his usual position next to the rear hatch of the APC. His rifle was between his legs. He leaned forward, resting his elbows on his thighs. That position kept his head from banging against the bulkhead behind him, which made it as comfortable as he could hope to get in a Heyer with fourteen other men.

There was no idle chat in the compartment. After the first hour, no one had any inclination to do anything but brood in silence. Nor energy to spare. Being bounced along over open country in a Heyer was, in some ways, more draining than marching the same distance in quick step.

The breaks were too few and far between, and too short. Colonel Stossen was pushing the 13th as hard as he dared. If he had thought that the men would be able to function without the periodic breaks, he would have eliminated them completely. A growing sense of urgency was driving the colonel, but he couldn't explain it, not even to himself.

Stossen or one of his senior staff officers was in constant contact with CIC on the flagship. As many of the sensing assets as possible were dedicated to providing current information to the 13th, but there were still gaps large enough to fly an entire wing of aircraft through.

Overhead, the five remaining Wasps of Red and Blue flights patrolled, landing when they had to for fresh batteries, getting back into the air as quickly as possible. In the various support trucks, men kept their own watch on the air, alert for any possible attack by enemy Boems. Through the formation, men had Vrerch rocket launchers ready. If enemy fighters appeared, the vehicles carrying men with Vrerchs would stop immediately. Those missiles were the only ground-based defense the 13th had against air attack. Five Wasps might not be enough.

It wasn't until mid-afternoon that Van Stossen started to relax, a little. The 13th was, if intelligence was right, far enough away from any Schlinal base for Boems to be a significant danger. They might be able to reach the 13th yet, but they would have no more than a few seconds overhead before they would have to leave to get new batteries.

"Ten more klicks, and we'll take a longer break," Stossen told his staff, who passed the news to subordinate commanders.

Ten kilometers stretched to nearly eighteen before the 13th found a place with decent cover available and the vehicles finally pulled to a halt, scattered over an area of nearly five square kilometers.

"Up and out," Joe Baerclau said over his platoon frequency. "Stay under the trees as much as possible."

He tripped the latch on the door and was the first man out. He stood next to the Heyer and stretched while the others piled out. "Remember who's got the duty on the splat guns," he said. "Get the essentials taken care of first. This is supposed to be a long break, but don't count on it. And keep your eyes open."

It was part of a noncom's duty to nag. Men whose minds were tired, or dulled by the sort of ride they got in a Heyer, were too apt to forget even the simplest things. It took the voice of authority reminding them what had to be done.

The regular driver was the last man out. He was groggy yet, and had to hold on to his machine to keep his balance. "What happened?" he demanded when he saw Joe. "Who slipped me the Mickey?"

"Colonel's orders," Joe said. "All you heroes. You needed the sleep, and a patch was the only way you were going to get it while we were on the move."

"How long?"

"Close to six hours, I'd say, and the patch was only for four. That should tell you how beat you were."

The driver growled. "Somebody could have said something."

Joe grinned. "I just did. Don't worry, we didn't damage your buggy."

"Where the hell are we?"

"Heading east." Joe pulled out his mapboard and showed the driver their location. "Way I hear it, we're heading a lot farther east, then south. Maybe."

"Back to our lines?"

"I imagine that's what the colonel's hoping. But we get out there, we might just as easily head the other way."

"Run and hide?"

"I don't make the orders, I just pass them on. And most of what I just said was a guess anyway."

• • •

If was conference time again for Colonel Stossen. He was sitting under a fruit tree with his staff.

"This is the layout, the best we know," Bal said. He punctuated his briefing by pointing to the relevant spots on the mapboard in the center of the group.

"By now, those Heggies who've been trying to get to us all along are riding again. No chance of striking at them since they seem to be running regular air cap over them now. The good news is that as long as we keep moving away from them, there's little chance that they'll catch us. No matter how hard they push, I don't see them narrowing the gap by more than ten or fifteen klicks an hour, and we must be close to three-hundred klicks ahead of them. There are two infantry regiments and a couple of battalions of armor coming our way from the perimeter southeast of here. They're moving north, more northeast, the last news we had of them. Depending on their speed and whether or not they, and we, stay on course, they could catch us sometime tomorrow morning. There are too many variables to be certain yet. They could put themselves in position to make it impossible for us to head south to rejoin the rest of our people, though."

"Where did they pull those troops from?" Stossen asked.

"From what Colonel Lafferty told me, from the center and south end of the Heggie containment lines."

Stossen frowned. "Nothing from the north end?"

"Not that've been spotted."

"Doesn't make sense. Why not take the troops from the near side, cut down on the travel time?"

"Maybe they're expecting us to head that way and don't want to weaken the lines there," Dezo suggested.

"That's the way I'd read it, Colonel," Kenneck said. "They must figure that we're going to try to get back to the rest of our people at some point, and that's where we'd have to aim."

"By now, they must have figured out where we've been," Teu said. "They'll find that we blew up the side of a mountain out in the middle of nowhere. That might give them some puzzling questions, but they might make good guesses. We went there for something or someone, then destroyed the evidence."

"Which has got to make them even more curious about us. There's a factor they can't ignore," Kenneck said. "They're gonna want us badly. Just to erase the question marks."

"The farther east we go, the easier it's going to be for them to bring up even more troops from the near end of their line," Parks said. "And the better angle they'll have to intercept us. I think we should head north, Colonel, farther off. Draw the Heggies as far away as we can."

"Use our displacement to try to sucker them into displacing even more troops?" Stossen asked.

"If they fall for it," Kenneck said. "At some point, all they'd have to do is ignore us until they take care of the rest."

Stossen stared at the mapboard for a moment. "Nothing's changed then, really, has it?" He glanced around at the others. "The only thing is, now we can see what sort of assets they're sending after us."

"Some of them, anyway," Kenneck mumbled.

Stossen nodded. "I think we'll put off any idea of changing plans a bit longer. East as far as we can, looking to head south, but with the option of going north if we have to."

"This is still our point of no return," Kenneck said, stabbing at the mapboard with an index finger. "East of this spot on the river, there are no more crossings we can make, all the way to the sea. Whichever side we're on, that's where we'll have to stay."

That spot was only four hundred kilometers from where they sat, perhaps no more than another eight hours of driving time.

CHAPTER 17

Night. The 13th was stopped again, twenty kilometers west of the last place where they could ford the river to the north bank.

"We're here for what's left of the night," the Bear told his men. "Set up defensive positions."

"Facing which way?" Pit Tymphe asked.

"We're supposed to be watching south. Start digging, then eat and get some sleep. One sentry per squad."

Joe waited until the men were working, then walked back over to the APC. Lieutenant Keye was sitting in the hatch, feet out in front of him, boots off.

"Why here, sir?" Joe asked. "And why now? With the drivers rested, we could go on the rest of the night, then dig in for the day." That, to Joe, would have made more sense. Move at night, in the dark. Hide from the light. For what little advantage it might give.

"Decision point, Joe." Keye closed his eyes and leaned back, resting a shoulder against the side of the hatch. "Colonel has to decide if we're going to stay on this side of the river or cross to the other."

Joe took a few seconds to think that over. "Whether we head back to the lines or keep running away?"

"More or less. Once we pass this ford, there's no place to get vehicles across, all the way to the ocean."

"If it's the only place, might be better to cross and dig in. Keep the Heggies from using it," Joe suggested. "We ought to be able to do that."

"Not our mission. Those civilians are still our job."

"Anybody find out what they're all about yet?" Joe asked.

"If they have, nobody's talking. Better if they don't. Best if the men don't even waste time speculating."

"Haven't heard much lately. These mixers don't make for much small talk."

"Colonel's called for all company commanders to sit in on some sort of briefing. I'll be leaving soon as I can squeeze my feet back into my boots."

"Be nice to know what's goin' on for a change, sir."

"It would that. If anybody knows to tell."

Joe let out a sigh. "I'd better go get myself a hole dug, I guess. See if I can work up the nerve to take *my* boots off. Been so long I can't hardly remember the last time."

It had taken eight hours of work and a lot of luck, but Dem Nimz finally stepped back and grinned. Surrounded by bombed-out and shot-up Schlinal trucks, Dem and his men finally had one truck running. They had been forced to cannibalize a half dozen vehicles to get parts, and even then it had looked as if they might not find a battery with enough juice left in it to start a fuel converter working. But the engine was running now, not perfectly, but good enough.

"Good thing we followed the same path the Heggies took," Fredo said. He sounded smug, as if that had been his idea. "This must have been the last place our Wasps hit 'em."

A dozen trucks, two tanks, and nearly fifty bodies had been scattered around. Two of the Heggie soldiers were still alive when the reccers arrived. Dem's men didn't help them—either way. They merely let their wounds take their course. Neither of those men was alive now.

"No point in standing here until the thing runs out of H_2," Dem said. "Let's get in and ride. Maybe we can catch up to the action yet."

"Long as we don't get bombed by our own people," one of the men from 1st recon muttered. But he was one of the first to climb into the back of the truck.

Dem got into the driver's seat on the right. He had never driven a Heggie truck before, had never even seen the controls of one, but he wasted no time. While they had been working on the repairs, he had traced out some of the control linkage. Most of it was obvious. And steering was steering. The truck went where he wanted it to go.

"How far behind you figure we are?" Fredo asked after they started rolling. He was on the seat next to Dem. The rest of the men were in the back.

"Not sure," Dem said. "If they sit still, we might be able to catch up in twelve or thirteen hours."

"If the Heggies let us drive right through them," Fredo said.

This was the longest that Zel had been out of his cockpit since Blue Flight had come out to operate from the 13th's moving position. All five of the Wasps were on the ground, and would be until the 13th got ready to move in the morning. The planes were under thermal tarps. The pilots had set up their ground cloths underneath, where they usually slept. The support vans and the ground crews were close enough to handle the planes.

Zel *had* slept, for a time. But after no more than two hours, he had been wakened by some noise in the night and hadn't been able to get back to sleep. After an hour of rolling from one side to the other, he had crawled out from under his Wasp. He knew that he couldn't roam *too* far. The mudders providing close security for the Wasps and their support vans knew that there were pilots "on the loose," but those farther off might not, and they might be nervous enough to shoot before asking questions.

Walking had helped take the kinks out, but after an hour of pacing, with occasional breaks, Zel was no nearer being ready to attempt sleep again than he had been before. The muscles in his forearm were taut, hard, as if he had just finished a long session on the weight machines in the gymnasium back at home base on Albion. Three or four times a week, when the air wing wasn't heavily engaged in training flights, Zel would work out on the machines until his muscles all felt ready to shatter. He felt that way now, without the workout.

Zel and Slee had usually worked out together, pushing each other to do the most repetitions with the most weight in the least time. Slee. Remembering his friend brought back the pain of losing him. Zel saw the explosion in his mind. Again. Almost anything seemed able to bring that back, except in the air, in action. Then, Zel was too intent on flying and fighting for remembrance and pain.

Squeezing his eyes shut didn't help. The image was still there, playing out infinitely slow, imagination now providing details that Zel hadn't seen at the time, bits of metal and structural composites spinning wildly away, jagged shards and geometrically perfect shapes, light and smoke curling and billowing, growing, then fading, a deadly flower for some giant's lapel. In Zel's mind, it was a ballet without music. The real sounds of the explosion were blotted out, with nothing to replace them. Silent pictures. Silent death. Not even an imagined scream.

Did he scream? Zel wondered. He needed time to recall that there had been an open radio channel. He would have heard anything up until the instant when the rocket tore the Wasp apart. After that, there could have been no scream.

Suddenly Zel became aware of himself. He was standing rigidly still—had been for some unfathomable time. His fists were clenched at his sides, so tightly that he could feel stubby fingernails digging into his palms. At first, he was unable to release the pressure. He brought his hands up slowly, until the balled fists were close to the face. Even in the dim starlight, he could see what had to be blood running toward his wrists. Finally, by staring at the fists and willing movement, he opened the hands and saw the gouges on each palm.

His hands started shaking violently. Arms, shoulders. It took—subjectively, at least—an eternity for Zel to realize that he was crying, sobbing loudly.

Too loudly. He did force himself quiet, but not before a figure got up and ran toward him.

"You all right, sir?" Roo Vernon asked, anxiety plain in his voice.

Zel needed another eternity before he managed, "I'm okay, Chief."

"What's wrong with your hands?" Zel still had both hands in front of his face, staring at them.

"I think I need a couple of small patches, Chief." Zel's voice sounded dreamy, distant, to him. Roo came a step closer, grabbed Zel's hands, and lowered them enough so he could see the cuts.

"Yes, sir, I think you do," Roo said. *An' then some,* he thought, wondering who he could talk to. Lieutenant Paitcher obviously needed more help than a couple of small soaker patches to stop up the cuts on his hands, and the 13th's flight surgeon was back with the rest of the Accord troops, more than seventeen hundred kilometers away. "Come over here, sir, to the truck. I'll see what I can find." He tried to find a better solution, but in the end, all Roo could think to do was to leave Zel with one of the mechanics while he went to get another pilot to talk to him.

Zel wasn't the only member of the 13th who spent a mostly sleepless night. Van Stossen found himself unable to sleep for long either. Self-discipline and a lot of years in the military gave the colonel a few extra tricks. He did take several catnaps, but he rarely managed to stay asleep as much as thirty minutes at a time.

Every time he woke, he unfolded his mapboard and stared. The scene was always the same, or nearly so. The display was zoomed out to show a wide stretch of the continent, from the position of the Heggie unit trailing them to the ocean, and south to the main battle lines. The positions of friendly units were shown, as were the positions of Schlinal units, when known. There was no way to tell, simply by looking at the display, how out of date the data was, particularly for the Heggie units that were on the move. The unit coming up from behind, in trucks again, was gaining. From the various sightings made by the spyeyes, it looked as if that convoy hadn't stopped. Certainly, they had never been seen stopped. Always moving, closer.

A couple of times, Van got up and looked out into the night through his helmet visor, staring off in the direction of the river and the last practical crossing for vehicles—broad and shallow with a rocky bottom and decent grades on either side.

North or south?

He had quickly dismissed a third option, splitting the 13th, sending part north with the researchers while the rest stayed on the south side of the river to accept—seek—combat with the Heggie forces moving toward them. He had split off part of his command once already in this campaign, with disastrous results. He wasn't ready to try it again.

If the 13th moved north, they would—most likely—escape any fighting. In the near term. If the Accord should manage to prevail, the 13th might not have to do any more fighting at all. Only if the Accord lost could the 13th anticipate that the Schlinal garrison would come looking for them, and they would have all of the odds on their side then, an overwhelming advantage in numbers, undisputed control of the air, and leisure.

I have the authority to make that choice, Stossen thought. No one would fault him. General Dacik had left the decision to him. He would be carrying out his primary orders—to keep the civilian researchers out of the hands of the Heggies.

It was well past three in the morning before Stossen asked himself the important question, *Can I live with that choice?*

When he had the answer to that, he had the answer to which direction the 13th would take. He called the exec on their private channel, waking Parks.

"We stay on this side of the river, Dezo. East, then south . . . if we can manage it."

He did not sleep better after making his decision. He didn't even try. He went back to his mapboard, looking for ways to maximize the 13th's chances.

Reveille came ninety minutes before dawn. The men were given thirty minutes to prepare for the day's march—ride.

"We're staying on this side of the river," Joe said when Lieutenant Keye gave him the orders.

"How do you figure that?"

"That thirty minutes, sir. If we were crossing, we'd wait till a lot closer to dawn, have at least *some* light while we're in the water. Colonel wouldn't try that in the dark unless the enemy was right on our butts. We wouldn't have thirty minutes then. It'd be up and move right this second."

Joe couldn't see the lieutenant nod. They were thirty meters apart and not even looking at each other.

"You must be right," Keye said, though there had been nothing about the direction in his orders. "You keep making deductions like that, somebody's liable to tap you for Intelligence, maybe bending over a compsole up in CIC."

"I would purely hate that, Lieutenant," Joe said. The shiver was entirely in his mind. "I'd go crazy in a week."

Keye chuckled. "I'll keep that in mind."

Joe switched channels to talk to the platoon's noncoms. Then, once he was certain that there were enough people moving to get the platoon ready, he sat down with a meal pack. Breakfast took less than five minutes. The packaged field rations did not invite lingering.

There were still eight minutes left on the thirty when Joe started moving 2nd platoon into their Heyers. He was the last man in, pulling the hatch shut after him. Lieutenant Keye was at the forward splat gun again.

"Everybody accounted for, sir," Joe reported. "We're ready to roll."

They waited. It had gotten chilly during the night, so in the first minutes crowded in the Heyer, before it started moving, nobody complained about the crowding. The warmth was welcome. Accord battle dress was supposed to be designed to keep a man cool in the heat and warm in the cold. It did, but only within very narrow limits. Nature never seemed to hold to those limits.

Finally, the APC started moving forward, late. The earlier vehicles needed time to get started. The 13th would attempt to maintain strict intervals now, sacrificing a little speed to make sure that every unit was just where Colonel Stossen wanted it.

"Coulda slept another twenty minutes," Wiz Mackey groused. "Hurry up and wait. Same old bull."

"Nobody's keeping you awake," Mort Jaiffer told him. "You're still tired, sleep. And give us a rest."

"Only way I'd sleep in this mixer was if you started givin' one o' your history lectures. That'd put us all out better'n sleep patches."

Joe lowered his head and grinned. He had his visor down, so no one would have seen him smile anyway, but the movement was instinctive. The men were feeling better if they were up to bitching at one another. Let them enjoy it while it lasted. The ride would wear them out soon enough.

It was, according to the time line on Joe's visor display, exactly thirty-eight minutes after the APC started rolling that it lurched to a sudden stop and the men inside heard the first explosions. The 13th had rolled into an ambush.

CHAPTER 18

The surprise was complete. The five Wasps had taken off just as the 13th started to roll. They had moved high and away, scattering to do some reconnaissance work, looking for the current positions of the Schlinal units that were known to be heading for the 13th. From as far away as possible. The pilots' eyes and instruments were focused away from the 13th. They weren't concerned with a near ground search.

The two remaining recon platoons had rolled right past the ambush without challenge or warning. In their Heyers, the reccers hadn't spotted possible trouble. Intelligence said that there were no Schlinal forces within two hundred kilometers except for the one unit that was chasing from dead behind. The 13th was racing east again. There was no time to stop and let reccers move through the terrain on foot ahead of the rest. Moving that slow, all of the Schlinal regiments the 13th knew about would have had more than enough time to catch them.

When the shooting started, the recon platoons were eight kilometers east of the fight.

George Company was the first unit of the 13th hit by the initial assault. It was the forward line company on the march this morning. A full salvo from a battalion of Novas hit among the fourteen Heyers that were carrying George. Three were hit. Two more were disabled by near misses that ripped treads. One was flipped on its side by another near miss.

In the initial confusion, the remaining Heyers of George Company scattered. Some simply stopped while their drivers shouted for orders. Others sped up, what little extra speed they could manage, while the rest veered to one side or the other, looking for cover.

Lieutenant Vic Vickers, George's commander, was in one of the lead Heyers. His wasn't damaged by the initial salvo. He had a flurry of calls from platoon leaders and noncoms, pleas for help and orders, reports of losses. After twenty seconds, he simply cut off the channels for his company while he tried to get information from Colonel Stossen.

Stossen was almost as busy as Vickers. The rest of the convoy was also coming under attack. The Novas switched their aim. They had stopped the point company. After that, their guns raked the convoy, each company of tanks targeting a different portion. Their fire was rapid but not overly accurate.

Closer in, there were rockets and RPGs hitting as well. The grenades could do little harm even to a Heyer, but the shoulder-operated rockets could bring down a Wasp or stop a Havoc. And the Heyers were less well armored than the howitzers.

The five Wasps were recalled at once. "Attack on the deck," Zel told the others. He *was* flying again. There had been no choice. All that the medic had been able to do was give him a sedative—not even a sleep patch. There hadn't been enough of the night left. If there had been a spare pilot along, Zel would have been grounded, but he either flew his plane or the plane would have to be abandoned. And Colonel Stossen had made the decision. "If he can fly at all, he flies. We need that Wasp in the air."

Back in the cockpit, Zel no longer felt troubled. He was where he was most comfortable, doing what he had trained to do, busy enough to keep extraneous thoughts away.

The Wasps had been at ten thousand meters. Coming in, they spotted a number of flashes from the attacking Novas, loosely clustered in three different areas, all along the right flank of the 13th.

The Novas weren't alone, though. As the Wasps dove in to attack them, surface-to-air rockets came up from the Novas' infantry cover.

Launch and evade. Zel held his course steady for the extra seconds it took to get good target locks on two Novas. As soon as his missiles were on the way, he swerved hard right, then up, putting the throttles all of the way forward as he started his electronic countermeasures against the SAMs.

For an instant, he came close to blacking out as the gee-load hit him. His vision dimmed, and he felt himself sliding toward unconsciousness. Just before the load could become too much, he dragged back on the throttles, only enough to clear his vision.

He took a deep breath, hurried, while he tracked the SAMs on his heads-up display. One had already veered off, heading harmlessly to the south. The other had lost its lock but was close enough to regain it. Zel continued climbing, trying to maintain his margin on the missile. He dropped a decoy, then flipped left, twisting the Wasp around 90 degrees.

When he dove again, the SAM kept climbing, closing in on the decoy.

Zel turned his attention to the tanks again. Two of the Wasps from Red Flight were already into their second attack. Another flurry of rockets came up from the ground, toward those two planes.

Two more tanks lined up in Zel's TA system. He locked them in, showed them to his next two rockets, and launched. One of the Red Flight Wasps, trying to escape a Schlinal rocket, twisted into the path of one of Zel's missiles. Zel hit the projectile's destruct button, but too late. It struck the Wasp, outboard, taking off the last drive nacelle.

The pilot managed to eject. The cockpit/escape module shot upward thirty meters before the parachute deployed.

As soon as the APCs stopped and men started to pour out of them, the 13th came under fire from rifles and splat guns as well. But the infantry could respond quickly. They didn't need directives or fancy target acquisition systems.

"Hit it!" Joe shouted, slapping open the latch on the hatch. He jumped out, ran three steps, and dove to the ground. With more than 150 ground vehicles scattered around, there was little chance of being hit by rifle fire. Echo had been in the center column, just in front of the colonel's headquarters detachment and the bulk of the support vehicles.

Most of the Heyers turned outward, so that both of the splat guns each carried could be brought to bear on the flanks. Lieutenant Keye was still at the forward gun in the Heyer that Joe had just jumped out of. The driver took over the turret gun, sending Olly Wytten out, the last of first squad to emerge from a vehicle.

"Get out a defensive perimeter" had been all the order necessary to put the eight line companies of the 13th into action. From that, company grade officers and their noncoms could figure out what to do.

Only the recon platoons and the rear guard had avoided coming under attack so far. The tail received a few tank shells, but there was apparently no Schlinal infantry that far west. The companies on either side of the formation consolidated the perimeter at that end and sent out heavy patrols to try to identify just where the Heggies were.

"Joe, you seen any fire coming in from the north?" First Sergeant Walker asked over his direct channel to Baerclau.

"Nothing. Are the Heggies all on the south?"

"That's what we need to find out. Take your platoon north, toward the river, then east. Cover as much ground as you can. First platoon will be heading west."

"You gonna keep the rest of the 13th from shooting at us?"

"Working on that now. Things are still a little balled up, but we're trying to get to all of the other companies on the northern side."

"We'll be moving in thirty seconds," Joe promised.

"Don't go any farther north than two klicks," Walker said. "We want you close enough to spot any Heggie mudders on that side."

"Roger."

Joe crawled closer to the Heyer while he called the platoon's noncoms and gave them the orders. Then he leaned inside the APC and tugged at the driver's leg. The driver pulled his head down out of the turret.

"We've got a patrol going out. Don't shoot us," Joe said.

"Just got the word," the driver replied. "Don't sweat it."

That's easy for you to say, Joe thought as he withdrew. Lieutenant Keye had turned to give Joe a thumbs-up gesture. *He* obviously knew about the patrol.

The platoon gathered by squad, sheltered behind two of the three APCs that had carried them. Even though there seemed to be no wire coming anywhere near them, all of the men stood hunched over, presenting the smallest targets possible. Joe took a few seconds to tell his squad leaders what he wanted, then sent first squad out on point.

Joe followed immediately behind with second squad. Third and fourth moved to the sides and started out almost even with second. The columns were eight meters apart. Within each column, the spacing between men was three meters.

Mort was out on point. He sought that duty more often than not, and both Ezra and Joe were happy to have him there. Mort was a good point man, cautious but not too slow. He did his job without bogging down a march. He concentrated totally on his surroundings, knowing what to look and listen for, any slight indication of booby trap or ambush.

Mort cranked the gain on his earphones to the maximum. With a little luck, and complete silence, he would be able to hear a man breathing softly ten meters away.

In the field, there was never any hint of the university man left in Mort. He stepped carefully, as softly as a cat on the prowl. In training, Mort had used the image of a cat to help him hone his skills. At the university, he had kept a pair of cats. They had been incredibly tame for felines, almost as easy to control as dogs. He could take them for walks, without leashes, and if they didn't always stay right with him, they never wandered far and always came back quickly—even, on occasion, at a whistle. Those cats had liked the park, a mostly wild preserve that bounded the university grounds on three sides. Mort would sit with his back against a tree, sometimes meditating, other times simply daydreaming, or watching the cats. For the cats, a trip to the park meant a chance to hunt. At some point, a century before Mort's birth, a pair of lab mice—of a strain brought from Earth by medical researchers—had escaped from the biochem labs. A hundred years later, the park was still infested with the descendants of that one pair of rodents. Numerous attempts to eradicate them had never been successful. The mice weren't native, so they weren't protected. They were fair game, and Mort's cats had delighted in that game.

Even moving through trees and tall grass, Mort needed only fifteen minutes to cover the two kilometers. There was no sign of Heggies. The sounds of battle had receded. There was clearly no firing on this side of the 13th.

At the two-kilometer mark, Mort knelt next to a tree and waited. Joe and Ezra both came up to confer face-to-face with him.

"We turn east now," Joe said, whispering. The three men had their visors up.

"How far?" Mort asked.

"Unless I hear different from the lieutenant or Izzy, until we make contact. We *know* there are Heggies out in front of the column."

"You heard anything new?" Ezra asked. "Like how many of them there are?"

"Not much. The Wasps spotted several groups of tanks, all with infantry support. No way to count mudders from the air. Must be quite a few, though, enough to keep most of the far side of the Team under fire."

"Where'd they come from?" Mort asked. "I thought we knew where they had pulled troops to chase us."

"I guess everybody thought that," Joe said. "That's the way it goes. Let's get moving again."

Dr. Corey and her people were in the center of the 13th. With all of the trucks and APCs around them, they too were in little danger from enemy wire. But there were still occasional explosions to worry about, RPGs and rockets as well as the cannon fire of enemy Novas. The civilians, with help from the SI team and part of the headquarters security detachment, were busy digging in.

Gene Abru stayed close to Philippa Corey, as he had from the beginning. She was digging with great vigor, if little skill.

Quite a head on her shoulders, for a civilian, Gene thought. She hadn't questioned his orders to get out and start digging. Most civilians seemed to think that any armored vehicle, even a Heyer, represented the ultimate in protection, instead of being merely a flimsy shell that drew heavy enemy munitions. Once, during the ride, she had even taken time to reinforce the orders that Colonel Stossen had given Abru.

"No matter what it takes, you can't let us fall into enemy hands, and you can't let them get the data cubes we're carrying." Holding his eyes with her own, she had repeated, "No matter what it takes."

"Those are my orders, Doctor," he had assured her, "and I *always* obey orders." The latter was, to say the least, an exaggeration. In the field, an SI team leader had extraordinary discretion about formalities like orders. But this order he *would* obey without hesitation. If it came to that point, it would almost certainly be the last order he would ever have to obey.

"How many are there?" Stossen asked. This conference was over the radio. With the 13th under fire, the colonel wouldn't cluster his staff together where a single shell or rocket could take them all out.

"Absolute minimum, call it two battalions of tanks, probably three, and at least one battalion of infantry, more likely an entire regiment," Bal said. "Not any of the groups we knew about. Either the Heggies managed to sneak more troops away from the lines than the general knew about or these were reserves, close enough to get here without being noticed."

"As far as we can tell, they're all east and south of us," Dezo said. "The patrols on the north have seen nothing, and the enemy infantry is just not getting in range of the rear guard, from the south."

"Trying to encircle us?" Stossen asked.

"Doesn't look as if they're up to anything that coordinated yet," Kenneck said. "Just trying to get us tied down until they get reinforcements. We stay in one place, we could be tied down permanently in another four hours."

"So if we want to keep some distance, we have to deal with this batch, however many they are, in two hours or less," Stossen said.

"Once we get a better idea what we're facing, we'll know what we *can* do," Ingels said.

"We'd better be able to do whatever it takes to bust loose, and soon," Stossen said.

"Takes more than that," Parks said. "It won't matter if we're on the move again if we've got all those Novas chopping us up."

"Our artillery is on them now," Ingels said after a hurried conference with the battery commanders. "The Wasps are finally getting them good targeting data. We've got patrols out, trying to circle around to give us good numbers on the infantry."

"We can't wait forever," Stossen said. "As soon as the tanks are fully engaged by our Havocs, we'll wade into them, infantry and Heyers. We'll get some use out of the splat guns on the mixers, use the rest to give the men what protection they can."

"East and south?" Parks asked.

"Right. The patrols that are out on foot now, tell them to keep at what they're doing. We'll pick them up as we can."

Moving east, Echo's 2nd platoon adjusted its formation, putting two point men out. Mort continued to hold the post for first squad. Twenty meters south, third squad had another man out front. He and Mort communicated directly. Behind them, the rest of their respective fire teams followed, and behind them, the rest of the platoon in a skirmish line.

Joe moved with Ezra's fire team, in communication with both point men. They weren't always visible. The platoon was in dense forest, a narrow band that paralleled the river but didn't extend right to the bank. In the floodplain immediately adjacent to the river, there was only tall, reedy grass mixed with a few stunted trees. The band of larger trees, a mixture of evergreen and deciduous varieties, was between three and eight kilometers wide, giving way to more open prairie broken only by occasional stands of trees. The 13th had been rolling through that more open ground. In the trees, the vehicles would have been reduced to a crawl and it would have been impossible to keep any sort of coherent formation.

Open ground was for vehicles. The woods were made for mudders.

Joe heard the 13th's new orders from Izzy Walker and passed them on to his squad leaders. Continue the operation. They'll pick us up. Be alert for any Heggies trying to get around to this side of the formation.

Once the 13th jumped fully into the fight, almost anything could happen. Joe had been in uniform long enough to know that.

We're away from the fighting again, he thought, but not with any particular relief. Combat was deadly. Battle took something out of a man, even if his side won and he wasn't hurt. But to miss a fight . . . sometimes, that could take just as much out of him, particularly if his mates came out on the short end.

There had been a lot of short ends for the Accord on Jordan.

The sounds of Heyer engines on the move finally reached the patrol. In an almost unconscious response, the two point men picked up their pace. Joe noticed, but didn't stop them. *The sooner we get our job done the better,* he thought.

As he could, Joe checked with Lieutenant Keye and the first sergeant, trying to keep informed. The reports were brief and usually covered no more than what the two men could see personally—not a lot. The Heyers advanced on the ambushing Schlinal troops, with the infantry in skirmish lines alongside and behind the mixers. The artillery was ranging about, shooting whenever they had targets. The Wasps—four left now—were in the air, also attacking when and as possible.

"Peel your eyes back a little more," Joe advised over his platoon channel. "Things might start popping any second." It had been five minutes since the Heyers had started leading the 13th's counterattack.

Once more, Joe glanced at the power indicator on his rifle. It was still at 100 percent, and Joe knew that he had a full spool of wire in.

"Hold up," Joe told the point men after another five minutes. "We must be close. Let's bring this back into a proper skirmish line. No sense leaving you two out to dry in front now."

The point men went down behind the best near cover and waited for the rest of the platoon to catch up. Joe pulled fourth squad back to serve as rear guard and reserve. They could be moved wherever they might be needed once any shooting started. If it did. Joe took up a position for himself just behind the skirmishers, in the center.

"Okay, let's get going again. Carefully now. We must be nearly even with where the point of the column was when the Heggies triggered the ambush."

For an instant, Joe flirted with the idea of having the platoon go to ground and wait for Heggies to come to them, a small counter-ambush. The idea was tempting. It would give the platoon a little edge, the defense waiting for the other side to come into range. Let the Heggies expose themselves first. But, reluctantly, Joe set that scenario aside. He couldn't fit it into the orders he had received.

Joe brought his rifle up a little more, at the ready, not quite at drill field port arms. The muzzle was too much to the front, a fraction of a second from being able to come to bear on an enemy . . . "out there"—in front.

The platoon was moving very slowly now, with hesitations after every step as the men looked for possible targets—and good cover. There would be little warning when—if—they did stumble upon an enemy that was down and waiting for them. Any clues would likely be subtle, easy to miss. The men moved at a crouch, rifles pointed more and more to the front.

The veterans in the platoon provided stability, both by example and by advice. By this point in the Jordan campaign, even the new men had *some* seasoning. People reacted differently to this kind of stress. Even when their overt actions were identical, drilled in over many long training sessions, inwardly each man had his personal response. Some, like Mort Jaiffer and Ezra Frain, became exceptionally calm, so totally methodical in thought and observation that they might almost have been programmed by rather primitive computers. Others, like Wiz Mackey, became extremely tense, ready to erupt into action like a spring suddenly released from tight bonds. Of the new men in first squad, Pit Tymphe seemed, so far, most like Wiz in his response to the stress. Carl Eames was already almost as calm about the business as the squad's two noncoms. Olly Wytten fell somewhere in between, to the surprise of the veterans. Mort had tagged him as another of the overwound spring types.

The platoon did get lucky. The last man on the right end of the skirmish line spotted a Heggie patrol perhaps a tenth of a second before he was spotted by them. He had time to call out a warning over the platoon frequency and start his dive to cover before the nearest of the Heggies—he saw three of them on his way down—could open fire. By that time, most of third squad was already shooting.

"Ezra, take your squad out and see if you can get around them," Joe said. "It doesn't sound like there's too many of them. Only a squad, or less. There's no way to tell yet."

Joe reported back to Lieutenant Keye and First Sergeant Walker that they had made contact and that a firefight was in progress.

"Push on as best you can," Keye replied. "We're a little busy here ourselves right now." He hadn't even stopped firing his splat gun during the short conversation. The 13th's advance into the ambushing Schlinal troops was turning into a real melee, confused small actions moving around one another.

"Trying to flank them now," Joe said before he switched channels. "Frank, take your squad around to the right. Try to cut them off there." Sergeant Frank Symes was fourth squad leader. "You run into any more of them, get down until we have some idea what we're up against."

"On our way," Symes replied.

Staying low—on hands and knees when he thought he had decent cover, slithering along on his belly when he didn't—Joe started to move toward where third squad was engaged. It still sounded as if there might be no more than a half dozen Schlinal wire rifles firing. The standard Schlinal weapon made a different sound than the Accord Armanoc. After very little exposure to both, a soldier could tell which was which.

Joe was still twenty meters from Sauv Degtree's position when new firing started, on the right, where fourth squad was moving.

"What is it, Frank?" Joe asked.

"Don't know yet. One of my men thought he saw something. No return fire yet. We're checking it out."

Joe waited for several seconds before he resumed his own movement. He was staying very low now. There was wire whizzing by overhead—not far enough overhead for comfort.

"They're pulling back," Degtree said when he noticed Joe. "That way." He pointed southeast.

"Frank, moving across your front from the left. The Heggies who've been doing the shooting," Joe said, relaying the information before he said anything to Degtree.

"I see them," Symes said. "We're taking them under fire."

The Schlinal soldiers went down. Although there was no immediate return fire from them, no one assumed that they had all been killed—or even wounded.

"Move in carefully," Joe told both squad leaders. "Second squad, move around up here. Don't let first get too far away."

Joe waited until second squad was moving before he made his next call. "Ezra, you found anything yet?"

"Not a sniff. You want us to bend around behind those Heggies you've got?"

"No. Wait until you link up with second. Then both of you echelon around. Unless something else happens first."

"Roger." There was a pause before Ezra said, "We're down and waiting. Where's second?"

"Low" Gerrent, second squad's leader, broke in to say, "I've already got you in sight. Ten seconds and we'll be ready."

That was when the shooting started on the left, from beyond the north end of first squad's line.

Mort felt wire pelting his helmet as he dove for cover. It wasn't the first time he had been dinged that way. The first time, after that fight was over, he had described it in almost whimsical terms. "Like getting hit with rice at a wedding," he told the rookies who joined the squad when the 13th got back to base. "Rice with a bad attitude."

He didn't waste energy on thoughts like that while he was being pelted with wire. He went flat, head toward the incoming fire. He waited for pain to come, the pain that would tell him that he had other hits, wire that had penetrated his net armor or found one of the gaps. When no pain came, he brought his rifle into position and fired off a couple of short bursts. He knew there was little chance that he would hit anyone. What he wanted now was either to draw more fire or suppress it. Either would help. If more wire came in, he might get a better idea where to aim. If no more came, that carried its own, more obvious reward.

"Anybody see where that came from?" Ezra asked.

There were no affirmative answers, and the squad was too well trained to waste air on negatives.

Joe redirected his attention to the left, where the heavier Schlinal fire was. First squad had gone to cover seventy or eighty meters from where Joe was. He heard the news that third and fourth squad had zeroed in on the lone squad that had started the firefight. There was another heavy burst of Armanoc fire over there, and then Sauv reported that the enemy squad had all been accounted for.

"Looks like we're facing at least a platoon," Ezra told Joe a minute later. "I think they were moving, trying to get around on the river side."

"You have any casualties?" Joe asked.

"Negative. The Professor may need a new bonnet, but he's okay."

"Keep 'em busy. I'll get help to you as quick as possible."

Joe pulled third squad back to go with him, around the left to get in front of the new Heggie contact. He sent fourth squad the other way, to try to get behind them.

The squads moved as quickly as reasonable, by fire team. Joe moved with third squad's second fire team. The groups leapfrogged one another. During the first several cycles, they didn't draw any Heggie fire. When wire did start coming their way, it was light, perhaps no more than two or three rifles aimed at them, and too far away for the wire to be especially dangerous.

Joe turned the squad more to the northwest, trying to keep the enemy far enough away to let them move quickly without taking serious hits. Then they bent back toward the east. As they closed in on where the enemy seemed to be, the fire team that was moving let loose with suppressing fire while they ran.

And drew more enemy fire in return.

Time seemed to speed up for Joe. Up and run, down and cover. Even the slight breeze seemed to double its velocity. Joe recognized the feeling of being pumped up as he moved toward danger. The sound of enemy wire flying past made the hair on his arms stand on end. First and second squads were firing into the enemy from cover to Joe's right. Somewhere beyond, fourth squad was still trying to get around to cover the third side of the enemy force.

Second platoon started to take casualties. Joe heard calls for medics from both first and second squad. He saw a man in third squad go down and called for that squad's medic himself.

But the enemy fire was diminishing at the same time.

"They're on the run!" Ezra reported.

CHAPTER 19

"It's like trying to catch rain in a net," Dezo Parks complained. "I've never seen Heggies play this game, breaking into small units and turning guerrilla."

There was little enemy armor still firing, but Parks was certain that no more than half of the Novas had been destroyed. At least a dozen were racing away from the 13th at the best speed they could make. Perhaps a few more were hiding, close, shut down, under thermal tarps. The Wasps all needed to land to rearm. None had any rockets left; only one or two had rounds for their forward cannons.

"No help for it," Van Stossen replied. "Let's make as much of a mark as we can in the next fifteen or twenty minutes. We'll try to disengage then, get the men mounted again."

"We haven't seen any trucks to haul these troops," Dezo admitted. "With their armor on the run, we might have a chance to put some real distance between us. Until the tanks come back."

"Start the Wasp support units moving now, with their security detachment. We've got to get them clear first. Those planes haven't got more than another twenty or thirty minutes of juice left."

"I've already alerted them. All of the support vans, Wasp and Havoc."

"What line company can we mount up fastest to cover them?"

"Howard. We've kept them close to their mixers and the trucks."

"Okay, they go along. Start them now. They'll need to get a good ten klicks to give them time to get the Wasps down and back up."

Echo's second platoon moved forward again, a little faster now with an enemy in retreat, but still not carelessly. They knew that there were still a lot of Heggies, somewhere close, and no one wanted to dash headlong into something too big for them to handle.

"Turn the corner," Joe ordered after five minutes. "We've gone too far east now." Their job wasn't pursuit of one small enemy unit. They needed to get behind whatever enemy was engaged with the rest of the 13th. If they could.

They didn't make much progress south before new orders came. Joe whistled over the platoon frequency. "Hold up. We've got to get back to our mixers." He had already given directions for the Heyers, through Lieutenant Keye. All the platoon had to do now was make it to the rendezvous.

"Back right over the path we took coming out," Joe told the squad leaders. "Don't let your men dope off just because they've seen it before."

Going out, Joe had stayed close to the point squad. On the way back, he lingered just in front of the rear guard. Where trouble was most likely. The conscious part of the decision was to avoid getting *too* close. As platoon sergeant, he wasn't supposed to be the first one involved in any fighting. He had broader duties.

Joe didn't walk backward, but he spent so much time looking over his shoulder that his neck started to ache. He had a nasty itch in his mind, an itch that worried that the Heggies would ambush them one more time before they could get to their Heyers.

This time, the itch was wrong.

It was a bumpy ride for beat-up reccers in the Schlinal half-track they had salvaged. Dem kept the accelerator all of the way to the floor. The vehicle lurched and bumped over uneven ground. At least Dem had the steering wheel to hold on to. On the other side of the bench seat in the cab, Fredo used both arms and legs to brace himself in position, and even that was sometimes insufficient to keep him from sliding, or bumping his head. In the back of the truck, where the rest of the men were, it was much worse.

"We've got a lot of ground to make up," Dem shouted one time Fredo complained.

"What good will it do if we're not fit to fight when we get there?" Fredo asked.

"If you can't handle a ride in the park, maybe you should transfer to C and B school," Dem suggested. C and B: cooks and bakers—the ultimate insult among reccers.

They *had* been making excellent time considering that there was nothing even vaguely resembling a road within a thousand kilometers. Dem's calculation, with a wide margin of error, showed that they had closed to within four hundred kilometers of the 13th. He hadn't stopped the truck for more than five minutes at a time, and that only twice since they started.

"Time we catch 'em, we might all of us be unfit for anything but C and B," Fredo suggested.

"Quit bitchin'," Dem said. "We coulda had to walk. Might yet, if our repairs give out. Don't know how good these Heggie buckets are anyway."

At the moment, the prospect of walking was not all that unappealing to Fredo.

Dem had been piloting more by guess than by map. He had headed east, then south, then east again. They were already past the point where the mudders had rendezvoused with their armor and support vans. A lot of traffic had passed. Even from a truck cab at fifty kilometers per hour, Dem could see how badly the terrain had been chewed up by so many tracked vehicles passing over the same sod. Farmer set up shop here, he thought, an' he wouldn't have to plow the first year. Straight furrows, heading east.

"Maybe we ought to move off this line," Fredo suggested. "A little to one side or the other anyway, just to avoid running into company we don't want. We do know there are Heggies between us and our people."

"Let's give ourselves another forty-five minutes," Dem said after considering it. "We must still be at least that far behind them, and this way, we don't have to worry about missing our people."

Fredo glanced at the time line on his visor. Forty-five minutes. He would try to hold Dem to that.

Only twenty of those minutes had elapsed before they saw a lone Schlinal half-track, the same type as the one they were riding in, sitting with its hood up and two men looking into the engine compartment. Another half dozen men were sitting in the bed of the truck, with several more standing by the side. One of them moved a couple of steps away and started waving with both hands, trying to get Dem to stop.

"Action on the left!" Dem pulled his visor down to talk to the men in the back. "Rake 'em as we go by. Any of them left, we'll stop to mop up."

"Dem!" Fredo protested.

"No choice. We don't get rid of them, they'll radio ahead and we'll have more to deal with later. Get your zipper ready."

Dem pulled his foot off of the accelerator. Slowing down served two purposes. It would make the Heggies think they were stopping—comrades ready to help them fix their truck or pick them up—and it made it possible for the reccers to get their weapons ready for action. It would have been impossible for the reccers to do any good at full speed. Even if they had been able to bring their rifles to firing positions, they would have been unable to hit anything smaller than the sky or the planet.

Even slowing down, Dem had to keep both hands on the wheel. There would be no drive and shoot for him, though he considered it.

"Watch it," he whispered into his radio. He was watching for the moment of recognition, when the Heggies realized that it wasn't help arriving but grief, when they noticed that the helmets and camouflage were wrong.

At fifty meters, the Heggies still seemed to think that the truck was carrying men from their own army.

"They must be wondering why we don't answer their calls by now," Dem muttered. Without a Heggie helmet handy, he couldn't know, but he suspected that they would be trying as many different channels as possible to explain their problem and what they needed.

"Get ready," Dem said, a little louder. Forty meters. He had the truck's speed down to 25 kph. His foot was back on the pedal, holding that speed, ready to increase it at need. If any of those Heggies had a rocket launcher handy, it wouldn't take long for him to get it into position.

The Heggies started to look at one another, uncertainly perhaps. Then one of them started to bring up his rifle.

"Take 'em!" Dem shouted. "Now, now, now!"

From behind Dem, six zippers fired at the stalled truck and the Heggies around it. Two reccers got ready to lob grenades, into and over the truck, to take care of any Heggies they couldn't see. On the left side of the cab, Fredo had his rifle out the window firing. There wasn't time for any of them to fire a full spool before they were past the enemy truck. None of the Schlinal soldiers had much chance to return fire. Twenty meters past the stalled truck, Dem shouted, "Hold on!" and spun the wheel in a hard left turn. "Make sure they can't radio ahead."

He hit the brakes. Before the half-track came to a complete stop, Dem had grabbed his own rifle and was out the door shooting. Fredo was out on the other side. Three of the reccers in the back of the truck were on their feet, shooting over the cab, while the rest dismounted.

"Grenades," Dem said. "Plaster them." He pulled a fragmentation grenade from a pocket and popped it straight into the back of the other truck. That half-track shook at the explosion. Dem was certain there would be no one left in it to radio ahead that they were coming. Six reccers advanced carefully toward the downed Heggies, rifles ready but no longer being fired. The other three stayed high, in their truck, covering the rest.

All of the Heggies—there had been nine of them—had been hit. One very short burst of wire from Dem's appropriated Schlinal rifle put the truth to his summary: "No survivors."

None of the reccers questioned what their sergeant had done.

"Let's see what we can salvage," Nimz said. "And get back on the move."

"Ain't there *any* way to get us better dope, Lieutenant?" Gunnery Sergeant Ponks pleaded over the radio. Lieutenant Ritchey was somewhere in the area, about two kilometers from Basset two. "There's Novas around, somewhere. I'd sure like to know where they are before I've got a one-thirty-five shell coming up my butt."

"We'd all like better TA," Ritchey replied. "But we're getting everything CIC and the Wasps can get for us now. There's no more to be had. Just keep your eyes open. Anyone sees anything, they'll sing out so the rest of us know."

"Will you, please, at least *ask* if they can get us any more?" Ponks was on a private channel with Ritchey, so he wasn't worried about how his pleading might sound to his own crew or any of the other gun commanders. As long as the conversation was private, he would do anything he could to—maybe—get what he wanted.

"I've asked, I've begged," Ritchey said, exasperation creeping into his voice. "Just make do with what you have."

"Yes, sir." Eustace realized that he could go no further.

"We're still on our own," he said after switching back to his gun channel. "They can't get us any more eyes."

"The Wasps'll be back in the air in a minute," Simon said. "We'll have them spotting for us again."

"Yeah." There was no joy in the word. "Jimmy, how we doing on ammo?"

"Still got six AP and three HE," Ysinde replied. "We'd best start looking for Rosey pretty quick." Rosey was Rositto Bianco, the crew chief for the support van that serviced them.

"Okay," Ponks said. "I'll give him a call, see if he's clear enough of the fighting to fill us up."

Since the support units had moved away from the fighting, as had the Havocs, it was just a matter of arranging a rendezvous and heading for it. Once the Schlinal armor had been driven off, the balance of risk and value had tilted against the Havocs. Infantrymen were poor targets, while the Havocs were easy pickings for any mudder with a rocket. Only once in a ten-minute drive was there a fire mission for the Fat Turtle. They altered course just long enough to shoot an armor-piercing round at a Nova that had been spotted by a Wasp.

A dozen men of the Havoc security detachment were posted in a loose perimeter around the support van before Basset two reached it. Jimmy and Karl popped their hatches and got out to help move ammunition from the truck into their ammo rack.

Eustace opened his hatch and stood but didn't get out. "Better top off our fuel tanks too, Rosey," Eustace called toward the crew chief. Bianco grimaced. Ponks had done his shouting into his microphone.

"You having any problems?" Rosey asked.

"Purring along. Growling whenever they find us something to growl at."

"Keep it that way," Rosey said as he waved two of his men toward the fuel lines. There were two tanks, one with hydrogen and the other with water. The H_2 would provide immediate fuel. The H_2O would keep the Havoc's converter supplied, separating hydrogen from oxygen. "I'd hate to have to do anything more than patch a tread. Hard to fix these beasts on the move."

"I heard that," Ponks agreed.

By that time, the work was done. Jimmy and Karl buttoned up the rear hatches. Rosey's men were recoiling their fuel lines.

"Good hunting!" Rosey shouted as Eustace lowered himself back into his seat.

Safe hunting, Eustace thought as he spun the lock on his hatch.

Zel hadn't *wanted* to watch his Wasp take off without him, but when the time came, he couldn't look away. The pilot who had been forced to eject from his own Wasp was flying Zel's now.

"We've got five pilots and four planes," Major Parks had explained. "In a way, that's a break. We can spell all of you fly-guys, get you a little rest and still keep all our birds in the air."

Zel hadn't said anything. He knew why he was the first man being spelled. Everybody thought he was coming unglued.

Maybe I am, he conceded after his Wasp disappeared from sight. *I certainly came close enough.* After it was over, his emotional outburst had troubled him. It was out of character. He wasn't surprised that he had worried Roo enough to send the crew chief looking for help.

If we'd had a spare pilot then, I'd probably have been grounded for the rest of the mission, Zel thought. Now . . .

"Better get in the truck, Lieutenant," Roo said. "We've got to get moving again."

Zel nodded and climbed into the support van. Being an officer did earn him the spare seat in the cab. And Roo had decided to take over the driving to keep from being relegated to the back of the truck. He was a sergeant and the regular driver a corporal. Rank still had its privileges.

"Where to, Chief?" Zel asked once the truck was moving.

"East, that's all they tell me, Lieutenant," Roo replied. "We're supposed to keep out of the way of any Heggie mudders."

"Sounds like a good idea." Zel was holding a carbine between his legs now. He knew how to use it. Pilots had never been required to master the Armanoc, but after the 13th's last campaign, Zel, and most of the other flyers, had made a point of doing so, spending time on the firing range whenever they could. A number of them had been turned into temporary mudders on Porter when they ran short of planes and, eventually, out of ammunition. It could happen again.

"Always a good idea," Roo said. "An' we've got to stay handy for the birds."

Several minutes later, Zel said, "I *hate* having somebody else fly my bird."

Roo turned his head just enough to look at Zel out of the corner of his eye. "Why not try to get a little rest, sir? That's the whole point of this. Lieutenant Carney'll take good care of her."

Zel closed his eyes, but he didn't sleep. He was too keyed up.

The men of Echo's 2nd platoon were boarding their APCs when they came under fire again. This time it was close. At least two squads of Schlinal infantry were within thirty meters. They had remained down when the Heyers arrived before the platoon. And they had waited until half of the men were inside the vehicles.

Joe Baerclau was standing next to the rear hatch on his Heyer, pushing men in, hurrying them along, when the shooting started. Carl Eames was between Joe and the shooters. Carl was hit, many times, and fell against Joe. Carl's weight almost carried the sergeant to the ground, but Joe managed to heave the private into the Heyer before he dove for what little cover there was available.

From the ground, Joe flipped the hatch closed. Wire ricocheting inside a mixer could be gruesome. Before he could get his own zipper into action, several of the splat guns were firing—two of the turrets and one forward gun. That cut down on the Heggie fire immediately. A grenade exploded in front of Joe's APC. A little dirt and debris showered down on him, but the Heyer's armor was enough to stop the shrapnel.

Then all three Heyers started to move. Joe and the other men who were still outside got behind them as the mixers headed toward the line of Heggies in the grass and trees off to the side. The rest of the splat guns on the vehicles started firing.

Joe looked from one side to the other to make sure that everyone was moving with the vehicles.

"Careful," Joe said. "Let's get this over with fast. You men in the mixers. Start coming out, one by one. We need your guns out here."

The APCs weren't moving fast enough to make that difficult. As the men emerged, Joe and the squad leaders directed them to places in the line. Not many had made it out before the Heyers reached the Schlinal line.

Most of the Heggies tried to run. Not many made it.

"Okay, turn it back," Joe ordered as soon as he saw that the firefight was over. "Medics, get to the casualties. Al, you've got one in here."

Joe got in and knelt next to Carl Eames. The big farm boy was conscious, but his net armor and fatigues had a lot of holes in them. Much of the camouflage pattern was hidden by the red of blood.

"Hang in there, kid," Joe whispered, but it didn't do any good.

Carl's eyes remained open, but he was dead before Al Bergon got to him.

CHAPTER 20

Disengagement was not simple for the 13th, and it was costly. Breaking away from the fight cost more men than all that had gone before in the series of skirmishes.

"Where did they come from?" Van Stossen asked his staff once the 13th was on the move.

"All we have are guesses," Bal replied. "Nobody saw them. Nobody reported another regiment missing from the lines facing the rest of our people. That means either we simply didn't spot them being pulled or they were never in the lines. I think that's the more likely answer."

"If intelligence missed one regiment, they may have missed more," Dezo pointed out.

"Hold on a second," Stossen said. "How confident are the two of you about calling this force a regiment?"

There was a long delay before Bal finally said, "Not at all confident, Colonel. We had no chance to get good numbers, except on the tanks. It seems certain that there were at least two battalions of tanks. In Schlinal TOs, that usually means a regiment of infantry." TO: table of organization, the bean counter's view of any military unit.

"We certainly didn't face *more* than a regiment," Teu said. "It might have been less. All small-unit engagements. A single infantry battalion could have handled that. Or two."

"Which means that even conceding that we faced a Schlinal

regiment, we didn't face all of it," Kenneck said. "In their TO, a regiment usually has three battalions of heavy infantry, one of light—not quite comparable to our recon units, two or three battalions of armor, and whatever ancillary units they might have along, like engineers or special purpose troops."

"Often one more battalion of infantry," Dezo said. "A Heggie regiment can come close to double the manpower of an SAT."

"Without an air wing," Kenneck said. "Their Boems are organized separately."

"What you're telling me is that we might be heading into another ambush," Stossen said. "That there could be from one to three more battalions of infantry and another battalion of armor we haven't even seen yet."

"That's about the size of it," Kenneck admitted. "We're doing what we can to get more information. The fly-guys are doing what recon they can, but Schlinal thermal protection is very good for their Novas. If the tanks are lying doggo under tarps, there's little chance for us to find them unless we know exactly where to look."

"We lost more than an hour back there, closer to ninety minutes," Ingels said. "That puts all of the Heggie units we knew about that much closer. We have another holdup like this one and we're caught, maybe not instantly, but if we lose more time, that will give at least two of the other units a clear shot at intercepting us."

"With no place to run," Bal added.

"I know." Stossen hesitated. "I suppose the important question is can we get far enough to put us in range of Wasps operating from behind the main Accord lines?"

"Touch and go," Parks said after a moment's calculation. "It depends on where they hit us next and how much time we lose."

"The Heggies will know just how close we have to be to get extra air cover," Kenneck said. "They can calculate that almost to the meter."

"So can we," Ingels said. "There, I've just put the line on the mapboards."

Stossen looked at his. That line, a thin yellow arc, seemed an impossible distance away.

Corgi Battery rolled almost into the center of a battalion of Novas ten minutes later. Those tanks had been hidden under camouflaged thermal tarps, which gave the Havocs a few precious seconds' advantage. Gun commanders used their 200mm howitzers in ways they had never been designed for, firing point-blank at tanks that were less than five hundred meters away. Five Havocs got off one round and had their second ready to go before any of the Novas had a chance to respond.

At five hundred meters, the velocity of a Havoc 200mm round was still so great that it was almost possible for it to penetrate both sides of a Nova before it exploded. But the destruction it caused with a hit was complete.

Those guns that were able to get a second round aimed fired those and turned to race away from the Novas at full speed. They were still outnumbered by nearly three to one, and a Nova was much more capable at close-in fighting.

The Novas were slow responding. Eight had been destroyed before they had a chance to get a round off, but that still left a dozen of them . . . and five Havocs running away at full speed, their cannons no longer able to bear.

Corgi two was hit by the first Schlinal shell.

A few kilometers away, to the north . . .

"Got those coordinates?" Eustace Ponks demanded.

"We're on line . . . now!" Simon replied.

"Ready!" Karl shouted.

"Fire!" Eustace ordered.

The Havocs of Corgi Battery might be running for their lives, but their TA systems were operating, feeding up-to-the-second data on the Novas to the rest of the 13th's artillery. Basset and Dingo batteries, and the one remaining gun from Afghan, all had fire missions on the way.

"Loaded!" Jimmy Ysinde called, no more than twenty seconds after the first round went out. The gun was aimed, the fire order given. The second and third rounds were on the way before the first shells from the initial salvo hit. Corgi one relayed information: two direct hits, two glancing hits that had stopped or damaged Novas without destroying them, and half a dozen near misses.

"Not bad," Eustace muttered. Basset Battery was racing closer to the enemy tanks, cutting across in front of the 13th's infantry. And still firing.

No one in Basset two saw what happened, but three minutes after the battery had started firing, there was a call from one of the other Havocs. "Basset three's been hit!"

Eustace swiveled his rear periscope until he saw the smoke rising from the hulk of Basset three, nearly a kilometer away. "What was it?" he asked over the battery channel.

"Must have been a rocket. Mudders."

"Another ambush." Eustace swore under his breath. "Keep your eyes open, Simon," he said over the crew channel. "It looks like we've got company close."

There was another explosion, ahead and to the left. The new Basset one swerved ninety degrees to the right and stopped.

Eustace had seen this explosion. "Mine!" he shouted. "We've rolled into a Heggie minefield."

"Stop?" Simon asked.

"No! If they've laid mines, they've got this area registered for their guns. Keep going. Bend the throttles!"

"I bend 'em any farther, they'll come off in my hands."

"New target," Eustace called, alerting the men in the rear compartment. "On the TA monitor now. Get it off, Karl." He switched channels.

"Lieutenant Ritchey, you all right?"

"We're okay, Ponks. You've got the battery for now. We're out of action." For the second time since leaving the main lines.

"There may be enemy mudders around, sir. I think a rocket got Four."

"We'll try to hold out until our people get here. Just get the others out of this minefield."

"We're all moving, sir," Eustace replied, checking the blips on his map console. *The three of us left, anyway.*

It took the four Wasps nearly two minutes to respond to Corgi Battery's calls for help. Once they arrived, the Havocs were able to proceed without further trouble. The Novas were unable to defend themselves against the air attack, and the way they had been stumbled upon in hiding had left them too far from their infantry cover.

Corgi ran south, and into long-range fire from one of the Nova units that had fled from the earlier battle.

The bulk of the 13th changed course, just enough to take them around the mined area that Basset Battery had found the hard way. They moved northeast for several minutes, toward the river that they could no longer cross, then turned east again.

Pinched closer together on the detour, the 13th ran into more trouble.

Alpha Company ran into the second minefield. Two APCs were destroyed. The rest ground to a stop and started disgorging their passengers as Schlinal infantry took them under fire. Rockets came in first, hitting one more Heyer.

Briefly, Colonel Stossen brought the entire 13th to a halt, except for the artillery and air, while the staff went through a hurried consultation.

"We've got to get around them," Stossen said. "Put Echo around on the left flank, George on the right. First opening we find, push the recon platoons through, on foot if necessary."

We're blind, Stossen thought while he waited for his orders to be implemented . . . and for the next stage of the Schlinal attack. There *would* be more. He was certain of that. A quick hit-and-run just wouldn't do it, and even liberal minefields could only slow them momentarily. Once the minefields had been spotted, they could be cleared quickly by specialists, as long as the fields weren't under direct covering fire.

Stossen sat in the APC that served as his rolling command post and stared at a mapboard. The positions of his own forces were marked, and those enemy units that had been spotted. The 13th couldn't reverse course. That would send them straight into the arms of the unit that had been chasing them almost from the beginning. They couldn't head south. There were two Schlinal regiments coming in from that direction, poised to intercept them. And the river meant that they couldn't go north. That was the most impenetrable barrier of all, at least for the vehicles.

"Bal, I need to know what we're facing here, and I need to know right now," Stossen said over the radio.

"Not much we can do but put mudders out on foot to test it," Kenneck said. "Wasps might find *some* of the enemy, but we're more likely to lose planes without learning enough."

"Dezo, what companies do we send, Bravo and Fox?"

"Those are nearest if we're just testing east," Parks replied. "But we can't forget our right flank. I think the next stage is likely to come from there, as before."

"We'll hold the rest of the line companies to meet that," Stossen said. "We've got to punch through as soon as possible." *If it's possible,* he thought as Parks acknowledged the orders.

Lieutenant Keye briefed Echo's noncoms while their APCs headed north toward the river.

Mines, Joe Baerclau thought. It sent a shiver up his spine.

Rolling into a minefield was a nightmare thought for any soldier. To do it in a mixer compounded the fear. There was no way to take counteraction, no way that individual caution could make a difference. For a moment, Joe sat with his eyes closed, trying not to hold his breath.

There was no chatter inside the Heyer after Joe passed along the news. "We're going to try to get around the enemy and hit them from the side or behind, just hard enough to let the rest of the 13th break through," he told them. "We don't know how many Heggies, or just where they are."

There was still blood sloshing around on the floor. Carl's blood. It had marked the boots of every man in the troop bay. Some of the men avoided looking down; others couldn't help but stare at the blood.

Two men in the Heyer had been slightly wounded in the last firefight, but nothing so serious that they wouldn't be able to fight again. Even Joe had a soaker over a pair of cuts on his right arm where long, thin strips of skin had been taken off by enemy wire. "Flesh wounds"—not deep or serious. But they had bled freely until they were treated, and Joe hadn't even noticed for several minutes. The sleeve of his fatigues had been soaked.

"I can see the river," Lieutenant Keye reported from the front of the APC. A few seconds later, the Heyer slowed down and turned east. Joe nudged Olly Wytten. Olly pulled his head down out of the splat gun turret.

"I want to take a look," Joe told him. He moved into the turret while Olly crowded around to get the seat that Joe had just vacated. There wasn't room for two heads in the turret at once.

Joe had to stretch to get a good view through the turret viewports. He eased the turret back and forth to give him a look at the terrain. They were 80 meters from the river, moving through trees.

That explains why we slowed down, he thought. The wooded stretch wasn't particularly dense, but the trees were too close together for an APC going full out. A Heyer was no tank or self-propelled howitzer. It didn't have the weight, or the armor, to bull its way through a tree. The drivers had to pick their way around anything thicker than a sapling.

"Be ready to bail out in a hurry if we have to stop," Joe warned the platoon. "We run into Heggies, we're going to have to react in seconds."

He pulled down out of the turret and gestured Wytten back into place. When he sat down again, Joe took another look at his rifle.

Not quite a full spool of wire, more than 80 percent of a full load in the power pack. Then he wiped sweat from the palms of his hands. Nerves. It never changed.

Five minutes. Ten. The Heyer turned southeast.

"Get ready," Lieutenant Keyes said. "We're going back to feet."

As the Heyers came to a stop, they turned toward the southwest, in line.

"Bail out," Keye ordered.

Joe already had his hand on the latch. He slammed it up and kicked the door open. He went out, to the side and down.

"Unless they've moved, there should be Heggies four hundred meters ahead," Keye said, dropping to the ground next to Joe. "The ones that ambushed Alpha when they rolled into the mines."

"We're going to move 'em out?" Joe asked.

"That's the plan. Let's get moving."

Joe turned his attention to his platoon. At the far end of the formation, the first sergeant was directing 1st platoon forward. The rest of the company moved as well. The Heyers followed, but slowly, letting the infantrymen get farther ahead. The APCs made too much noise. If they stayed close, they would simply announce their presence.

Joe took a series of deep breaths as he moved forward. There was more relief than tension in him now. It felt *good* to be out of the mixer and back on foot, where an infantryman belonged, where he could respond instantly to whatever came.

Not much cover, for them or us, Joe thought. But it would do. They would see any enemy before they were close enough for wire to do real damage.

Four hundred meters. On a track in camp, any man in the platoon could run that in a minute or less. With a full load of gear and an enemy at the end of it, four hundred meters might take ten minutes. Or an hour.

"Watch the ground," Joe warned. "They might have mines here too." *Maybe, maybe not,* he thought. It was dumb to bar your own retreat with mines.

There was a thick layer of wet leaves and moss on the ground. Joe scuffed at one place. The dirt was a couple of centimeters down. It would have been easy to hide mines in that.

At least walking men made virtually no noise on the damp ground. There was even little danger from the proverbial snapping twig. So much rain had fallen recently that even the dead wood on the ground was saturated.

Three squads of the platoon walked the skirmish line. Fourth squad followed behind. The other line platoons assumed the same formation. The heavy weapons platoon came in back of the center with the headquarters detachment. There was only one "noncombatant" slot in a line company's TO—the senior medtech. And even Doc Eddles was out walking, back with the APCs.

Joe glanced over his shoulder when the Heyers turned off their engines. They were close enough, for now. If their splat guns were needed, the drivers could fire up their engines again and close the gap quickly. In the meantime, they wouldn't give away Echo's advance.

"Narrow the line," Lieutenant Keye ordered. "Two squads up and two back."

Joe quickly pulled his third squad back with the fourth. The forward advance slowed as the flanking platoons eased in toward the center.

"Keep a close watch now," Joe said on his platoon channel. "We should be closing to within two hundred meters soon. When we get closer, don't forget that there are friendlies on the other side of the Heggies. Keep your head and your aim low."

"A little more space between the first and second ranks," Keye said over the radio. "Interval!"

Once more, Joe rearranged his platoon, and looked to make sure that his men were lined up with those on either side.

"First man to spot Heggies, give me a whistle," he told the platoon. "Don't shoot until you get the order, unless we're being shot at. And if we're being shot at, be damn sure you know it's Heggie wire before you cut loose." In this type of action, it would be all too easy to get into a firefight with a friendly unit.

"Slow it down." This order came from the first sergeant. Echo was within 150 meters of where the Heggie ambush had been located. The sound of rifle fire was louder now, and the sound of Heggie guns predominated.

"Sarge, Mort." An anxious whisper over the platoon noncoms' channel.

"Yeah, Prof."

"Ten degree's right from me, out about 120 meters, low next to that tree trunk with the cockeyed branch on its right."

Joe spotted the tree by the branch rather than by the bearing. The branch angled sharply down while the rest of the branches on the tree went sharply up. The branch was bent again about two meters out from the trunk, and it ended almost on the ground.

Joe stared for thirty seconds before he saw the trace of movement. The figure was wearing camouflage, but the pattern wasn't Accord, and the lines on the helmet were wrong. Joe switched channels.

"Lieutenant, we've spotted our first Heggie." He explained where. "He's facing away from us, and cutting wire."

"Right. Have one of your men lay a grenade close to the position," Keye said. Then, switching to his all-hands channel, he ordered, "Cover!" The men of Echo went down almost as if they had all been tripped by the same wire.

Joe passed the word to Mort to lay a rocket-propelled grenade as close to the Heggie as possible. As soon as it exploded, Lieutenant Keye gave the order to fire.

At first, most of Echo's wire went into that one narrow area. It wasn't until some of the other Schlinal troops turned around to return fire that Echo really had a good sense of just how dispersed the enemy was . . . and more targets to shoot at.

At least company strength, Joe thought. He had gone to his knees and ducked behind a tree with the order to go to cover. Once wire started coming back, he got flat on the ground, still behind the tree. The near end of the Heggie line was considerably closer than 120 meters, perhaps even close enough for their wire to penetrate net armor.

Joe started sliding forward. Flat on the ground, he didn't have a clear avenue of fire at the Heggies. First squad was directly in the way. He had only gone about two body lengths before he heard the engines of the Heyers fire up behind him. The APCs started forward, but they didn't open up with their splat guns until they were close enough that they could be certain of firing well over the heads of Echo. By that time, the Heggies were starting to withdraw, moving away to the left, east, at an angle, away from Echo and from the company they had initially ambushed.

"Into the mixers as they come by," Lieutenant Keye ordered. "It's express time again."

CHAPTER 21

South and east of the 13th, the main Accord perimeter was shrinking again. During the night, and on past dawn, a Schlinal attack pushed the northern end south by nearly twenty kilometers. The pressure was constant, with full coordination among infantry, armor, and air. General Dacik had no choice but to withdraw the troops in the northern end of the semicircle before they could be cut off. Even then, a few units were isolated and either neutralized or captured.

"If they break through," Dacik reminded his staff, "there's nothing to stop them simply rolling up our entire line."

It was mid-afternoon, and they were gathered in the general's basement headquarters, now no more than forty kilometers from where the heaviest fighting was going on.

"There's a Heggie column—forty Novas backed up by at least two regiments of infantry—trying to advance along the ocean now," Colonel Lafferty said. "They're not having much luck. We're holding them at the Galilee River."

"For how long?" Dacik demanded.

"For as long as they insist on keeping tanks on the point, General," Lafferty said. "We blew the approaches to the only place they can possibly get tanks across. They'll have to bring in engineers and waste a lot of time repairing the damage, and we're able to keep their heads down. There's no alternative crossing for fifty klicks inland."

"I'm afraid that's not good enough." Dacik looked around the table, moving his glance slowly from one officer to the next. "It's time to throw all the dice at once."

That brought heads up. Through the last day and a half, Operations and Intelligence had been trying to find holes in the Schlinal defenses and a plan to exploit them. Every alternative they had managed to come up with had more holes than a colander.

"Which option, General?" Colonel Ruman, Dacik's operations officer, asked.

Dacik got up from the table and walked to the large mapboard hanging on the wall. "A variant of Zero-Three," he said. "Variant mostly because of the changed circumstances on our right." He shrugged. He was looking at the map now, not at his staff. The others waited for him to continue. They waited for several minutes before he did.

"On the right, we'll stage an orderly withdrawal, but as fast as we can manage without letting it turn into a rout. Get as many of the support units moved ahead of time, beginning as soon as this meeting is over. Get them back, and get engineers preparing new positions. Just before sunset, we make it look as if we're being routed, but again, we have to make sure the appearance doesn't become the reality." He turned away from the map just long enough to make sure that he had everyone's attention.

"As soon as the Heggies respond, and even *they* shouldn't need more than thirty minutes to pour in after us, we start the breakout. Here, and here." The first point Dacik indicated on the map was nearly to the southern end of the Accord foothold. The other was almost precisely in the middle of the flattened semicircle that represented the perimeter.

"Ninth SAT will handle the punch on the left. We'll use both of the other SATs in the middle, and follow them through with everything we can spare. Left and right. We try to roll up the Heggie lines before they rip us apart." He turned and looked at the others again. After a pause, he said, "Questions? Comments?"

"It looks like about even odds who rolls up whom," Lafferty said. "If we slip up on this, even a little, there won't be any second chances."

"I'd suggest that you move your headquarters prior to the attack," Colonel Ruman said before Dacik could respond to Lafferty's comment. "Besides the obvious fact that this site will probably fall within an hour after we start this, command and control is going to get . . . dicey, at best. We need to be located somewhere where we can avoid getting bagged by the Heggies and yet stay close enough to the main action to respond to whatever happens."

"A mobile CP has already been set up, ready to move, Colonel," Captain Lorenz said.

Dacik nodded. "We'll move here." He turned and pointed to a spot on the map again. "Right behind the central breakout. It might not be any safer there than here, but it will sure keep us on top of the situation."

"When do we move?" Ruman asked next.

"Local sundown, which will be 1907 hours tonight, according to CIC. That's the time for the staged retreat on the right. The exact timing for the breakout may change, depending on how the withdrawal goes, but—temporarily at least—it should start exactly one hour later, 2007 hours."

"Preparatory bombardment or air strikes?" Ruman asked.

"Nothing to give them any warning. We'll have Wasps up and Havocs in position covering the withdrawal from the north, but no site preparation at either of the breakout locations."

"Diversions?" Lafferty asked.

Dacik glanced from Lafferty to Ruman. "Ru, I think we'll pull in the left end, just a little, beginning fifteen minutes after the start of the movement on the right. They have secondary positions prepared?"

"They should have, General," Ruman replied. "I'll check."

"Just that little bit then, and maybe"—he turned and stared at the mapboard again—"a patrol in strength . . . here." He stabbed at the position. "That's about halfway between the two places where we're actually going to attack, and it's where the Heggies pulled out one of their units."

"How much strength for the patrol?" Ruman asked.

"A battalion. With cover from a single battery of Havocs if they run into trouble."

Dacik walked back over to the head of the table but didn't sit.

"It's not going to be pretty, gentlemen, and . . . well, Lafferty might have been optimistic with the odds. But we have to do something, and there won't be any cavalry to the rescue to bail us out. Anything gets done, we've got to do it ourselves."

"What about the 13th?" Ruman asked.

Dacik frowned. He had *almost* forgotten them. "They're in deep trouble. There's precious little we can do to help them but win this fight here tonight, or make such an effort that the

Heggies *think* we might win." He stared down at the table and his frown deepened. "It looks as if the Heggies have turned at least four regiments against the 13th—ten, maybe as many as fifteen thousand men. That's really the only thing that gives us a chance. Even if we mop up everything here, we might still lose the 13th."

He turned away. In his mind, that "might" was already "will."

The 13th ran into one ambush after another. Although they no longer let themselves be bogged down by firefights, each ambush did cost time, even if no more than a few minutes. One company, sometimes two, would be detailed to stop long enough to allow the rest of the 13th to bull through. Until the next one. Each minute that the 13th lost to these delaying actions allowed the other three Schlinal units trying to reach them to get a minute closer to interception.

Just before sunset, the enemy massed all of the Novas it still had in the area for a determined bombardment of the 13th. A half dozen APCs and several support trucks were lost before the 13th's Havocs and Wasps drove the Novas off again. Not more than 10 percent of the men in the hit vehicles survived to be picked up by other vehicles.

The two Heyers carrying Dr. Corey's research team and their SI "minders" were kept near the exact center of the 13th. Gene Abru was with Philippa Corey. They spoke little but stared at each other most of the time.

Dem Nimz was driving slowly as sunset approached. Somewhere, probably very close, was the Schlinal convoy they had been following. Dem had turned the captured Schlinal truck away from the track at the first distant hint of the enemy, hoping to circle around them without being spotted. The Heggies had stopped for what Dem suspected would be a very short break. The few rest stops that the column had made had all been very short, never more than ten minutes.

At Dem's side, Fredo sat with his rifle muzzle out the left-side cab window. The safety was off, and his finger was over the trigger guard, lightly, ready to move at the slightest provocation. He stared toward the north as if he expected to see the trucks carrying the Schlinal force. They were too far away for that though, *if* Dem had taken as big a loop around them as he thought.

"You still plan to curve back in front of them?" Fredo asked.

"Yes. They're on the shortest track to the 13th. All we have to do is stay in front of them and follow the 13th's tread marks. That way, the Heggies'll never know that there's another vehicle out in front of them."

"They wouldn't know if we stayed a couple of klicks over to the side either," Fredo pointed out. "We know where everybody's at, as long as that mapboard still works."

"That couple of klicks might make the difference in our catching up in time."

"In time for what? You think that nine of us are going to affect the outcome?"

Dem just glanced at him for an instant. "We belong there, Fredo. We *belong* there."

An hour after sunset, the 13th turned slightly toward the north, closer to the river. Thirty minutes after that, 4th recon left their APCs and moved away from them on foot, into the forest. As the rest of the 13th reached the first group of parked Heyers, they too stopped and disembarked. The running was over.

"This is probably the best defensive position we're likely to find," Stossen told his staff when they gathered near his command post. "We've lost too much time to keep running. We've got a fight on our hands. All we can do is choose the ground."

The colonel had already issued his preliminary orders for the various components of the 13th. Everyone was moving into position as quickly as he could. It would take some little time for them all to get situated. Fourth recon was out to try to make sure that the rest *had* that time.

"We're at the extreme range for Wasps operating from behind our lines," Teu Ingels said. "But we can't look for any help from there. It looks like all hell's broken loose back there."

"I talked to General Dacik two hours ago," Stossen said. "Crunch time." He let that hang for a moment. None of the others broke in with any comments. "The next twelve to twenty-four hours will likely tell the tale. Win or lose, the Jordan campaign is near the end. Our job now, besides making sure that those scientists don't fall into enemy hands, is to keep as many Schlinal troops occupied for as long as we can. We do our job right, maybe the general will manage to pull Jordan out of the coals."

There were a handful of trucks that had backhoes or scraper blades. They couldn't possibly do enough excavation to provide sound cover for every vehicle with the 13th, but they did what they could. Men with shovels worked as well, as many as half of the regiment at a time. More was needed than simple foxholes for the infantry. Positions were arranged close behind the perimeter for the Heyer APCs. Their splat guns could contribute materially, as long as the APCs could be protected. Trenches were dug for them, with the dirt piled up in front and on the sides, lessening the amount of surface accessible to enemy rockets or tanks shells. Camouflaged thermal tarps might help them escape detection as well, for a time. The support trucks for Havocs and Wasps were camouflaged and bunkered also, farther back, in the last stands of trees before the river. The 13th's remaining Havocs were split. Only half were kept with the perimeter that was being hastily established. The three remaining guns of Basset Battery, the one left of Afghan, and one from Dingo were sent on farther east with their support and orders to "get lost"—avoid detection—but stay close enough to help when the fight came.

Joe Baerclau dug his foxhole between first and second squads, working fast even though he took time, frequently, to look up and down the line to make sure that everyone was working, and doing the job right. "We don't have all night," he warned—among other banal cautions. *What* he said wasn't all that important. Every man in the platoon knew what was needed. The platoon sergeant's voice was enough to keep anyone from slacking off.

As soon as he had his own position prepared, Joe started walking the platoon line. There were faint sounds of firing by then, in the distance, where 4th recon was operating. Several of the line companies also had men out beyond the new perimeter, to set mines and listening devices along the most obvious approaches to the 13th's positions. Joe spent as much time looking out beyond the platoon's line as he did inspecting the foxholes the men had dug and the other preparations they had made. Somewhere out there was the enemy.

"First and third squads. We need a line of mines and bugs across the platoon front. Mines at 80 and 120 meters. Bugs at 200."

The two squad leaders got their men up and moving out. The rest of the platoon waited, ready to provide covering fire should that prove necessary. In the meantime, the men continued working. Joe walked back the length of the platoon's section of the perimeter, then walked back to the three Heyers that were dug in behind it. Lieutenant Keye had his command post slightly behind and off to the right, behind the junction where first and second platoons met.

"Your men ready?" Keye asked.

Joe lifted his visor and nodded. "Soon as the men get back from laying out greeting cards, Lieutenant. Any word on how close the Heggies are?"

Keye shook his head. "The ones who've been playing tag with us can't be far. The rest . . . just take a look at your mapboard. One regiment could be here in less than an hour, the other two not long after that. Within two hours, we're going to be ass-deep in them, maybe four or five to one against us."

"We're gonna stay right here and slug it out?"

"Far as I know," Keye said. "That's the current plan, anyway."

"How 'bout we haul some of the reserves up to the line, ammo and food?" Joe suggested. "I'll feel a lot better if I'm not worried about running short of wire again."

The lieutenant's hesitation was minimal. "Get your working parties out." He turned to the first sergeant. "Pass the word to the other platoons, Izzy."

Joe gave the lieutenant a casual salute, lowered his visor, and headed back to his men. On his way, he paused to look at the three Heyers. All were dug in so that their front splat guns were just barely above the earthen berms in front of them. That fire wouldn't be far above the heads of men in foxholes on the line. The turret guns would be less of a hazard. Except to approaching Heggies.

"While they last," Joe whispered. He had no illusions. The Heyers would draw heavy fire from the start. They were unlikely to survive for long, even dug partially in.

Zel Paitcher almost hyperventilated. He was back in his Wasp for the first time since being relieved. It felt so good that he started breathing, deeply and quickly, until he started to get light-headed. By that time, he had trouble slowing his breathing again. A slight pain developed in his forehead over the left eye.

He took his hands off of the control yoke one at a time and flexed them. He had also been gripping the yoke too tightly.

I am nervous, he thought. He scanned his heads-up display and the monitors below it. They told him everything he needed to know about the Wasp, and everything that was known about its surroundings. Irv Albans was flying off his right wing. Jase

Wilmer and Roy Carney were flying together, some distance away. The latest data on enemy locations was on the map monitor, some of the information hard, most of it guesses based on outdated intelligence.

The Wasps were looking for the enemy now, not just to update the data.

"That one vehicle moving by itself, that must be those reccers they told us about," Irv said when the single infrared blip showed on his TA system.

"I'll go down for a closer look," Zel said. "You stay up here to make sure I don't find more than I expect."

He hardly waited for a response before easing back on the throttles. The Wasp started down like an express elevator. Zel turned the nose to come up on the truck from behind. He wasn't worried about being spotted from the ground. It was dark enough for invisibility, and with the engines throttled back, he couldn't possibly be heard over the sounds of a truck engine.

Zel came down below fifty meters, an equal distance behind the truck. At that range he could distinguish the individual heat signatures of seven men in the rear of the truck—at that range, clearly a Schlinal half-track. The truck was moving too fast for foot soldiers to keep up, and there were no other vehicles anywhere close.

A smile played over Zel's face as he thought, *I could almost get close enough to make sure those are Accord helmets.* But he wouldn't. At *that* range, his Wasp would occult enough of the sky to be noticeable, and he didn't want to spook the reccers into firing at him. Instead, he eased the throttles forward and started to climb.

"It's them," he told Irv. "Now, let's find the Heggies who're chasing them. They can't be far."

Twenty kilometers.

"In and out," Zel reminded his wingman. "We're just here to slow them down."

"And pare them down," Irv replied. "The more we zap, the fewer there'll be to hit our mudders."

In the dark, the Wasps had every advantage. There was nothing visible of them until they fired their first rockets at the lead trucks. Then, before anyone in the half-tracks could respond, they allowed themselves a four-second strafing run before they split, one to either side, and climbed as rapidly as they could without blacking out from the gee-load.

Three Schlinal SAM rockets came up into the night sky, blind shots. None achieved target lock. They rose harmlessly, then fell back after they exhausted their fuel and momentum.

For their second run, Zel and Irv came in from straight behind, almost at ground level, too low for their Wasps even to show up by occulting stars. Missiles and cannon. Once more the two fighters split, left and right, and climbed away from the enemy column.

"Now let's see if we can find the next batch of 'em," Zel said. The other pair of Wasps was already looking for that next collection of Heggies.

The crew of Basset two was out of their gun. They were hiding under bushes some twenty meters from it. They had stretched a thermal tarp over the Fat Turtle. Now all they could do was wait.

"I feel like my butt's hangin' out the window," Simon muttered after they had been in position for fifteen or twenty minutes. "Out here all alone, nothing but a pistol in my hand."

"Shut up," Eustace said, mildly. "It could be worse. The guns shut up inside the perimeter got no room to maneuver. Not enough, leastwise. The shooting starts, they won't last long if the Heggies bring up Novas or Boems. Out here, we got a chance."

"Chance for what?" Simon asked. "To be the last ones bagged by the Heggies?"

Eustace growled. "If it comes to that. Even that's somethin'." *We'll give 'em what-for even then,* Eustace promised himself. As long as they had the Fat Turtle and rounds to fire, they would keep fighting. And after that, they still had their pistols.

Eustace grinned. *Bloodthirsty bastard I've become.*

He cleared his throat. "If the dope we got was good, we've got an hour, hour and a half, before we have to worry too much. Unless the Heggies have more Novas lying doggo in close."

"Like we're doing," Simon said.

"Yeah." *They ambush us, we ambush them. Helluva way to run a war.*

"Peekaboo, I see you," Karl Mennem said in a falsetto.

"We didn't play it with 200mm howitzers when I was a kid," Simon said.

"Enough," Eustace said. "You guys try to get a few minutes' shut-eye. It might be a long time before we get another chance."

CHAPTER 22

The noises in the night might almost have been nothing more than distant thunderstorms. More rare than the muted crump-thump of explosions were the brief flares of light that the infantrymen manning the 13th's perimeter saw. More rarely yet, a man might hear an artillery shell whizzing overhead, outbound. There was fighting going on, but it wasn't close. Not yet. In fact, the obvious distance of the enemy—marked by the muted sounds of Havoc shells and Wasp rockets exploding—had a calming effect on many of the infantrymen waiting in their newly dug foxholes.

A lullaby was how Joe Baerclau thought of it. One man per fire team was left on watch. The rest tried to get some sleep. Nearly everyone was exhausted enough to sleep now, if only fitfully. Joe might have wakened a half dozen times in the hour he permitted himself to sleep, curled up in his foxhole. Sometimes it was one of the distant noises that woke him. At other times, it was a brief message over the radio, or someone moving close by. But each time he woke, he would listen for a moment to satisfy himself that the danger wasn't imminent, and then slide back into sleep for another minute or five. Until the next time.

It was a little more than an hour before Ezra Frain called and told him that his time was up. Joe took several deep breaths and went through a stretching routine. He stood and looked around. The flashes were no longer quite so far away.

"They'll be here before long," he told Ezra over a private channel.

"Last word from the lieutenant was that we might have another hour. The Heggies that have been chasing us have been slowed down quite a bit. All we've seen lately is a few sniping incidents from the Heggies right around us. I guess the rest of them are waiting for reinforcements."

"They might wait until all of them rendezvous," Joe said. "Now that we've gone to ground to wait for them. They don't have to slow *us* down any more."

"Sounds logical to me," Ezra said. Then, after a pause, "Joe?"

"Yeah?"

"This is gonna be worse than Porter, isn't it?"

"Could be, Ez. Nobody's going to come in-system to rescue us this time."

"This last hour, just sitting here waiting—there's been too much time to think. I'm scared, Joe, more scared than I've ever been before." When Joe didn't say anything, Ezra continued. "I mean, there really hasn't been time to get deep scared before. All that crazy riding in the mixers. No time to think there. Even back on Porter, we were too busy for fear most of the time."

Most of us, Joe thought. "Don't let it eat at you, Ez. Nothing we can do about it now. Try to get a little sleep. I'll look after the squad."

"I managed to catch some sleep in the mixer earlier. Don't know how, but I did. It would take a patch to put me to sleep now, and we don't have *that* much time."

"Probably not. When's the last time you talked to the lieutenant?"

"About twenty minutes. I think he's trying to sleep now. I was over there. He looked like he'd aged ten years the last coupla days."

"I'm going to take a short walkabout, and get something to eat," Joe said. "Call me if you see anything."

He checked his rifle, then climbed out of the foxhole, careful not to damage the berm he had piled around it. After taking a minute to do more stretching—his knees had gotten stiff curled up in the foxhole—Joe walked along behind the platoon's section of the line, warning each squad that he was coming as he neared it. He talked to the men who were awake, looked over the defensive emplacements again, and stared out into the night quite a lot. He went to one end of the platoon, then back to the other, and finally he dropped behind the line to the APCs. There was only one man in each of those, the assigned driver. They would also operate the splat guns. The mixers were too vulnerable in the kind of battle that was almost certain to develop to put two men in each.

The first sergeant was manning the company's CP while Lieutenant Keye slept nearby.

"Anything new?" Joe asked.

Iz Walker shook his head. "Not really. Still no sign of enemy aircraft. That's the only real good news we've had. They don't seem to have too many tanks left either, far as we can tell. The bad news is that it looks as if we're going to be facing four regiments of Heggie mudders in an hour or two." His chuckle was mirthless. "None of them are anywhere near full strength anymore." He paused before he added, "They probably still outnumber us by four to one."

"What about the rest of our people?" Joe asked.

"Can't make much sense from what we're hearing about that," Walker said. "They're up to their earholes in trouble. A real set-to, no lines left. Heggies attack in one place. We attack in another. They've broken in and we've broken out, different places. Trying to turn each other's flanks. A real nightmare."

"Who's winning?"

"No idea. I don't think anybody has any idea. Maybe in the morning we'll know. One way or the other."

"You think it'll end that fast?"

"Maybe, maybe not. No damn way to tell."

"What about the civilians?"

Walker stared at Joe for a minute or more before he answered. "All I've got there is scuttlebutt. Last I heard, they're stuck in a hole, a bunker, with an SI team. Abru—you know him?"

"We've met."

"If it looks as if there's any danger of the Heggies getting the scientists, Abru's got orders to give them the whack."

"He'll do it, too, if he has to," Joe said.

Walker nodded. "Those SI guys are all loons, and he's one of the worst."

"Or best, I guess, depending how you look at it," Joe countered.

"There's *women* in that research team," Walker said.

• • •

It does *make a difference,* Joe thought as he walked back toward his foxhole. But, right at the moment, he could not tell himself exactly *why* it made a difference that there were women in the research team. Why was it more repugnant to kill them than their male counterparts? They were all civilians, highly trained professionals making an important contribution to the defense of the Accord of Free Worlds. At least, they *would* make an important contribution if they, or their research data, ever made it to a safe Accord world.

Joe doubted that any of them signed up for their project thinking, *I may have to be killed if we do good work and the Heggies come along.* He doubted that any of them *wanted* to die. *Any more than* I *do,* he thought. But he had accepted military duty willingly. He had always known that there was a chance it would kill him, and he had seen too many other soldiers die to have any illusions left. But those deaths had always come as a result of a free choice those men had made, knowing that death was a risk.

I wonder what they're thinking now? It was a question Joe couldn't answer, and he decided, without too much difficulty, that he really didn't want to know the answer to that question.

Dr. Philippa Corey, her team, and their SI guardians were already in what was nearly a tomb. A Heyer had been buried. One of the backhoes had been used to excavate a trench deep enough, and after the APC was driven into it, the dirt had been backfilled. The only exit left uncovered was the top hatch. Two air vents in that provided circulation. Above the hatch—propped open just a few centimeters to provide additional air until the fighting started—there was a circular hole surrounded by a low dirt rampart. From outside, that hole looked like any other foxhole, except up close. The Heyer was safe from just about anything short of a direct hit by a large rocket or a Nova shell right in the hole.

Gene Abru sat quietly on one of the bench seats in the troop bay. The mixer wasn't quite as crowded as it would have been with as many soldiers in full kit. The civilians weren't burdened by weapons, ammo, and all of the other field gear that a soldier would be carrying. Nine civilians and five SI men.

No one in the Heyer had said anything for more than thirty minutes. Most avoided even looking at any of the others. They sat almost motionless, their eyes staring at the floor, or at their knees. One dim red light gave the Heyer some little illumination. The soldiers with their night-vision visors could see fairly well, the civilians less so.

Gene could see most of the others without turning his head. He did watch, because he *always* watched. But, mostly, he paid little attention to what he was seeing. More important was what he was hearing, a running commentary from Colonel Stossen's headquarters. Abru and his teammates were linked to the command staff channel. They heard all of the intelligence as it came in, heard the radio conferences among Stossen and his staff. If the 13th were overwhelmed, or about to be, the SI men would hear it over the radio.

And know that they had to execute their final orders.

Before the Heyer had been fully buried, Gene had decided how he would do that. Fourteen people in a small, confined space with metal walls and dirt all around. Two or three fragmentation grenades set off in those confines would leave little of anyone. Even the battle helmets and net armor of the SI men would do little to stop shrapnel like that. But first, by no more than a second, a phosphorus grenade would be detonated in the small box that held the data cubes with all of that important research data. Those cubes had to be destroyed as well as the people who had created the data.

If they go, we go. The decision had been easy for Gene: no leftover guilt to worry about afterward. If there were time, he would take his helmet off before he detonated the grenades, just to be absolutely certain that the end was quick.

It will leave a pretty little puzzle for the Heggies, Gene thought, and he managed a thin smile at the prospect. A buried armored personnel carrier crammed with people who had just sat there and turned themselves into sausage meat. What would the Heggies make of that? *I hope it drives the lot of 'em out of their friggin' minds.* Gene felt considerable satisfaction at that prospect.

Roo Vernon could do just about anything possible with a Wasp, and not a few things that the technical manuals said were impossible. He could take a Wasp apart and put it back together. He could even rebuild one of its antigrav engines, almost blindfolded. And, although he had no formal training in engineering, he was absolutely confident that he could design a better fighter than the Wasp, or make significant improvements to the machine.

He was comfortable around his planes and tools. He definitely wasn't comfortable around officers, though, except for pilots. They were a different breed. But Roo had left his van and his crew to seek out Colonel Stossen's command post. What he had to say had to be said face-to-face. He couldn't adequately do the job over the radio. Another man might have been able to, but not Roo Vernon.

"Colonel?" He found Stossen sitting inside a Heyer, alone at the moment.

"Yes, Sergeant?" Stossen set his mapboard aside and turned more toward Vernon.

Roo identified himself. "Me and the boys been thinking, Colonel. We've got plenty of spare 25mm cannon pods and ammo, and a lot more rockets than our four Wasps'll be able to use. We got to thinking, there oughta be a way to put all those spare munitions to use here."

Stossen blinked rapidly, several times. It was something that hadn't occurred to him. "Did you come up with anything?" His voice was casual, belying the unexpected excitement he felt.

"We think so, sir." Roo waited for the colonel to tell him to proceed. "Wouldn't be the work of but maybe two minutes to rig a manual firing system for the cannons. We put two together, just to see would it work. Takes a bit longer to rig a tripod strong enough to handle the cyclic rate, but we carry parts that'll do it, from level to about 40 degrees elevation, 360 rotation."

"How many can you put together in an hour?"

"Put all of us on it but what's needed to service the birds, maybe five of 'em, Colonel."

"Get to it. What about the rockets?"

"Can't fit any TA to 'em. But let a target get close enough for a man to eyeball it so's the rocket's video system can lock on, we can set up a remote launch switch from spare radio circuits. That don't take hardly any time at all. Manually arm the rockets one by one, then use the radio clicker to launch."

Stossen came out of the Heyer. "Get with it. Grab any help you need. I'll send people to collect them and put them where they'll do some good."

"Aye, sir. We'll get right on it." Roo saluted and started to head back toward his truck.

"Sergeant Vernon?" Roo stopped and turned back to the colonel.

"You may have just saved the 13th. We get through this, I won't forget."

Roo was too embarrassed to do anything but salute again and run off toward the work he had just volunteered for. He still didn't *know* that any of it would really work. He wouldn't know that until somebody actually pulled the trigger on one of the devices.

There was no warning before the first salvo of Schlinal 135mm shells dropped into the 13th's position, but it was still no great surprise. Anyone who had given it any thought assumed that the Heggies must still have some armor in the area, close, just waiting for the right time. And it came in heavy for five minutes. The best estimates that the Accord had suggested that a Nova with its automated loading equipment could maintain a sustained rate of fire of slightly over five rounds per minute, as accurate as the available targeting data permitted.

Target acquisition was a weak point for both Accord and Hegemony on Jordan, though. Each side had been knocking out the other's spyeyes as quickly as they could be tracked and attacked. The Accord could attack Schlinal satellites from space. The Schlinal garrison had to work with ground-launched missiles. They had no fleet in orbit around Jordan.

"Here it comes," Joe Baerclau told his platoon—an unnecessary gloss since everyone could hear the exploding shells. "Watch for their mudders."

The Nova fire didn't seem to be particularly well directed against specific targets. The bursts were spread, seemingly at random, throughout the area that the 13th had secured.

They must still be quite a way off, Joe thought. Had the enemy tanks been closer, or had accurate ranging from infantry observers, the line of Heyers behind the frontline foxholes would certainly have been among the first targets.

After five minutes of concentrated fire, the rate of incoming rounds slackened off considerably. That too came as no great surprise to Joe. A Nova had a limited capacity for ammunition, and the Novas would be moving rapidly now, putting as much distance as they could between themselves and their last firing points, scurrying to get out of the way before counterbattery fire or Wasps could get to them. The barrage did not completely end, but it grew much lighter and would likely stay light until the tanks had a chance to take on more ammunition from their support vehicles.

Several more minutes passed before Joe heard any small arms fire, off to his left, the east, and—apparently—well out in front of the lines.

"Lieutenant, we got any reccers or other patrols still outside?" Joe asked. The patrols he had sent out to plant mines and bugs had been back for quite some time. As far as Joe knew, all of the patrols doing that work had come back to their holes an hour or more before.

"I'll check." No more than a minute passed before Keye was back on the channel. "There's a reccer squad out yet on this side. They shouldn't be in front of us, but who knows. Tell the men to be careful who they shoot at until the reccers get in."

"Why aren't they on the visor display?" Joe asked.

"Reccers." It was almost a curse the way Keye said it. "Probably got their position markers turned off so the enemy won't spot them."

"I thought that was impossible."

"Far as I know, it is," Keye said.

Joe passed the word to his men that there might be friendlies coming into their field of fire. "So be careful. Those reccers *are* on our side."

After another long look out beyond the foxholes, Joe felt around on the ledges he had carved into the sides of his own "nest." There were grenades close at hand, spare spools of wire for his carbine, even meal packs and one of his two canteens, all within easy reach, and where he would know exactly where to reach for whatever he wanted. Two extra power packs for the rifle were in his tunic pockets. He wouldn't need either of those soon.

He opened a meal pack and waited the few seconds it needed to warm up, then ate, slowly, hardly looking at what he was doing. His eyes continued to scan the forest and tall grass beyond the perimeter. The trees were thin, but only in a few narrow areas facing the platoon did his men have really clear fire zones. There had been no time to cut trees and haul them out of the way. In a few spots, there were even what might prove to be dangerous avenues, allowing enemy soldiers to get within twenty-five or thirty meters without exposing themselves. Maybe. The platoon had done everything they could to cover those approaches.

"Keep a sharp watch now," Lieutenant Keye said over the company channel. "The enemy is close, maybe within two hundred meters in some areas."

Joe dropped his empty meal pack to the bottom of his foxhole. It bounced down into the grenade sump, out of the way. He switched the safety off on his zipper and settled himself into firing position. The waiting was almost over. That nearly made up for what might follow.

CHAPTER 23

Major General Kleffer Dacik was in his mobile command post, *beyond* what had been the Accord front lines in the sector no more than twenty minutes earlier. He was on the move, following the battle. His aide and intelligence chief were with him, along with two clerks, the driver, and one man to handle the turret splat gun. All but the latter two were busy on the radio, jumping from one conversation to the next, trying to keep in touch with what was happening in a dozen different firefights and three distinct sets of troop movements.

Basically, no one knew just what was happening. Information was starting to come down from CIC, but that data was always at least three minutes out of date, and the situation was so fluid that those three minutes might have been three hours.

"Hold to the orders you were given," Dacik told one SAT commander. "As long as you can move, move. And try to keep the information flowing."

The general was in the process of switching to another channel when an enemy tank round hit, too close. The explosion was enough to pick the APC up off of its tracks and flip it onto its side. Power went out inside. The force was such that even the helmet electronics of the men inside were cut.

It was more than a minute later before Dacik could even think that far. He had been tossed and rolled. At least two of the others had dropped on him before the Heyer came to a halt.

I'm blind was Dacik's first—almost—rational thought. He could see nothing at all. It took a few more seconds for him to realize that he couldn't hear anything either. So close to an explosion, the blast could easily block hearing—temporarily or permanently.

Fear ran through the general, numbing fear, at the prospect of being blind on a battlefield, and trapped. For an instant, he was completely paralyzed by terror. Only gradually did it occur to him that his blindness might well be the result of a total lack of light inside the troop compartment. He felt his face. The visor was gone from his helmet. Then he fumbled his way to the rear of the Heyer—once he'd figured out which direction that was. He had to crawl over one of the others, an unconscious someone, to get to the hatch. He got both hands on the latch but couldn't budge it at first. He had to shift position and work up, against the weight of the door.

When it did start to open, there was some little light, enough to let him know that he wasn't really blind.

The general wedged himself in the hatchway, sighing deeply, too relieved at being able to see again to do anything else. He was still there when someone came over from outside and pulled the hatch up the rest of the way.

"General, you okay?" It was Colonel Ruman, the operations officer.

Slowly, Dacik nodded. "Get someone to check on the others." He half fell out of the Heyer and got up slowly, slightly dizzy, uncertain on his feet. After fighting with the vertigo for just a few seconds, Dacik sat down. Before he could fall.

Other soldiers were rushing over now. A medic stopped to check the general, but Dacik waved the man off. "I'll be fine. Get to the men still inside there." He pointed at the vehicle—or not quite at it. He was still too dazed to get it right.

At some point, not more than a minute or two later—though Dacik himself had no idea how much time had elapsed—someone put an open canteen in front of the general's face. He took one long drink, then another. His head was beginning to clear.

"Thank you." He looked up to see who had given him the water. An enlisted man, someone he didn't know by sight.

Dacik turned to look at the overturned Heyer. The other four men who had been inside had been brought out. Hof Lorenz, his aide, was sitting with his back against the APC. The others were all flat on their backs. Medics were working on two of them. After taking a deep breath, the general tried to get to his feet again. He was still light-headed, but he did manage to stand. After waiting to see if he could stay there, he walked—slowly, uncertainly—over to Captain Lorenz.

"You okay?" Dacik asked.

Lorenz nodded. "Yes, sir. Just banged up a bit. But Colonel Lafferty's dead."

Dacik turned so quickly that he got dizzy again. He reached out to support himself against the Heyer.

"The clerks will both be okay. One's got a busted leg, the other a dislocated shoulder. Maybe head injuries on both," Lorenz said. "I think the gunner's dead, though, and the driver looks to be in real bad shape."

"Your radio working?" Dacik asked.

"No, sir. Blast must have zapped it. Yours?"

"Gone. You up to a little work?"

Lorenz took a deep breath. "I'll try. I think I can navigate, but don't look for any speed records from me, General." He got up almost as slowly as the general had. He started flexing and stretching, testing his limits. The pain in the back of his head was the least of his concerns at the moment. Hof Lorenz certainly didn't look like a parade-ground soldier now.

"First thing, we need working helmets. Then"—Dacik hesitated—"for the time being at least, I guess you're going to have to fill in as my intelligence officer, at least until you can get to Captain Olsen." Olsen was Lafferty's deputy.

"I think he's somewhere out with the point, General."

"Soon as you've got working helmets for us, give him a call. I'll want him back here as soon as possible. But radios first, working helmets. I need to know what the hell's going on."

There had already been a number of brief exchanges of wire along the 13th's perimeter as Schlinal patrols, up to company strength, tested the Team's defenses. None of those probes had come close to Echo Company yet, but twice men in one or another of the platoons had fired out into the woods, at some real or imagined sight or sound. Nervous men. Frightened men.

Joe Baerclau was nervous himself. Little information filtered down to him about what was going on around the perimeter. Most of the time, he could only try to guess based on what sounds he was hearing and how distant they seemed to be. In some ways, the waiting was always worse than the fighting that followed. It was certainly more difficult mentally. Once a fight started, you could respond more or less automatically, based on training and experience. Silent waiting took a different toll.

More than once Joe had to caution men to be quiet and to keep their vigil. Useless chatter over the squad radio channels might help ease the tension, but it could also be a deadly distraction. Joe had to fight his own urge to call Lieutenant Keye or First Sergeant Walker for information every few minutes. When there was something he might need to know, one or the other of them would call him. Joe smiled at the thought of having to fight the temptation to do almost exactly what the most inexperienced of the soldiers in his platoon were doing.

"Half and half," he told the squad leaders after forty-five minutes of the tense waiting. That meant one fire team in each squad on watch, the other to rest. As if rest might be possible. "Half an hour each, for now," he added. Echo's "peace" might end at any minute, or it might continue for hours. The longer the men were staring down their rifle barrels out into the night, the duller their minds, and their vision, would become. The less use they would be in the first seconds and minutes of the fight . . . when it finally reached them.

It *would* reach them. Joe had no doubt of that.

"Joe, come back to the CP for a minute," the first sergeant said.

Joe warned the squad leaders that he was leaving, then climbed out of his hole and trotted back toward the command post. He was one of the first to arrive, but in just a couple of minutes, all of the platoon leaders and platoon sergeants were there.

"I'll keep this brief," Lieutenant Keye said. Even though they were gathered together in a tight cluster, the lieutenant spoke over his helmet radio. That way he could whisper and still know that everyone would hear.

"We think we've got all of the major enemy positions around us charted now." Keye pointed to the mapboard open on his lap. "We might be missing some infantry units, but what we have is better than anything we had before."

"Helluva lot of red on that board," Joe said. Red marks indicated Schlinal units.

"The estimate is four short regiments of infantry, possibly three companies of Novas left," Keye continued. "Right now, it looks as if they're trying to make sure that we've got nowhere to go except—maybe—into the river. There've been no reports of Heggie movement on our north yet except for a couple of small patrols."

"They're setting us in the center of a horseshoe," Iz Walker said. "Putting in strongpoints, digging foxholes, the works. They're going at this carefully, as if they've got all of the time in the galaxy to work with."

"What about the shooting we're hearing?" one of the other platoon sergeants asked.

"Just keeping us occupied," Walker said. "Making sure we know they're around, trying to keep us thinking, and in place. That we don't mount any sorties. That line of crap."

"Which is why we're going to put out a patrol," Keye said, taking over again. "Baerclau, I want you to take your platoon on a little walk. Out a kilometer, unless you meet resistance sooner. Then take a left and give this outfit here"—he pointed at one of the red blips on the mapboard—"something to remember us by."

"How long do we keep at it, sir?" Joe asked.

"In and out. Give them a couple minutes' of everything you've got, then beat it back in. Don't let your men trip over any of your own mines."

"In and out through our own zone?"

"Right. Too many mines out there to try it any other way. Jump off as soon as you get back. Like now. The rest of you, have your men ready to provide cover when they come back in. They might need it."

Joe hurried back to the platoon's area. He alerted the squad leaders and assistant leaders while he was moving. By the time he reached his foxhole—just long enough to pull out most of the things he had stashed on the various ledges he had dug along the sides—the platoon was ready to move.

"First squad on point," he whispered into his helmet radio. First squad expected to be sent first. They certainly received that "honor" more than their fair share of the time, but no one in the squad, certainly none of the veterans, ever complained. A couple of the men had been heard to brag, "We go first because we're the best. The platoon loses fewer men when we're opening the way." The truth of that might be open to debate.

With first squad in the lead, it was their second fire team and Mort Jaiffer actually on point. Mort threaded his way through the mines that the platoon had planted earlier. He didn't assume that there were only Accord mines in the area, though. Heggies *might* have sneaked in close enough to lay a few of their own.

Until the platoon got out beyond the lines where they had planted mines and bugs, they were forced to travel in single file, with narrow intervals between men. Each soldier watched exactly where the man in front of him stepped. That was more important than watching for Heggies in the woods to either side. Enemy soldiers would make their presence known quickly enough. A land mine, friendly or hostile, would only make its presence known if someone tripped it.

At the front of the column, Mort breathed easily, pacing himself as carefully as he always did. After each step forward, he would look through a 180-degree arc, searching for heat signatures or any trace of unnatural movement. Then he would look at the ground just in front of him, choosing where he would next place a foot. Despite his caution, the platoon made good time. It always did with Mort on point. He didn't stop for longer than his routine required until he was far enough out that even the last man in the platoon would be beyond the lines of bugs and mines they had planted.

Joe followed first squad, less than forty meters behind the point. He tried to avoid thinking about anything but the demands of the instant, but a couple of times a worrisome thought invaded his mind: *I'm leading twenty-four men out into the middle of what might be close to eight thousand of the enemy.* Each time that happened, he would stop for a second, blink a couple of times, and swallow. It helped to clear his mind.

Once past their own early warning devices, the platoon shifted to a different formation. Joe put second and third squads out on the flanks. First platoon stayed in front, and fourth brought up the rear. Joe took up his position almost in the middle, actually staying with the trailing fire team of first squad. The intervals between squads, and among the men in each squad, were increased. Echo's 2nd platoon was getting closer to the enemy, and farther from friends.

Joe kept a close watch on the distance gauge on his helmet display. Just below the time line, the distance he had walked from the lines was marked. He had to glance up and to the left to see the display clearly. It had to be out of the way to avoid being a dangerous distraction. At 750 meters, Joe stopped the platoon again, just long enough to take a good look to either side.

"When Mort gets to a thousand meters," he warned, "we'll shift to a skirmish line and move to the left. First, second, and fourth squads will move into line. Third will trail behind to cover our tails and pick up casualties. Mark where we make the turn.

We've got to get back in over the same trail. We don't, and we could walk into friendly fire. Or mines."

He took another long look at his mapboard. The red blips representing the enemy unit they were supposed to attack hadn't moved, but that didn't mean much. It was an infantry unit. They might easily have moved just about anywhere. Until they were spotted again, the mapping system couldn't update their position.

Out so far beyond the perimeter, the night was almost silent. The sounds of fighting were muted, all at a considerable distance. It was even possible, on occasion, to hear some of the normal night sounds of this wilderness, small animals moving in the underbrush, birds in the trees. Joe listened for the patterns. If he could mark those, he would be quicker to hear the exceptions, the altered patterns that might indicate trouble.

Mort reported when he reached the one-kilometer limit. Joe gave the platoon two minutes for a quick drink while they realigned themselves. He moved forward and to his right, between second and first squads, closer to second. He was right up on the skirmish line when the platoon started moving again.

The first hundred meters on the new course went as easily as the kilometer out from the lines. They did seem to be moving closer to the sounds of war again. Somewhere, ahead and farther out, a couple of artillery rounds exploded. Joe stopped the platoon while he tried to gauge the distance. At least a kilometer. Havocs throwing shells at something, probably an enemy tank. That brought a new tightness to his throat.

"Keep the Vrerchs handy," he whispered over the platoon circuit. "There might be more than infantry ahead."

A few seconds later, he said, "Slow it down. We should be almost in range. Watch for Heggie trip wires and bugs. First man to spot anything, sing out. We go to ground then and give them something to remember us by."

The squad leaders already had their orders: hand grenades and RPGs, Vrerchs if there were anything to use them on. The rest of the platoon would lay down covering fire with wire, whether or not they were close enough for the wire to do any good.

It was Frank Symes, fourth squad leader, who made the call. "About ninety meters straight ahead of me. Three men, too close together."

The men of 2nd platoon went down, carefully, making certain that there were no nasty surprises. Ninety meters. That was almost close enough for wire to be fully effective. Joe only hesitated for a second.

"Let's see how close we can get without being spotted. Another ten meters, at least." *I hope,* he thought. At eighty meters, wire would penetrate net armor with some reliability.

Flat on his stomach, Joe edged forward, his zipper across his forearms. Scuttling along like this was one of the first things a recruit learned in basic training. Besides being a skill he might need, it worked a lot of muscle groups.

The platoon didn't make the ten meters. Joe had moved no more than three meters himself before wire started coming toward them from the Schlinal positions—first from just a single rifle, then from too many to count. Second platoon stopped moving forward without command.

"Hit 'em," Joe ordered. He brought his Armanoc into firing position and started squeezing off two-second bursts, working back and forth across a 30-degree zone. Leaves and twigs were shredded by wire heading both ways, quickly clearing the zone of underbrush and low-hanging leaves between the two forces.

Rocket-propelled grenades went out. Each squad had one man equipped with an RPG launcher. One of the men with a Vrerch launcher let loose one missile as well. He hadn't seen any target really worth a Vrerch, but the ground blast did put a hole in the Heggie line and slowed down their fire for several seconds.

Joe was inserting a new spool of wire in his rifle when the Vrerch went off. "Damn it, don't waste those on dirt," he warned. He lifted his head just enough to see down his rifle's sights. This time, he let off the entire spool of wire in one long burst, working to one side of where the rocket had exploded.

Two minutes. Joe put another spool of wire in. *This one and one more,* he decided. When he put the next spool in after that, it would be time to disengage. There was time for him to toss one grenade of his own. The range was extreme. There was little chance that anyone could lob a one-kilo hand grenade eighty meters from a prone position, but it didn't need to go all of the way. If it went fifty meters, it might do some damage, and if it went sixty, it would put the nearest Heggies in the kill zone.

Then it was back to the rifle.

Joe heard someone grunt heavily. Glancing to the left, he saw one of the men in second squad flop over onto his side, hit by wire. There were a couple of short calls from medics.

There were other casualties as well. Joe kept firing until he reached the wire total he had decided would use up the two minutes.

"Pack 'em up," Joe said. "Third squad, get ready to cover us as we pull back past you. Maybe it's time to use a couple more Vrerchs."

Withdrawing under fire was always dangerous. No matter how well trained the troops were, there was confusion as men tried to move in one direction while firing in another, and trying to avoid being hit themselves.

The first thirty meters, most of the men moved flat, on their stomachs, one fire team in each squad moving while the other kept popping away at the Heggies with wire and RPGs. The Schlinal troops were starting to get a few RPGs out themselves.

The rest of the platoon moved through third squad as the latest Vrerchs exploded among the Schlinal positions. Second platoon had a half dozen wounded men being helped along by their buddies now. Two men wouldn't be making the trip back at all. Their bodies had to be left behind. If the 13th somehow managed to survive this fight and there was a later, the dead would be retrieved. Attempting to bring them back now could only cause more casualties.

"Up and out of here," Joe said, getting to his feet and spraying wire toward the enemy. He was close to 120 meters from the Heggies now, out of the greatest danger zone from enemy wire. "Third, you've still got rear guard. We'll stop and cover you from another thirty meters back."

The platoon moved faster now. Men ducked around trees, trying to keep as much wood as possible between them and the enemy. Three squads covered thirty meters and stopped to let the remaining squad rejoin them. Third had one wounded man of its own to deal with now.

"I want the rest of the RPGs out," Joe said. "We've got to keep them from following us too soon." Carrying wounded, they would be too easy for any pursuit to catch.

Third squad moved past as the men with the grenade launchers started firing as quickly as they could load. Four at a time, over and over.

"First, we'll take the rear now," Joe said. He sent the other squads on after third and stayed back with third. Pit Tymphe, the only wounded man in first, was still firing wire as rapidly as he could load new spools.

Joe waited until the rest of the platoon had covered twenty meters before he started to pull first squad back. "Let's start it out slow," he said. "Keep 'em occupied."

There was no sign of any Heggies coming out from their lines to pursue. Yet. That was good news, but there was always a chance—a good chance—that the enemy commander would be doing whatever he could to get troops in from one side or another, circling around to ambush the Freebies while they retreated.

Joe put himself right in the center of the first squad's line. Ezra Frain anchored one end, Mort Jaiffer the other. Those three set the pace, and they kept it dead slow until the rest of the platoon was nearly back to where they had to turn for the final kilometer-long leg back to the 13th's lines.

After checking with the other squad leaders, Joe said, "Okay, let's beat it," on first squad's channel. The six men turned and ran through the woods, making for the rest of the platoon.

First squad had nearly reached the turn before there was any sign of pursuit by the Schlinal unit they had attacked. Joe and the others could hear men running through the underbrush, beneath the trees. It was a surprise to hear fire coming from up ahead also, on the other side of the path leading back to the rest of the 13th. Heavy fire.

"It's not coming at us," Sauv Degtree reported. "They're shooting at the main lines. Looks like the Heggies are finally getting around to attacking our sector."

That's all we need, Joe thought. He switched channels. "Lieutenant, we're coming in, right down the path we followed going out. There's Heggie activity on both sides of us."

"We're monitoring you, Baerclau," Lieutenant Keye said. "The men know you're coming."

Just so they don't get trigger happy anyway, Joe thought. He took a deep breath and started running again.

CHAPTER 24

Reports came in from every company of the 13th. *We're under attack.* Van Stossen and Dezo Parks both took calls, talked to company commanders. There was no change in orders. *Do what you can. Hold at all costs. We don't have anywhere to go.*

With very little time to work, the headquarters security detachment had dug and built a solid command bunker for the colonel and his staff, well camouflaged and as solid as possible working only with the materials at hand. There were two separate sections, secure enough that even a direct hit might take out only one of the two. Stossen was in one. Parks was in the other. The rest of the staff circulated between the two as needed. Some thought was given to keeping approximately half of headquarters apart from the other half to insure some sort of continuity even in a disaster.

Around the command bunker was a last line of defense, a place for the security detachment and other headquarters personnel to make a last stand, if—or when—it came to that. There were splat guns and men with Vrerchs and RPGs.

Even Colonel Stossen kept a loaded rifle close at hand. He had a full bandolier of wire spools and power packs slung over a shoulder, and several hand grenades hanging from his tunic and web belt. He looked very little like a regimental commander now, except perhaps for the harried look on his face.

Bal Kenneck came over to the colonel, waited until Stossen finished a call and nodded to him, then said, "The last of our patrols is back in. We've just lost another Wasp." Kenneck shook his head. "On the ground. Hit by a tank round, I think. The pilot's okay."

"Three planes left," Stossen said. It wasn't a question.

"They're all back up, freshly charged. There's still no hint of shortages for them, either batteries or munitions, but if the assault gets much heavier, we might have trouble getting them in and out safely."

"Has that crew chief, Vernon, got his weapons ready for us?"

"They're being humped into place now, fast as he puts them together. I wouldn't put too much faith in them, Colonel. Eyeball-aimed rockets, and those cannons. The guns are made to be held securely under a Wasp. Makeshift tripods aren't going to give them the stable platform they need. They start shooting those, there won't be any safe places to hide."

Stossen smiled for the first time since Roo Vernon had made his proposal. "Don't sell the chief short, Bal. If Vernon says they'll work, two'll get you five they do."

"I hope so."

"Anything new from General Dacik?"

"Not a thing, for nearly an hour now. Nothing anyone can make sense of. The general's mixer was hit. They've got headquarters back up and running, after a fashion, but no one seems to know what's going on. They've got it even more hectic than we do."

"Small comfort in knowing other folks got worse problems than we do," Stossen said. "What about our Havocs?"

"We've lost three of the ones we kept within the perimeter. The ones roaming free seem to be intact so far."

"I more than half wish I'd turned 'em all loose," Stossen muttered, more to himself than to Kenneck. "Should have. Too late to do anything about that. Keep them moving around as much as possible."

"Yes, sir. They're doing that already. The ones outside. Basset is engaging this latest batch of Novas now."

"Right twenty degrees!" Eustace Ponks shouted. "Turn us *right*!"

"I am!" Simon shouted back.

For the last five minutes, the crew of the Fat Turtle had been moving so fast that they were all getting a little confused. Simon had started to turn left instead of right, but he was already correcting his error before Eustace shouted.

"Karl, you got those coordinates punched up?"

"Ready." Karl sounded relatively calm.

"Keep laying it in. We're not likely to get any updates for several minutes. The Wasps all had to land."

"Doesn't make a hell of a lot of sense shooting at old ghosts," Karl said. "Be a lot better off to save it for when we know where they are."

"We're coming up on the firing vector now. Soon as you can get us aimed, get another AP off. Then we put some distance between here and the next place."

The turret slid two degrees to the right. Karl hit the firing switch, and the sound of the shot was the only thing audible in the Havoc for a moment. Before Simon could hear the order, he had already swerved the Fat Turtle another 20 degrees right and he had the throttles all of the way to the spots. Although it was speedy enough once it got moving, a Havoc didn't accelerate with any particular haste.

"Five minutes," Eustace told him. "Three Wasps are just now taking off."

"Three? We lost another?" Simon asked.

"I guess, one way or another."

Zel Paitcher wandered around the center of the 13th in a daze. A medic had treated the minor injuries Zel had received when his Wasp was overturned by a near miss. The plane was wrecked beyond any hope of repair in the field. Zel had been lucky. He had lost consciousness for only a few seconds after striking his head against the side of his canopy. There were a couple of muscle strains. His right wrist was sprained—not severely. The medic had needed no more than five minutes to treat the obvious injuries.

"You gonna be okay?" he asked Zel, watching the pilot's eyes closely. "Get yourself back to the field hospital, over by the colonel's bunker. I'll tell the doc to expect you."

Zel had nodded, and had even managed to repeat the instructions before the medic left to treat another casualty, one hurt worse than Zel. For several minutes then, Zel had merely sat on the ground where he had been, scarcely aware of anything going on around him. No one else paid any attention to him. They were busy, or looking for deeper holes to crawl into to escape any additional shelling.

Finally, Zel stood up. He held himself erect, as if he were at attention on the drill field. He turned through a complete circle, in slow steps, stopping after every one to survey the area. It was dark and he didn't have an infantry helmet on. At the moment, he didn't have any helmet at all. His vision was severely compromised by that. But not as much as it might have been. The sky was clear. There were plenty of stars in the sky. And there were a number of minor fires around. There was *some* light, certainly enough to let Zel find his way to the field hospital.

For a time, though, he completely forgot about that. He was hardly aware of where he was, what had happened. He started walking around, casually, hands in his pockets, with no thought of the fighting that was going on. Every once in a while, he stopped and called out.

"Slee?" He would wait for an answer. When none came, he shouted again, "Slee, where *are* you? Enough is enough. The game is over." And, just once, he sang out, "Come out, come out, wherever you are."

He had been wandering in circles for thirty minutes before he noticed the flash of intense white light in front of him. But he didn't hear the explosion of the shell that went off some forty meters from him, didn't feel the shrapnel that hit.

There was light, and then there was darkness as he lost consciousness, bleeding from a dozen small wounds.

So far, there had been no wild charges. The Schlinal troops had been content to work themselves as close as they could with reasonable safety, exchanging wire with the 13th while they gradually tightened the ring around the Freebies. Here and there, a Heggie squad or platoon would find an avenue that let them sneak close enough to do real damage for a few minutes. There were plenty of trees to give cover. The 13th hadn't been able to pick the best defensive terrain ever seen. And there had been no time to prepare extensive artificial enhances out beyond the lines of foxholes.

Sometimes, the lines of bugs did give early warning, but not always. The sensors could not cover every meter of the perimeter. The same could be said for the lines of mines laid closer in. Some exploded when a Heggie tripped a wire. Others were spotted and disarmed. And still others weren't meant to be tripped in that manner. They were controlled by men of the 13th, to be triggered when the infantrymen had good reason to think that there might be Heggies in the kill zone.

Echo's second platoon got back to their foxholes just ahead of one of the fiercest of the exchanges. The Heggies had started advancing toward Echo's section of the perimeter while 2nd platoon was on its patrol. Only luck had kept them apart.

The dead had been noted. The wounded received treatment. Those who could still function were back in their foxholes. There could be no "excused duty" for a wounded man who could still pull the trigger on an Armanoc.

"Take it easy on wire," Joe reminded the platoon. It was an almost unconscious litany. There was no immediate worry of running out of wire for the zippers, but the experience of Porter had made Joe's personal habit of being stingy with wire something of a mania that he tried to enforce on the entire platoon.

Although there was no way for human eyes to see the tiny snippets of wire coming, it *was* sometimes possible to estimate where a flow of wire was coming from, particularly when it was cutting greenery. And, sometimes, a Heggie got close enough, and exposed enough, to show up as a clear image on night-vision gear. Joe saved his wire for those occasions. Behind him, the splat guns on the APCs were putting out more than enough to hold the enemy down. The mudders in their holes could wait for better targets.

Some of them could.

Pit Tymphe was using a lot of wire. He felt no pain from the wound he had received. A soaker had taken care of that. But he *remembered* the pain. *The guy who shot me might be somewhere out there,* he told himself. Twice, Ezra told him to slack off, then gave up. His shouting never held Pit back for more than a couple of minutes.

Olly Wytten, the other new man left in first squad, was very stingy of his wire. He waited with cold determination for targets, then squeezed off only the shortest effective bursts. If he had thought it possible, he would have tried to zap each enemy with a single cut of wire. When he *did* shoot, his fire was accurate. Even at distances up to 150 meters, he would aim for the weak spots in a mudder's defenses—neck, hands, and wrists—and at places where net armor tended to weaken due to flexing, such as the elbows and knees. Most of those sites were unlikely to produce fatal wounds, but anything that cut down on the number of Heggies shooting back was worthwhile.

It was an hour short of midnight when the fighting on Echo's front suddenly increased in fury. A half dozen tank shells burst in front of the lines, a couple of them within twenty meters, causing some casualties in third and fourth platoons. Several Schlinal splat guns opened up, the first time in this fight that the Heggies had used the heavier crew-served weapons on Echo. Several rockets came in, targeted against the APCs, destroying one and putting another out of commission.

At the same time, the volume of rifle fire increased dramatically. To Joe it seemed as if there were suddenly four times as many rifles firing, and firing longer bursts.

"Watch out," he warned the platoon. "Sounds like they're getting ready to move on us."

RPGs came in next, poorly aimed but close enough to make men duck deeper into their foxholes to avoid shrapnel. Almost simultaneously, two of the mines that second platoon had planted went off.

"Eighty meters out," Joe reminded his men. "Time to use some wire."

A distance, a line. Enemies close enough for wire to do real damage. And movement. The Heggies were coming forward now, squad by squad.

Another mine went off. This time, Joe saw one of the bodies being hurled away from the explosion. Accord grenades went out, hand- and rocket-propelled. And wire from every rifle on the line. Another salvo of 135mm shells landed, these behind the lines. Three Heyers were hit, though one of them kept firing.

Joe ducked down for a moment and looked back toward the center of the 13th's ground. There were more than a dozen fires that he could see. Two of them were fierce, as if fuel tanks had been ruptured. Those fires burned down quickly though, even as they spread to damp grass and brush.

It seemed forever before friendly artillery rounds started landing out beyond the Accord lines, as the Havocs got targeting data. The 200mm shells came in in volleys of three. That had to be apparent to almost anyone. The suspended plasma HE rounds chopped the forest apart. To a radius of fifteen meters from impact, all but the thickest of trees would be felled by the blast. Trees fell, some taking smaller neighbors down with them. Branches were quicker to fall. Fires started, hot enough to incinerate even wet wood and leaves. Or human flesh.

For a moment, the Schlinal wire stopped coming in at Echo. The heat of fires gave the Heggies better camouflage than the night and their uniforms, blotting out half of the night-vision gear of the Accord soldiers. Behind the fires, men could advance or retreat.

"Hold off," Joe ordered, shouting over the radio, against the noise of another volley of Havoc rounds. "Let's see if that's taken the fight out of them."

The Havoc fire moved off to the right, from Echo's front to Fox's, still coming in three rounds at a time, eighty to a hundred meters out. To the left, somewhat more distant, Joe noticed more rounds exploding out beyond the perimeter. He couldn't be certain because of the distance, but he thought that those were coming in pairs.

I wonder how many Havocs we have left? He blinked several times. There was no way he could know, and speculation was wasted energy. He looked back out directly in front of him. There was still no enemy wire coming from beyond where the barrage had fallen. The enemy, if they hadn't fled, at least hadn't regrouped enough to resume the attack.

"Lieutenant?" Joe asked over his private channel to Keye. He waited, and when there was no reply, he repeated the call. When there was still no answer, he switched channels.

"Izzy, Baerclau. Where's the lieutenant?"

"Out of action," Walker replied. "Had his helmet blown clear off."

"Dead?"

"Naw. Medic's still working on him but says he'll be okay. Concussion most like."

"We have no enemy activity at all in front of us right now," Joe reported.

"Yeah, those Havocs gave 'em something to think about. Keep your eyes open and your heads down. No sign that they're pulling out."

Dem Nimz and the survivors of two recon platoons had abandoned their commandeered truck an hour before, as soon as they saw the flashes of the battle going on northeast of them. As a parting thought, Fredo Gariston had wired an explosive charge so that anyone opening either of the truck's doors would be greeted by two kilograms of explosives and white phosphorus.

"Long as it's not us," Dem whispered. He had his visor up. The other men were around him, waiting for orders.

"While we're out here, we might as well do some good. We'll split into two squads. I'll take one and Fredo the other. Circle round, left and right. We're reccers, so let's do some reconnoitering. Find out how many Heggies there are, where they're at, and locate any armor they've got with them. You all know the drill. We've got about four hours till first light. Use that time. We'll try to meet on the far side by dawn."

"Who goes which way?" Fredo asked.

"You go north, then east, round on the river side. We'll take the south," Dem said.

With no more than that, the two men separated, each gesturing to those he would be leading. They moved apart without a look back. No one complained about the orders. They *were* reccers. They would do the job as long as one of them was left alive.

Bal Kenneck had blood on his neck. An eardrum had been damaged by concussion on one of his periodic trips out of the command bunker. Blood had flowed out of the ear for several minutes before he came back inside and someone else saw it and called a medic.

"We've got a fight in the air now, too," Bal reported while the medic was still working on him. Kenneck shouted because he couldn't hear himself speak. "Six, maybe eight, Boems came in and engaged our Wasps."

"Results?" Van Stossen asked.

"Not good," Kenneck shouted, "but not as bad as it might have been. I think we've lost the last of our Wasps, but they accounted for four, maybe five, Boems first. The rest tore out as quick as they could then."

Stossen turned away. The last of the Wasps. No air cover at all left. But he quickly turned back to Kenneck. "What about the pilots? Did any of them make it out safely?"

"I don't . . ." Kenneck didn't finish the sentence. He passed out.

Stossen moved closer. He could see that Kenneck was still breathing, and he waited while the medic went through a flurry of activity before he asked, "How is he?"

"Pretty rough, sir," the medic said. "He should be okay, but I'm going to have to keep him out to let the nanobugs do their work."

"How long?"

"Four hours minimum, sir. I won't know beyond that until then. If it still matters four hours from now."

Once more, Stossen turned away, this time from the medic's brief glance. *If it still matters four hours from now.* There was that. Almost anything could happen in four hours. Not quite to sunrise.

"Just take care of him the best you can, lad," Stossen said. "If we're still here in the morning, we'll need him."

"Yes, sir." The medic's voice was blank. He didn't even bother to show resentment that the colonel might think he would do any less than his best for anyone.

The first serious attempt to breach the 13th's lines came at the junction between Echo and Fox companies. There was another flurry of RPGs—but no tank rounds—followed immediately by the assault. A full company of Schlinal infantry made the advance, laying down considerable wire as they moved.

At first, the action was too far away for Joe's platoon to have any real part in it. The angle across the front, and the Heggies' distance from the line, put them out of reach of any of the platoon's weapons except for the Dupuy cough guns. The snipers armed with those were able to contribute in a minor way, but even though the rocket-assisted guns were accurate to ranges over four-and-a-half kilometers, it was difficult to hit a moving target at even a tenth of that distance.

"Stay put," the first sergeant told Baerclau. "Keep your men watching their own front in case this broadens."

Joe leaned the barrel of his rifle against the mound of dirt in front of him. Just for a second, he took both hands from the zipper and flexed his fingers. They were stiff.

"We're watching," he told Walker. "The Heggies are too far away for us to do much good anyway."

A protracted blink helped Joe clear his mind of anything but what was right in front of him, his men and the section of forest they were responsible for. He had wanted to ask about Lieutenant Keye again, but this wasn't the time. Izzy would be too busy for anything but the immediately essential.

Joe looked at the power indicator on his rifle. It was down to 50 percent—still an hour of firing time left. Too soon to replace it. Once more he checked the location of all of the things he had stowed on the ledges of his foxhole—wire spools, canteens, rations. Everything was where it belonged, ready for him whenever he might reach for it.

Let's get it on, he thought. The sudden burst of impatience surprised him. Too much waiting. The earlier skirmish hadn't been enough.

Joe pulled back into his hole. *Am I getting to like it?* he wondered. The possibility was frightening. He had seen men who thrived on combat before, men who only seemed to be happy in the middle of a fight, the bigger and bloodier the better. Men like that scared him.

He glanced toward Olly's hole. Wytten was next to Ezra, some meters away. Only the back of the new man's helmet was visible. Olly was good at all of the skills of a soldier. Maybe he was too intense. Combat hadn't changed him noticeably. He went about his business with quiet efficiency.

Maybe he likes it too much, Joe thought, unconsciously adding another *too.*

Too much thinking. Joe took a new grip on his rifle, consciously keeping his hands loose on the stock and pistol grip. One hand at a time, he pulled loose again, flexing, trying to keep the fingers limber. It was too easy to tighten up.

Waiting.

CHAPTER 25

"I like it," Eustace Ponks said. He was grinning in satisfaction. "This is the way we were meant to fight." He transferred another series of coordinates to Karl's targeting computer, straight from the reccers who were out in the middle of the Heggies. They weren't even going through CIC or the 13th's headquarters now. This information was accurate right up to the second that the Fat Turtle received it, without any delays at all. What made it even better was that there was no sign of Novas or Heggie infantry close enough to be a threat.

"Locked on," Karl said from the rear compartment.

"Fire," Eustace said, already concentrating on the next set of numbers.

The big gun shuddered in its suspension. Simon started moving the vehicle again. Jimmy ejected the spent shell casing and slid the next one into place. By the time Simon had eased onto the new target vector, Karl was ready to shoot again . . . and Eustace had three more targets for them.

"That last one was right on target," Eustace reported to his crew. Actually, he was talking two shots back, but it didn't matter. With accurate, and current, sightings, they were doing pinpoint shooting—all of the Havocs operating outside the 13th's perimeter.

Forty minutes earlier, the Fat Turtle had rendezvoused with its support van to replenish the Havoc's supply of ammunition. That transfer had taken fifteen minutes, with most of both crews out in a perimeter of their own, just in case. There weren't many Novas left to the opposition, for all appearances. Those that were seemed to be operating on the far end of the engagement, out of range. But there was no way to be certain that there were no Heggie mudders around.

The big worry for the gun crews was that the enemy might send in more Boems.

"This rate, we'll have to stock up on ammo again before long," Simon said.

"Already laid on, my boy," Eustace replied, in rare good spirits. "Another forty minutes."

"Cutting it close, aren't we?" Simon asked. "The way we're pumping it out, we could run dry long before that."

"We'll be taking a break in a minute. Two more sets of targets. The reccers are on the move again, looking for more targets. We've already done for the ones they've seen so far."

The silence that followed after the last shell was out left a hollow ringing in the ears of all four crewmen. Working artillery was like that. Between campaigns, they would all have to take time out for medical treatment of their hearing. If they made it off of Jordan.

Dem Nimz wasn't grinning. He had watched the systematic destruction of an enemy infantry battalion with considerable satisfaction, but it wasn't something he could smile about. A few words of praise for the accuracy of the Havoc fire, a promise to get back on the line with the three Havocs he was personally directing as soon as he had new targets for them.

Then it was back on the move, gliding through the night, absolutely silent. Reccers liked to boast that they could move within fifty meters of any enemy even during the day without giving any evidence of their passage. Dem and the three men with him were doing everything they could to stay farther away than fifty meters. The forest area wasn't dense enough to give them any real feeling of security. And although Accord battle dress provided some thermal concealment, it wasn't enough. They would be visible to infrared snoopers, a lot farther out than fifty meters. The enemy might have a picket line out on this side, even though they had to think that virtually all Accord strength was on the other side, penned up neatly by four Heggie regiments.

Dem would have had posts out on the back side, even if he were absolutely convinced that there was nothing to worry about there. He was surprised that they hadn't found any Heggie sentries yet. And a little worried.

Although Dem communicated by radio with the Havocs, he still limited himself to hand signs with the men right with him. The habit of silence was strong, to be broken only at absolute need.

The four men moved in line. As far as possible, each man stepped precisely in the same places as the man before. If this was done right, and reccers on campaign almost always did it right, the enemy would be unable to guess how many of them had passed. One man or fifty.

Dem took the point himself. Although he trusted the other reccers with him—that was essential in any recon grouping since survival too often depended on reccers being confident of the abilities of their companions—he trusted his own senses more. Eyes and ears, and, as much as anything else, intuition. He prided himself on being able to know when a place, a situation, just didn't *feel* right, and his hunches had been correct often enough to support that confidence.

Shadows. Dem watched them, used them, moved from one to the next. Shadows would provide no defense against observation by anyone with infrared gear, but against available-light multipliers, shadows did help. A toss of the coin. Where Accord night-vision gear used both systems, most standard-issue Schlinal gear used only available light. But they did have IR scanners and sights as well.

As long as most Schlinal eyes were facing the other way, the odds favored the shadows.

In the silence, the reccers heard the tank several minutes before they saw it. One tank: the interval between shots was proof enough of that. It was firing and moving, of course, but it seemed to be maneuvering in a remarkably small area. Dem motioned to his companions. They didn't have any anti-tank weapons with them, so all they could do was locate the tank and call in Havoc support.

"Basset two, this is 1st recon," Dem whispered into his radio once he could see the tank. "I have a fire mission for you—one Nova, on the move." He had his mapboard out, held low and only half-open so that the soft glare of its screen wouldn't give him away. He read off the position of the tank and used his helmet's ranging capacity to provide a speed and course for the Nova.

"On the way," Eustace Ponks replied after feeding the data to Karl and the targeting computer.

Dem counted the seconds while he continued to watch the Nova. If the tank took a sudden turn, it could defeat the incoming shell. Time. The flight time for the 200mm shell would be at least thirty-five seconds. Dem wasn't absolutely certain where Basset two was.

He had reached thirty-eight in his count before the shell exploded. It wasn't a turret hit, but the shell did impact on the cover of the Nova's engine compartment. It was enough to destroy the tank. There was an instant of intense light in the night. Dem didn't get turned away quickly enough to miss all of that. He squeezed his eyes shut, hugging the ground, waiting for the aftereffects to fade from his vision.

"Bull's-eye," he reported when he could see again. "Good shooting. Be back to you when we've got something else."

The tip of the Schlinal wedge was still being blocked at the intersection of Echo and Fox companies, but the attack was still being pressed, and broadening gradually as additional Schlinal companies moved forward on either side of the initial point.

Echo's 2nd platoon was finally directly involved. They had Heggies on their front. The Schlinal advance remained deliberate, cautious, but it was determined. At eighty meters, the Heggies were stopped by the sudden flurry of Accord wire, but the pause was brief. The advance continued, with the Schlinal infantry moving by squads and staying low, moving in, trying to get close enough to do damage of their own.

"There on the right," Joe said, wasting a moment with the unnecessary warning. Sauv Degtree had already seen the men moving there. His entire squad shifted their fire, stopping the Heggie attempt to sneak closer.

A second line of Schlinal soldiers started to move up behind the first, and then a third.

"Izzy, this is Baerclau. It looks like we've got a whole battalion looking to walk over us."

"Three battalions hitting us and Fox. Hang on. Colonel's sending some sort of secret weapon up."

"What?" Joe asked, but Walker had already switched to a different channel.

Roo Vernon was used to carrying heavy objects, but he wasn't used to *running* with them, certainly not over any distance. But he was running now, and carrying more than a hundred kilos of cannon—more weight than he would have dreamed that he could possibly carry for more than a step or two. A hundred-plus kilos was *his* share of the load. One of his mechanics was under the gun assembly with him, and others were carrying the makeshift tripod and several canisters of the gun's 25mm ammunition. With every step, Roo thought that he couldn't possibly go one more without dropping his end of the gun, or just dropping. But the colonel had said that the gun was needed to stop a Heggie breakthrough, and the gun was needed a half kilometer from where Roo had assembled the mount.

In the 13th, mechanics and crew chiefs got just as much physical conditioning as any of the line soldiers, but they rode most of the time when the infantry walked. Roo had had more than a decade in the military, all of it doing maintenance work. He wasn't in the best shape of his life. Still, somehow, he kept going, though not at anything vaguely approaching breakneck speed.

Until he tripped over something and fell. Roo did twist aside so that the cannon assembly didn't fall on top of him, but the gun went down and so did the man who was helping to carry it. The rest of the team came to a stop as well, trying to see what had happened.

For a moment, Roo could do nothing. The breath had been knocked out of him, and he needed time to get it going again, and to make sure that he hadn't hurt anything seriously.

"You okay, Chief?" the other man who had been toting the weapon asked.

"Yeah. You?"

"Damn near put this thing through my gut. What happened?"

"Tripped." Roo felt around for what he had tripped over. His hand closed over a leg. "What?" He scrambled over onto his hands and knees. A leg. A body. He got up to the head. "Lieutenant Paitcher!"

Roo bent closer. Paitcher was still breathing, but he was unconscious. "Medic!" Roo shouted, switching to a radio channel that—he hoped—someone would be monitoring. He flipped on an emergency locator as well, which set off a flashing yellow blip on mapboards and visor displays.

"You guys get that gun in place. I'll be along as soon as a medic shows up. Leave a couple of cans of ammo. I'll bring them."

As the others started to pick up the cannon assembly, Roo said, "Be sure there's no dirt in any of the barrels. That gun'd blow sky high."

He turned his attention to Zel again. Roo had never served as a medic, but he did know enough to look for injuries without moving the lieutenant. Heartbeat and respiration: both were low and weak, but steady. No bones were obviously broken. Paitcher had clearly done a lot of bleeding, but there were no gushers, and the trickles that remained *looked* minor. Nearly five minutes passed before a medic arrived and did his own examination.

"You just found him here?"

"Tripped over him. Haven't seen him in a couple of hours, so I don't know how long he's been here. He gonna be okay?"

"Looks like," the medic allowed. "I'll take care of him, Chief."

"Thanks. I got work to do."

Running was a lot easier without the weight of a cannon to carry.

The civilians in the buried Heyer were all showing the strain. Twice in the last hour, Dr. Corey had asked what was going on. Gene Abru had answered her, as well as he could, each time, honestly. Mostly that meant saying that things were a mess and there was no way to tell yet how it would end.

Gene was more than a little nervous himself, but he didn't show it. He remained almost as motionless as a corpse the whole time. There were no twitching muscles, no nervous mannerisms of any sort. His throat was dry. *Four enemy regiments. The 13th is completely encircled.* There *was* good news—few enemy tanks left, no new attacks by Boems, but it still didn't look to even out the disparity in numbers. Four to one. Maybe even *five* to one. And the rest of the Accord in no position to help. By morning, they might be lost as well.

A conscious blink. *I hope the colonel makes it long enough to tell me when it's time,* Abru thought. *If I lose touch with headquarters, I'll have to go ahead and act.*

He would do what he had been told to do, but he would hate for it to be a mistake caused by faulty communications.

Joe Baerclau had lost count of the number of spools of wire he had used. That was unusual. There was no time, or real need, to count them, but it bothered him that he had lost count. He had just tossed the empties, some out over the side of his foxhole, the rest into the sump at the bottom of it. All that really mattered was that he still had a comforting stack of fresh spools to slip into the Armanoc. The power pack was down below a quarter full. He took the extra couple of seconds needed to replace that. When it went absolutely dry, he might not have those seconds to spare.

No Heggies had actually reached the line of foxholes, but some had come uncomfortably close. There were Schlinal bodies within twenty meters of 2nd platoon's first squad. Just bodies, no wounded. If any of those soldiers *had* only been wounded when they fell, the continuing fire past them—in both directions—had finished the work. Once in a while Joe would see a body jerked around as it was hit by misdirected wire. Once upon a time, that would have bothered him. *Had* bothered him. But he had seen it happen too many times for it to continue to have any effect.

The only bodies that bothered Joe anymore were those of his own men. There were more of those now, in their foxholes. The platoon was down to nineteen effectives, with two wounded men still returning Heggie fire. They weren't in any immediate danger from their wounds. There was no need, yet, for Al or any of the other squad medics to get out of their own foxholes to treat anyone.

The Heggies started another line of men forward out of the forest. That was something else that Joe had nearly lost count of—the number of times that a new company of Heggies had advanced into the killing zone. No sooner was one assault wave stopped than the next formed up and came on behind them.

"What have they got against *us*?" Ezra had asked Joe during one all-too-brief respite, some twenty minutes earlier. "Why don't they pick on somebody else for a while? There's enough of us to go around."

Joe hadn't answered. Ezra wouldn't have spoken like that if he had had fresh dead or seriously wounded men in his squad. But Joe had an entire platoon to think of, and the platoon had both dead and wounded.

Again, Joe thought as he spotted the newest skirmish line beginning to pick its way closer. This time, there seemed to be more of them, and they were moving cautiously again, doing more crawling than anything else, even back while they were still beyond the effective range of the Armanocs and the splat guns. With all of the bodies in front of them, these Heggies had plenty of cover as long as they stayed low.

Joe lifted his head a few millimeters, just enough to give him a slightly broader view of the new attack.

A *lot* more of them, he decided. "Izzy?"

"Yeah?"

"Baerclau. Looks like they're doubling up this time. I think they mean to get through here whatever it takes."

There was a pause before the first sergeant replied. "I see what you mean. We're getting hit hard all around the perimeter now."

"Where's that secret weapon you promised?"

"They're setting it up now. A Wasp cannon module on a tripod."

"Will it work?" Joe asked.

"I hope so," Walker said. Then he clicked off.

The Schlinal infantry continued to move forward, very slowly. Some died. Replacements moved up to take their places.

"Get ready, they're going to be on us in a minute," Joe warned his platoon. "Get fresh wire in now, while you can."

He took his own advice. Unless *something* happened very quickly, the platoon was going to be in for hand-to-hand combat within the next few minutes, and the Armanoc wasn't equipped for a bayonet. Bayonet fighting was obsolete in the view of the movers and shakers who decided on army weapons and tactics, "a relic of the Stone Age." "In close combat, should the occasion actually arise," the manual said, "the soldier should be prepared to use a quick burst of wire as the *modern* equivalent of the bayonet. It is, of course, preferable to use that equivalent before the enemy actually closes."

"The last few meters they'll have to stand up and charge," Joe said over the platoon frequency. "Be ready for that." There was only one APC-mounted splat gun still in operation behind the platoon. The rest had been knocked out. "You'll only have a few seconds. Make them count."

Joe revised his estimate of the number of Heggies moving forward this time. It looked more like an entire battalion—maybe six or seven hundred men—moving forward in waves, one right behind the other, just in front of 2nd platoon and the platoons on either side of them.

"Izzy, Baerclau. No way we can stop this mob," Joe reported. "They'll walk right over us."

"Just tell your men to keep their heads down," Walker said. "We're on our own, us and this Wasp cannon, if they ever get it going." *And if it works,* he thought.

• • •

Roo was sweating and shaking. The five cannons in the pod had to be individually loaded. When the gun was firing, each barrel could spew out sixty rounds a second, with the 25mm projectiles separating in flight into five slivers some 15mm in length. The unit could put fifteen hundred deadly hypersonic darts into an oval five meters by three at a range of five hundred meters—every five seconds. No body armor ever devised could stand up to that pounding.

His men were reinforcing the legs of the tripod, burying them thirty centimeters deep, packing anything they could find up against them. The recoil of the cannon might be extreme without the mass of a Wasp to absorb it. Roo wasn't at all certain that his rig would stand up to the shock, and there had been no chance to test it in advance. It shouldn't work, he thought, but there was no other way. It had to.

If nothing else, he would use the men with him to lean against the tripod and steady it. He had five men, close to four hundred kilos of extra weight.

Roo intended to man the trigger himself. The electrical firing device had a two-meter cable running to it. That would let him stay out of the way of the men holding the gun in place. A hand on the side of the housing, near the rear of the module, would let him direct the fire. If he had his design right, there would be no significant travel of the gun while it was firing.

"There, that's the last canister," he said. "Get in place."

For the first time in several minutes, Roo actually looked toward the front lines, not more than eighty meters from where he had set up the gun. He could see the Heggies clearly now, moving up behind the growing mounds of their own dead. Getting far too close.

At least I don't have to worry about hitting anything five hundred meters away, he thought. This would be simple point and shoot . . . and hope that the gun didn't upend itself with the first burst.

The Wasp cannons made a noise unlike any infantry weapon used by either Accord or Hegemony. The shells were powder-fired, and the sound was deeper than any of the wire or rocket-assisted weapons, and it was continuous, as long as the trigger was held.

Roo held his first burst to less than two seconds, the briefest touch he could manage on the unfamiliar setup. The gun did not turn itself over backward, and the barrels remained pointed where he had aimed.

"Any trouble with that?" he asked the men who were leaning against the legs of the tripod. None of them answered.

"Okay, let's see what we can do," Roo said, a whisper that was almost missed by even the sensitive microphone in his helmet.

The men of Echo's 2nd platoon were aiming more up than out. The Heggies were starting their final push, within the last twenty meters. Already they were closer than any of the early attempts had managed. There were so many that they couldn't help but take heavy casualties. It was almost impossible to miss hitting Heggies once they stood up to make that last charge. But they kept coming. There were too many for the zippers of one platoon, or company, to stop them all.

Even after the aircraft cannon opened up, the Heggie line continued to advance. For just a few seconds.

Heggies started falling by the dozen, from right to left as Joe looked at them. They tumbled like dominoes as the 25mm fire raked across them. Many of them were shredded before they hit the ground.

Those who were still standing stopped—for an instant. Some were frozen in place by what was happening. Those were felled either by the murderous cannon fire or by wire from the infantrymen in the foxholes just in front of them. A few, a *very* few, had the presence of mind to fall flat, to try to get below the new assault. A couple even dove toward Accord foxholes. The rest of those who weren't killed on their feet tried to turn and run.

The metal slivers chased them down.

Ezra Frain got a live Heggie in on top of him. The man had dove two meters or more, taking wire as he hurled himself away from the other fire. In the foxhole, he was still able to try to defend himself. The Heggie had abandoned his gun when he jumped. Ezra's rifle was knocked to the side, not out of his grip, but with the muzzle away from the Heggie. The two men wrestled for a minute. Ezra responded blindly, even while he was stunned from the impact of the man colliding with his chest. He was underneath the Heggie. They fought for control of Ezra's rifle. Neither could wrest it from the other.

Finally, Ezra heaved upward, trying to get all of his weight into the other man's middle. "Help!" he called over the radio. There was a burst of wire, close, and the Heggie went limp. The men in the foxholes on either side of Ezra had both pumped wire into the man.

By that time, the horizontal hail from the aircraft cannon had moved away from 2nd platoon's area. Joe lifted his head again to look. There were no Heggies left on their feet within a hundred meters of him. The makeshift cannon rig was now moving Heggies down off toward the center of the attack, where Echo and Fox joined.

And the assault was failing.

When the one gun fell silent for a time—for reloading, Joe assumed—he could hear similar sounds coming from farther off. Ten minutes later, all of the guns of the 13th fell silent. They no longer had any targets in sight.

Dawn was still an hour away.

CHAPTER 26

It was difficult to tell where the smoke ended and the fog began. Dawn was little more than a gray luminescence in the forest.

The daybreak was not silent, though, even in the fog. Noises that had been lost in the din of war could be heard now that the guns were silent. The cries of the wounded were faint, and growing fewer as medics got to everyone and administered analgesics or anesthetics, and tended to wounds. The more seriously wounded, both Accord and Hegemony, were being treated by company medtechs and by the 13th's surgeons.

In their haste to withdraw, the Schlinal forces had merely left behind their wounded—anyone hurt too badly to keep up with their unit.

Around the Accord lines, the stacks of Schlinal dead lay uncounted. The earliest estimates, made from a distance, were that there had to be at least twenty-five hundred dead, perhaps more than twice that number. Until the bodies were moved to graves—large, common graves—there could be nothing but estimates.

In the center of the 13th's area, men walked about as if in a daze. Most of them were aware that the battle was over—for the moment at least—and that was enough. More than a few men had simply gone to sleep in their foxholes, or next to them, too exhausted to do more.

In the exact center of the area, the top hatch had been opened on the buried Heyer APC. The people who had been confined inside for more than a dozen hours came out, as dazed as the men who had been out and fighting. Gene Abru and his SI team remained with the civilian researchers—close, alert. The colonel hadn't countermanded his orders. The civilians were still Abru's responsibility.

The Heggies might return.

Van Stossen had more immediate concerns than the civilians and their minders. Casualty reports were still coming in, still being totaled. The count of dead and wounded was too high to give Stossen much time to think of anything else. Nothing less than a renewed enemy attack would penetrate his awareness now. He sat alone in his command bunker. Alone. He acknowledged reported. He stared at his mapboard.

Mostly he thought . . . or, rather, tried not to. The numbness that accompanied the end of a major engagement helped. His mind was somewhat dulled by that, and by the long lack of sleep. During the night, he had kept alert by popping stimtabs in his mouth every fifteen minutes or so—far too often. Once he stopped, the physical reaction was inescapable.

Three different times—when he happened to think of it—he had called General Dacik, trying to find out what was happening back in what was, after all, the *main* engagement between Accord and Hegemony on Jordan. This affair, bloody as it had been, was no more than a side show. The first two times Stossen called, Dacik hadn't even answered. There had been no response at all on either of the channels that were supposed to connect Stossen with the local commander in chief—the channel shared by all of the regimental commanders and the private channel between Stossen and Dacik. The first, at least, should have been monitored by someone on the general's staff if he was sleeping or otherwise occupied.

On the third call, Dacik had answered, but the conversation had been even shorter than Stossen had envisioned.

"I can't talk now, Stossen. I'll get back to you. Your *guests* secure?"

"Yes, sir."

And then the general was gone.

Wait, Stossen told himself. The general said that he would call.

There was really nothing else to do in any case, nothing for him, personally. The necessary chores were being attended to by others.

Stossen let out a deep sigh and leaned back against the wall of the bunker. His eyes closed, mostly of their own accord, and he didn't fight it. Sleep did not follow, though. There was too much banging around in his mind for that, even with exhaustion. But rest . . .

"Up and on 'em," Joe said over the platoon frequency. He hoisted himself out of his foxhole with some difficulty. His joints were all stiff, and his mind was logy. "Up and on 'em. Patrol."

The groans were weak but undeniably sincere. No one was awake enough for volume or passion. Half an hour, forty-five minutes—Joe was uncertain just how long they had had to rest. To sleep or just to stare blindly ahead with eyes that would no longer even blink. There had been *some* time, though. It was nearly dawn before Lieutenant Keye came on the radio and said that they had to mount a patrol to make absolutely certain that there were no Heggies lurking in the neighborhood. Nearly a quarter of the 13th was being sent out to scout. Every other line company was around the perimeter.

Joe hadn't bothered to ask, "Why us?" He didn't have the energy, and in any case, he didn't care to hear the answer. No reason would have served to make him feel good about another trek in the woods.

The next call from Lieutenant Keye didn't help as much as it should have, either. "Be ready to take prisoners. I just got the word from Colonel Stossen. The Heggie warlord here has surrendered all his forces to General Dacik. He's ordered all of his troops to lay down their weapons. The fight's over on Jordan. We won."

That didn't cheer Joe in the least. Even if the news was true, there would still be another fight somewhere ahead. This battle might be over. The war continued.